Witch S

GW00858761

PART 1
(The First Half)

Books 1 - 3

Katrina Kahler

Table of Contents

Book 1

I'm a Girl Witch!

Chapter One

The shrill sound of the ambulance was deafening as it pulled up outside. But at least it had drowned out the sound of the panicked mothers as they hovered around the boy frozen stiff in the middle of the room.

Fortunately, Charlotte's mother had narrowly beaten the ambulance to the birthday party. She took in the scene and knew exactly what to do.

This is the moment that Charlotte's life changed forever...

It all started at Charlotte's next-door neighbor's birthday party and the silly thing is that she didn't even want to be there.

There were bunches of balloons scattered around the room, all in varying shades of pink. A banner with the message 'happy birthday' on it took up half of the far wall, and a group of adults stood to the side of the room, sipping on tea and stuffing their faces with leftover sandwiches.

Charlotte Smyth sat crossed-legged on the floor, in between a girl who kept rubbing her nose onto the back of her sleeve and a flat-haired boy who'd already won at apple bobbing and musical statues. She felt foolish being there, playing party games at the age of eleven, but it was a family friend's party and she didn't want to upset the birthday girl, so she went along with it. Charlotte took the pink wrapped parcel off the nose-rubbing girl and that's when the One Direction song stopped playing.

'That's not fair, SHE CHEATED!' the flat-haired boy screamed.

'No I didn't,' Charlotte replied, before she ripped the layer of paper off the parcel, revealing another layer of paper and a lollipop.

'You held onto it for ages,' he said as he snatched the lollipop out of the paper.

'Hey, that's mine.' Charlotte tried to get the lollipop back but he kept moving it out of her reach.

'Ed give it back, the music stopped on Charlotte,' a girl who sat opposite them said.

'Yeah, give it back Ed,' another boy said.

'It's okay, I have spares,' one of the viewing adults came tottering over and pulled a lollipop from her cardigan pocket then passed it to Charlotte.

The boy smirked at Charlotte before the music restarted, and he snatched the parcel out of her lap and reluctantly passed it to the poor child who sat next to him.

Pass-the-parcel finished and Charlotte stood up and was about to walk away when this most annoying boy sarcastically wisecracked. 'Your hair is so curly.'

Charlotte looked up to see the flat-haired boy smirking at her. 'It's stupid, you look like a giant fuzz ball.'

'Shut-up,' she growled back.

'What was that, fuzz ball? I couldn't hear you under all that fuzz.'

Charlotte stared at the grinning boy, annoyed and angry by his comments.

'Yeah well, you're a...' It was then that she realized that the boy wasn't moving, he was still grinning but his entire body was still. She waved her hand in front of the boy's face but he didn't blink.

'Stop messing about, it's not funny,' she poked his arm with her finger and watched in alarm as his rigid body fell backwards onto the floor.

A nearby girl let out a scream and a couple of the adults came rushing over.

'Edward, Edward darling, say something,' a woman gently shook him. 'He's not moving. He's rigid!'

'Musical statues is over, buddy,' a man bent down by the boy and tried bending his arms, only they would not move. 'What the fudge,' he let go of Ed and took a step back. 'He's frozen solid, he's a statue.'

'Don't just stand there Keith, ring an ambulance,' the woman snapped at him.

The man fiddled in his pocket for his phone, finally finding it and calling for emergency help. Within minutes they could hear the ambulance approaching and just as it pulled up outside...a pretty, well-dressed woman, with hair as frizzy as Charlotte's rushed over to the boy and bent down in front of him.

'He's quite alright, he just needs a glass of water,' she said to the boy's mother.

'He's not all right, HE'S FROZEN SOLID!' she sobbed.

'Please, a drink,' the frizzy haired woman forced a smile.

Ed's mother asked another woman to go and get the water and to be quick as her precious son was dying.

'Some space please,' the woman said to the crowd of onlookers, and they all took a reluctant step backwards. She bent over Ed and whispered some words.

With a cough and a splutter Ed sat up, he shook out his limbs and repeatedly blinked his eyes before focusing them on Charlotte.

'Her, it was her!' he pointed straight at Charlotte.

'I didn't do anything.'

'Yes, you did, you did this to me. I saw you do it!'

The woman hurried back over with the glass of water and held it up to Ed's lips.

'It's okay sweetie,' his mother wrapped her arms around him.

'It was her, Mother, I saw her do it.'

'With the utmost respect I don't see how my daughter could have caused such a thing to have happened,' the frizzy haired woman stood-up and walked over to Charlotte. 'We're leaving,' she whispered to her.

As Charlotte followed her mom across the room she felt everyone's gaze on her as they gossiped amongst themselves. She'd been angry with Ed and she'd wanted him to stop teasing her but she didn't see how she could have caused him to freeze.

She came to the conclusion that he must have eaten something funny, as people didn't just freeze solid for no reason.

Her mom was silent as they walked home, but Charlotte didn't mind this. As they walked, she wondered if she'd ever be invited to a party again.

It wasn't until later that day that Charlotte's mom called her into the kitchen and gestured for her to take a seat next to her at the circular table.

'Hi sweetie, I want to talk to you about what happened earlier at the party,' her mom said, her voice gentle.

'I didn't touch him Mom, he was teasing me but I didn't do anything.'

'I know that you didn't intend to do anything but that doesn't mean you didn't,' she sighed before continuing. 'Your father doesn't know this because he's an ordinary, a human, but I'm a witch.'

'A w-what?'

'When I was a child I found that I could do things, extraordinary things and it appears that you also have powers,' she placed a hand on top of Charlotte's. 'It's nothing to be afraid of, actually it's exciting, but you need to go somewhere where you can be properly trained so that nothing like what happened at the party ever happens again. As I said before, your dad knows nothing about witches. He is an ordinary. So this has to be our secret.'

'I didn't mean to do anything to that boy, although he was horrible. I'm not a w-witch,' Charlotte pulled her hand free from under her mom's and folded her arms.

Her mother glanced around the kitchen to confirm they were alone before she looked at the unlit candle in the center of the room, then clicked her fingers. A bright flame immediately appeared and gently flickered. Charlotte stared at it open-mouthed before turning her gaze to her mom.

'You're a witch, Charlotte, just like me. Ever since you were a toddler, I have watched you manipulating objects,' she gently grabbed Charlotte's shoulders and looked directly at her. 'There's two possible boarding schools where you can go to learn to control your powers. Witchery College and Miss Moffat's Academy for Refined Young Witches. My preferred choice for you is the latter, I contacted them earlier and they have a space. You're very lucky to have this opportunity, you will make lots of friends and learn so much,' she smiled.

'Then why don't you go to it,' Charlotte snapped. 'Sorry, it's just all a bit much.'

'It's okay sweetie, I understand. We'll talk more about this tomorrow but remember what I said about your father, he doesn't know about witches. He thinks that you're going to a normal boarding school, so please don't tell him otherwise. Ordinaries have a hard time grasping the magical world, which is why we like to keep it a secret from them.'

'Okay,' Charlotte nodded.

That morning she'd been a normal eleven-year-old girl but now everything had changed. She thought back to all the times in her life when odd things had happened, like the time when the broken nib of her pencil reappeared so that she could finish her school exam. There was also the time when the only yoghurt left was a loathed cherry flavor one, but when she went to eat it, it tasted of strawberries.

But she'd never turned someone into a statue before, maybe she really was different to the other children, maybe she really was a witch.

Chapter Two

It was muggy in the car and Charlotte's hair was stuck to her damp forehead. She wanted to open the window but her mom didn't like the noise that it made when the wind came through the gap. The air-con was on but this didn't seem to help much and Charlotte knew better than to open the window. Her mom was almost as anxious about today as she was, the fact that she'd caught her re-washing the dishes for the second time after breakfast verified this.

For the last few weeks Charlotte's mom had been dropping the new school into conversation wherever she could. A fact which had made Charlotte more apprehensive, it was also hard not being able to discuss it properly with her mom when her dad was around. She felt as if she was being thrown into a snake pit with no knowledge of which ones were poisonous.

They were on their way to Miss Moffat's Academy and Charlotte knew that there was no going back.

'Will we be there soon?' she asked, wiping back a strand of hair off her sticky face.

'In about an hour sweetie, we'll stop off and grab a drink on-route.'

'If I don't like this school do I have to stay there?'

'You will like it, you're fortunate to have been offered a place.'

'Maybe they should have given it to someone else,' she said under her breath.

'Charlotte, it will be fine, you just have to be yourself and you'll settle right in.'

'Okay,' she sighed, the concern still sitting in the pit of her stomach.

Charlotte turned her head and stared out of the window, watching as her old life blurred past her and her new, unknown one drew evermore closer.

***

After parking the car and her mom yet again going on about how great the school was, they both got out of the car. Charlotte followed her mom down a pathway surrounded by trees and they soon arrived in a clearing where a large maze of green lay in front of them.

'This is the furthest I can take you,' her mom said, as she leaned down and hugged her daughter.

'B-but it's a maze, I don't know where I'm going,' Charlotte looked at the narrow path between the high walls of greenery.

'It's the Entry Maze. It's part of the initiation process.'

'I'll get lost Mom, I can't do it.'

'Yes you can,' her mom grabbed her arms and looked directly at her. 'You can do this Charlotte, just follow your instinct.'

'But it's so big and I don't know where I'm going,' tears dripped down Charlotte's cheeks.

'You'll know when you find it,' she wiped away one of the tears before she squeezed Charlotte tight. 'Now go before you set me off,' she forced back her own tears as she kissed her on the top of her head.

'Okay Mom, I love you,' Charlotte forced a smile before she nervously walked towards the maze entrance, looking back once at her mom and giving a wave before she continued up the path and into the unknown.

Charlotte had never been keen on mazes, not since she'd ended up separated from her parents in a crop maze when she was five. A random family had stumbled upon her, led her out of it, and reunited her with her parents. She knew that this time no one would come to rescue her and that she was in this on her own.

She came across yet another dead-end and looked around her, a panicked feeling growing in her stomach. The midday sun was beating down and she didn't know where to go or what to do. Sitting down on the ground, she regained her breath as she tried to calm herself and figure out what to do next.

'You can do this,' she said to herself, before she closed her eyes tightly and murmured a desperate plea. 'Please, I don't know where to go, I need some help.'

Charlotte opened her eyes to see a ball of light in front of her. At first she wasn't sure if it was the heat or her anxiety causing her to imagine things but upon blinking, the ball of light remained in sight. The light began to move forwards, so she followed it as it weaved through the passageways, eventually stopping at another dead-end. Only this one wasn't like the other ones she'd previously found, as it contained a large tree. It was so large that Charlotte wondered how she hadn't seen it above the maze walls. It was as luscious green in color as the hedgerows were.

The tree shook which made Charlotte jump off her feet and then six green faces appeared amongst the foliage.

'Hello child,' the first face said, which caused Charlotte to become even more alarmed. This wasn't like one of the normal trees that were in the park near her house as she'd never heard them speak.

'We will ask you a question each, answer them correctly to gain access to the Academy,' the second face said.

'Don't worry, I'm sure you'll pass with flying colors,' the second face gave a friendly chuckle.

'Let's begin with an easy one. What's your name?' the first face asked.

'Ch-Charlotte Symth,' she croaked out.

'Correct,' the first face boomed.

'What is the color of a witch's hat?' the second face asked.

'Erm, black.'

'Correct.'

'What is the best mode of transport for a witch?' the third face asked.

'A broomstick,' she said confidently, beginning to think that these questions were a breeze.

'What is a witch's preferred pet?' the fourth face said.

'Erm, a frog, no an owl.'

'Incorrect,' the voice boomed and Charlotte felt the tears well up in her eyes. She wondered if that was her only chance and she'd failed? 'Don't worry child, you can try again.'

She thought hard about what it could be and then she recalled the books her mom had read to her as a kid, about a clumsy witch and her magic world.

'A black cat.'

'Correct.'

'What do witches brew potions in?'

'Erm, a pot, no a cauldron.'

'Correct.'

'Nearly there, only this question to go. See if you can solve this riddle: What is a witch's favorite subject?' the sixth face asked.

Charlotte bit on the side of her lip as she thought about this. She'd never been good at riddles as she tended to over-think them. She took a deep breath and tried to think carefully, hoping that she'd be allowed a few chances to get it right.

'Potions.'

'Incorrect,' the sixth face boomed.

'Oh, erm flying.'

'Incorrect.'

'Okay,' she rolled her eyes back as she tried to think what it could be. She thought about what witches were famous for liking; magic, their pets, turning people into rodents and spells. They liked spells. 'Is it spelling?'

'Correct,' the sixth face said and all the faces began to laugh in unison before the tree shook and the leaves flew into the sky, reforming as large leafy elephants.

'Cool,' she mouthed.

The maze vanished in front of her and in its place appeared a large field.

'Follow us,' the elephants said, before they began to plod along in front of her.

Charlotte did as they said, wondering what she'd have to do next. Suddenly a hole appeared beneath her and before she could do anything about it she felt herself falling. She landed on her feet in front of four life-sized stone statues of warriors on a platform. Behind them was a large castle. Could this be the Academy? She found herself annoyed at the elephants for coming across as nice and then luring her down that hole. They could have at least given her some warning.

'Is anyone home? Please can you let me in?' she shouted out, as she looked around for a door.

There was a loud clacking sound and Charlotte looked up to see the four statues pulling themselves down from their platform and walking over to her in their armor, with varying weapons in their hands as they circled her.

'What are you doing here?' one of the warriors asked, as he pulled his sword out of its case.

'I am, erm, I am a student here. I was in the maze and now I'm looking for the entrance.'

'An entrance,' the warrior laughed, before he turned to the warrior by him. 'You hear that Lancelot; she's looking for the entrance.'

'Please, the elephants, they brought me here. Well, they led me to the hole and I fell and-'

'Enough, you're giving me a headache,' a warrior holding a shield said.

'I can't hear myself think,' the third warrior said.

'Come on, this is enough,' the warrior known as Lancelot said.

'Spoilsport,' the first warrior said.

'Come on, you know if he doesn't get his way he will go on and on and on and on about it,' the fourth warrior said.

'Yes, you're right,' the first warrior sighed. 'Very well, go on.'

'We've been expecting you,' the fourth warrior laughed, which caused the others to laugh too.

'Ignore those fools,' a squeaky voice said. She looked up to see several bats flying above her head. 'Follow us,' they squeaked.

By this stage she didn't even question the fact that the bats were talking. She simply followed them, eager and grateful to escape the stone warriors.

'Follow us, follow us,' they squeaked, as they flew straight through the solid stone wall beside the warriors' platform.

Charlotte abruptly stopped and stared in disbelief, not understanding how they traveled through the wall. She thought that only ghosts could travel through walls, not witches. She wondered if the bats were tricking her and if perhaps they were ghosts instead. She didn't want to bash into the wall and then be laughed at.

'Hurry up and follow us,' the bats squeaked out as they flew back out of the wall and then flew back through it again.

Taking a deep breath, she took a few steps forwards before she paused in front of the mass of concrete and stared up at it, hoping that a door would appear and make things simpler.

'I can do this,' she said under her breath, before taking another step forwards so that she was almost touching the solid looking surface. She was about to reach out and touch it when one of the bats flew back out and flapped its wings beside her.

'No, you have to walk through it.' It's squeak was decisive. 'Hurry, hurry, you have to come now.'

Charlotte took one last look around her. She knew that she had to do it then or not at all, so she stepped through the wall.

Chapter Three

Pink Persian carpets covered the central part of the marbled floors that were under Charlotte's feet as she stood in the large, high ceilinged entrance hall.

She stopped by her bags that were there waiting for her and looked at the various spiral staircases that were in front of her, the banisters gold. Huge portraits of women in witches' hats and holding broomsticks were hanging on the grand looking walls and there was an overwhelming smell of rose petals.

Charlotte had never been anywhere as impressive as this before and she found herself staring at it open-mouthed.

'Follow us, follow us,' the bats squeaked, before they flew down and picked up her bags with their feet and flew them up one of the staircases.

Charlotte wondered how they were strong enough to carry her bags but then again they could talk, so being extraordinarily strong seemed minor in comparison. She followed them up the staircase and past a large gold bust that was standing by the wall.

They led her through a gilded golden door and into a room that was about four times the size of her bedroom at home.

There were four large, bronze framed beds in the rooms, each with an array of pillows in creams and golds and an ivory blanket folded at the end of the light grey colored duvet.

The bats placed her bags down in front of the bed furthest from the door, before they fluttered out of the room, closing the door behind them.

An owl appeared and perched on the windowsill by the open window and it watched Charlotte intently as she looked around the room.

Apart from the beds, the only other items in the room were an intricately carved ornate gold mirror and an enormous wooden wardrobe.

'Don't open the wardrobe,' the owl hooted.

'Why not?' she asked, wondering why the wardrobe had been put there if she couldn't use it.

'Don't open the wardrobe,' the owl repeated, before it flew off outside.

Charlotte sat down on her bed and wondered what she was supposed to do next. The castle was so massive and daunting; she decided that she'd just wait there until someone told her what she should do. She certainly did not want to try exploring and risk getting lost.

The door opened and the bats flew in carrying bags, followed by a girl in a creamy white dress, with chin length, wavy dark-blonde hair. The bats flew over to the bed by the window and put the bags down in front of it.

'Hi, I'm Stef,' she smiled, as she studied the room.

'Charlotte. Pleased to meet you Stef.'

'So, we're going to need rules for this bedroom gig to work. No sitting on other beds or touching each other's stuff!'

The door opened and again the bats flew in carrying bags, this time followed by a smiling girl, with curly blond hair.

'Hi, I'm Gerty,' she looked around excitedly. 'This place is so cool! I've never seen a castle this big before. And the bats actually talk.'

'How old are you?' Stef put her hands on her waist as she looked questioningly at the young girl.

'They don't normally accept students until they're eleven but they let me in a year early because I'm good at magic,' she said without pausing for breath.

'That's cool,' Charlotte said.

'I don't think it's a good idea for a ten-year-old to be here, from what I hear the lessons are challenging and a ten-year-old doesn't have the same maturity as an eleven-year-old.' Stef commented with a smug expression.

'It's only a year's difference,' Charlotte said.

'I'm so excited,' Gerty continued, ignoring Stef's comment. 'I've not been able to sleep properly in days. I wonder what lesson we'll have first?' Gerty fell back onto her bed and began to pull her body up with her hands as she bounced on the firm surface.

'Do you think anyone else will come and take that bed?' Stef asked curiously, as she gestured to the spare bed.

'I don't know,' Charlotte replied.

'Hopefully it's just us because it'll give us more space,' Stef walked over to the wardrobe. 'At least we have this to put our clothes in.'

'I wouldn't open that, there was an owl here and it said not to open it.'

'Whatever,' Stef rolled her eyes before pulling open the doors.

A black hole of intense force sucked Stef forwards, she grabbed onto the inner side of the wardrobe and clung on tightly as her body was turned horizontal.

Charlotte and Gerty both rushed over to her and each grabbed one of Stef's arms, pulling as hard as they could.

A pretty girl with long blond hair tied into a high ponytail and wearing a knee length satin black skirt and a fitted white blouse that emphasized her slim waist, stepped into the room, a long silver wand in hand.

'Newbies,' she tutted, before she waved her wand in the girls' direction. 'Entario.'

Stef was thrown back into the room and she landed on the floor with a loud thump, her hair a mess and her dress blown up around her waist so that her old knickers with a hole by the waistband were on show. She immediately jumped up onto her feet, her cheeks flushed as she flattened down her dress and then tried to smooth down her hair.

Charlotte and Gerty both giggled and Stef stared at them sternly, which caused them both to fall silent.

'I am Molly McDonald, the head prefect,' she tapped the small silver triangular pin on her blouse, the words 'head prefect' written on it in italic black font. 'I am here to welcome you all to Miss Moffat's Academy, we are renown for being one of the most successful schools for witches in the world and you're all very lucky to be here. Don't squander this opportunity that you've been given. Also, it is of the utmost importance that you always follow the rules and instructions that have been given to you.' She glanced towards Stef who was looking embarrassed.

'Oh, there's still one more girl to come to this room,' she turned and said after she'd reached the door. 'Alice Smithers.'

'What's she like?' Gerty asked.

'You'll have to wait and see,' she shrugged, a smirk on her face, as she left the room.

'Are you okay?' Charlotte asked Stef.

'Yeah, fine,' she said defensively.

'Wasn't Molly so pretty? I want to be that pretty. Do you think I'll be able to cast a spell to make myself look like her?' Gerty asked.

'I think it'll be awhile before you learn powerful spells, I mean you are only ten,' Steff replied.

'You're already pretty, Gerty, you don't need to look like Molly,' Charlotte said.

'Thanks, I think you're both really pretty too and I love your hair,' she replied, which caused Charlotte to instinctively pat down her hair.

'Yeah, I suppose you look okay,' Stef shrugged.

'You guys are so nice. I hope Alice is nice too.'

'Yeah, me too,' Charlotte said, not wanting to be stuck in a room with someone she didn't like. Gerty was giggly and excitable and Stef was confident and blunt but Charlotte liked them both and hoped that the other girl would fit in as well.

A loud bell rang out which startled Charlotte as she looked at the other girls. Just then the owl swooped into the room.

'Follow me to the meeting room,' the owl hooted and the girls nodded before following it out of the room.

They were led down the spiral staircase and along the wide hallway until they got to an arched doorway. As they walked closer, the doors opened inwards and the owl flew off. They stepped into the meeting room that was full of rows of chairs, most of which had students sitting on them. The room was alive with excited voices and Charlotte and Gerty followed Stef over to some free seats in one of the middle rows.

There was a raised platform in front of them with an impressive burgundy and gold armchair. The chair had an oval backrest that had massive dragon's wings attached to the sides.

'I've never seen this many witches before,' Gerty said, as she peered over her shoulder. 'It's so exciting.'

'How long do you think we'll have to sit here for?' Stef asked, as she restlessly tapped her fingers against the frame of her seat.

'It shouldn't be long,' Charlotte replied, looking up at the grey-bricked walls that had a row of colored shields displayed on them.

This whole experience was a new one for Charlotte and she wondered what was going to happen next. She was curious to find out what it would be but really hoped that she wouldn't have to solve any more riddles.

Chapter Four

The doors into the room opened and the room fell silent as dozens of bats flew up the aisle in-between the seats. Behind the bats flew a beautiful woman who was on a black handled broomstick with flickers of gold flashing vividly along its length. She hovered by the armchair and elegantly stepped off her broom, before making it float beside her.

Her long chestnut colored hair sat in cone shaped funnels at the sides of her head and her pale skin was clear of any blemishes. She stared towards the girls with eyes as dark as black sapphires, clutching authoritatively to her fur trimmed luxurious looking cloak.

Then, with a welcoming smile, she sat down on the chair and placed her arms elegantly on the rests.

'Hello students, new and old, I am Miss Moffat, the head-witchress and founder of this academy. I established it over four-hundred-years ago and regard it as my greatest achievement. Many well-renown witches have attended here, including Ivy Glossington who developed the famous chant to ward off trolls and Fiona Fitzgerald who wrote the best-selling *Witches Of The World* books.

This school is notorious for being one of the best of its kind, so for all the new students here today you should feel very privileged to have been offered a place here. I advise you all to make the most of this wonderful opportunity and not waste it. Each and every one of you now represents this school and what we stand for. Knowledge is what this school feeds on and from it can come greatness…but don't be fooled into thinking this can be achieved without hard work and one-hundred-per-cent effort. Many longed for a place here and didn't succeed. They're now forced to attend Witchery College, most-famous for its long line of witches who dabble in the dark arts, something that is thoroughly frowned upon at this academy.

When you have finished your education you will graduate with the finest moral upstanding and most advanced skills in the magical community, skills which are considered-'

The doors creaked open, followed by footsteps. Miss Moffat was scowling so everyone else turned to see what had happened. Standing there in a green and yellow sequined dress and with her mousy brown hair under a witch's hat, was a young girl.

'Good afternoon, sorry I'm a tad late. My bags are outside, could you ask the servants to collect them for me.' Her voice was confident and assured and she was clearly unfazed by all the eyes on her. Everyone stared open-mouthed, amazed at her rudeness.

'And who, are you?' Miss Moffat asked.

'I am Alice, Alice Smithers. I presumed you would have known that.'

'You presumed wrong,' Miss Moffat replied.

Alice was about to say something else when Molly rushed over to her and led her over to Charlotte and the others.

'These are your room-mates,' Molly said.

'Oh, I'll be wanting my own room.'

'You have to share, everyone else your age shares a room,' Molly said, before she walked back over to her seat, leaving Alice standing there looking begrudgingly at the girls.

The only empty seat was next to Stef and that meant Alice would have to squeeze past Gerty and Charlotte to get to it, but it was clear that she wasn't willing to do this. Aware that everyone was staring, Charlotte gently nudged Stef's arm and motioned for her to move along. At first Stef shook her head and folded her arms but Charlotte furrowed her eyebrows with insistence. Stef let out an exaggerated sigh before she moved onto the next seat. Charlotte and Gerty both shuffled along as well which meant that Alice could sit down at the end of the row.

'As I was saying, it is at this Academy where you shall learn skills which are considered greatly valuable in the magical society. Your final goal for your education at this esteemed Academy is for all of you, even those of you who are rude enough to interrupt me, is to develop your powers in order to become refined young witches and learn to use your powers for the good of everybody, including ordinaries.

'There is a strict code of conduct at this Academy that you must follow.' Miss Moffat continued in a strict tone.

Dozens of scrolls flew in the door and floated in the air before the students.

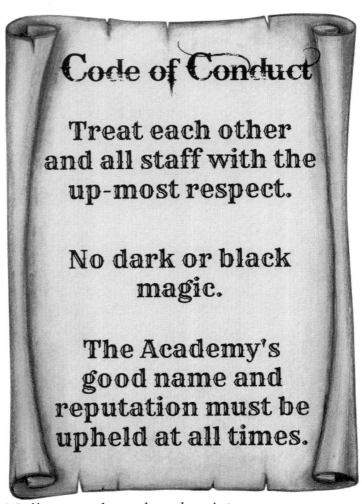

Code of Conduct

Treat each other and all staff with the up-most respect.

No dark or black magic.

The Academy's good name and reputation must be upheld at all times.

Miss Moffat went through each point.

'You must all treat each other and the members of staff with respect.' Her eyes focused on Alice as she made this statement.

'No dark or black magic will be tolerated in this Academy.'

'The Academy's reputation as a school for refined young witches is to be upheld at all times.'

'It'd be easier if she just laid down the rules, you know like lights out at 9pm and no running in the hall,' Gerty whispered to Charlotte, which caused her to giggle before putting her finger to her lips to signal for her to be quiet. It was then that Alice stuck her arm into the air but didn't wait to be asked to speak.

'Excuse me miss, those rules are fairly general, do you have any more specific ones?' she blurted out what everyone else was thinking, but that no one else dared to ask.

'This is not a day nursery for babies, you need to live by this code of conduct and make wise choices in the things you do and how you conduct yourself whilst at this Academy. There will be consequences for anyone who disobeys these rules. I was hoping that I wouldn't have to point this out today but it appears that it may be necessary.

1st offence- a wart will appear on your face.

2nd- Your nose will grow, by how much is determined by the severity of your misadventure.

3rd- Your laugh shall change to that of a witch's cackle.

4th- Your skin shall turn green.

5th- Your eyes shall turn bright red and bloodshot.

6th- The final warning. The word naughty shall appear on your forehead and will remain there for an entire month.

The severity and timing of these punishments will depend on the code of conduct violation. In other words, the naughtier you are, the worse the consequence.'

Alice once again lifted up her hand.

'Yes Miss Smithers?' Miss Moffat said in a sarcastic tone.

'What happens if you are naughty after the sixth consequence?'

'Then you shall be expelled from this Academy and shall have to attend the lowly rated public school Witchery College, headed by Mistress Ravenshawk,' she shuddered.

The girls all looked around at each other and exchanged knowing glances. It was clear that no one wanted to mess up, especially if it meant the consequence that Miss Moffat had threatened. Charlotte noticed that even Alice had gone quiet and lowered her gaze at the mention of Witchery College.

Charlotte found herself wondering how many students had been expelled and if Mistress Ravenshawk was as terrifying as she sounded, although she hoped that she'd never end up as a student at her school to find out.

'Go back to your room and unpack and get ready for dinner. If you're new here and unsure of the way back to your rooms then call for a bat and one will promptly arrive to guide you,' Miss Moffat stood up and got onto her broomstick. All the girls watched as she flew towards the now opened doors and left the room.

The hall instantly erupted into noise as all the girls began talking to each other.

'I know the way to the room,' Stef said, as she stood up and pushed her way past the others to get to the end of the row.

'Mind where you're treading with your big feet, these shoes are one-of-a-kind,' Alice demanded.

'Come on guys,' Stef ignored Alice's comment.

They all stood and joined Stef, following the crowd of girls out of the hall, excited at the prospect of their futures in this school.

Chapter Five

It turned out that Stef did remember the way back to the room and Charlotte tried to memorize the route, hoping that she wouldn't get lost when she was in the castle alone. The four of them walked inside and Gerty fell down onto her bed and swung her legs out over the side of it.

'Did you know that Miss Moffat is over four-hundred-years old? She looks amazing doesn't she and her hair, it's so beautiful and shiny. I think I might grow my hair that long and maybe when I'm older I'll dye it the same color as hers,' Gerty said excitedly.

'How can she be that old?' Charlotte asked.

'By magic of course,' Stef snorted.

'I'm new to this magic world so I didn't know.'

'That's okay, I can teach you,' Gerty smiled.

'Thanks, I'd like that.'

'I'll have that bed by the window,' Alice said, as she walked over to Stef's bed and sat down on it.

'Erm, no you won't, that bed's already been claimed by me. First come, first served,' Stef said.

'I should have my own room. Don't the staff here know who I am?' Alice was looking like she was going to be a king sized pain!

'Clearly not,' Stef rolled her eyes.

'If I can't have my own room then I should at least get to pick which bed I have and I want this one.'

'Well you can't have it because it's mine,' she strutted over to her bed, her hands on her hips. 'That one's yours, over by the bathroom.'

'I'm not having that one, it's the worst placed bed in the room,' Alice argued.

'Your bags are by it, see,' she pointed over to the large pile of bags that were by the bed. 'So that one's yours and this one is mine. You're currently sitting on my bed,' she smirked.

'This is ridiculous, rest assured that my parents will be hearing about this,' she abruptly hopped off the bed and stormed across the room and out of the door.

Stef sneaked over to the door and peered around it, followed by Gerty and Charlotte. They watched Alice storm off down the hallway.

'Where's she going?' Charlotte asked.

'Probably to ring up Mommy and Daddy and complain about the awful treatment she's been receiving here,' Stef put on a posh voice.

Gerty and Charlotte shared a look as if to say that Stef had gone too far and Stef caught sight of it.

'Relax, she'll be back but she needed to know her place,' she walked away from the door. 'Don't worry about Alice, she'll be fine.'

Charlotte went back over to her bed and rummaged through her bags. She wanted to unpack but didn't know where she was supposed to put her clothes…seeing as the wardrobe was off limits. She wondered why the wardrobe was there when it couldn't be used. It was annoying as it was so huge, all four of them would have been able to fit their clothes into it.

She looked over at Stef who had pulled a separate draw from out under her bed and was filling it with piles of her clothes. Charlotte found that there was a draw under her bed too, so she pulled it out and began to sort out her clothes. She found herself wondering where Alice had gone and when she'd come back. She didn't want any more bickering to happen between Stef and Alice but they were both strong personalities so she doubted their room would become a calm zone anytime soon. At least all this drama kept her distracted from thinking about home and about how much she was missing her mom and dad.

Charlotte was still unpacking her belongings when Alice huffed her way back into the room, followed by two similar looking girls, one wearing black and the other had a white tunic on and both of them wore a triangular silver pin boasting the word 'prefect'. The most noticeable difference in their appearance was that one girl was a couple of inches taller than the other one.

'I'm Sonya and this is my sister Silvia, we're prefects here at the Academy. According to Alice, someone's stolen her bed,' the taller girl said.

'Erm, no they haven't,' Stef folded her arms. 'Alice was the last one into the room and therefore she should have the bed that's left.'

'I am from a very important witching family called The Smithers, who I'm sure you've heard of, so I should have priority. And according to my measurements I have 29 and a half inches less space than the rest of you and that is NOT fair!

'If you were last in the room then you'll have to put up with the bed that's left, I don't see the problem,' Sonya said, as she flicked her long blonde hair behind her ears.

'The problem is that it's not the bed I want,' Alice complained.

'Well you should have got here earlier then,' Stef said.

'Alice, we suggest that you calm down and try to fit in,' Silvia said, before they both turned around and headed out of the room.

'But that's not fair. Don't you know who I am?' Alice shouted to their backs but neither of them turned around.

'Fine,' she said under her breath, as she walked over to her bed and lifted her bags on top of it.

'Where are the servants? It's positively awful that I'm expected to unpack this myself.'

'Just get on with it.' Stef rolled her eyes. She'd finished her own packing and was now lying on her bed.

Alice grabbed a handful of clothes and walked over to the wardrobe. Stef smirked in Charlotte's direction at the sight of what Alice was doing. Charlotte looked from Alice to the wardrobe and knew that she should say something. However annoying Alice was, Charlotte didn't think that she deserved to be sucked into that black hole. As Alice got closer to the wardrobe…even Stef's grin faltered, and Charlotte opened her mouth to warn her.

'Don't open that, it's like a wind tunnel in there, it'll suck you in,' Gerty blurted out.

'Don't be ridiculous. Why would they put a dangerous wardrobe in my bedroom?' Alice said smugly.

'It's not your bedroom, it's our bedroom and Gerty's right, so don't open it,' Stef said.

'Why should I believe you?'

'Because you don't want to end up with a first offence and a wart on your face, do you?' Stef grinned.

Alice rubbed her freckly nose before she walked back over to her bed and put her pile of clothes down onto it.

'There's a drawer under your bed,' Charlotte said.

Alice nodded before sitting on her knees and pulling the drawer out. She studied it before reluctantly unpacking her case and placing her clothes inside.

Once everyone had finished unpacking an awkward silence fell over the room and no one seemed to know what to say or do.

'Why don't we all tell each other a little bit about ourselves?' Charlotte suggested nervously, breaking the silence. The other girls all nodded.

'Okay, I'll start. My name is Charlotte Smyth, I'm eleven and I only recently found out that I am a witch. I knew I could do special things that my friends couldn't do but I didn't put much thought into it, at least not until I went to a party. There was a boy who was teasing me about my hair so I unintentionally froze him. My mom showed up and unfroze him and then she told me that she was a witch and so was I. You see my mom kept being a witch, secret from my dad, he's an ordinary and he thinks that I'm at some *normal* boarding school. Mom says he can't ever find out because he wouldn't understand. So all this is new to me but I'm really happy to be here and have you all to share a room with,' she smiled.

'I'll go next,' Gerty said, as she hopped up and bounced from one leg to the other. 'Hi, I'm Gertrude Baggs, Gerty for short'

'What a horrible, ugly name,' Alice interrupted.

'Shush,' Stef shot Alice a stern look.

'I like your name,' Charlotte said.

'Thanks,' Gerty smiled, unfazed by Alice's comment. 'I am ten but was accepted into this Academy a year early because I developed the skill of levitation at a very young age. Both of my parents have powers and at home I was encouraged to practice witchcraft. Up until now I've been home-schooled as I didn't fit into a normal school. It was so hard not using magic there, especially when the boys used to tease me about my last name. I may have turned a couple of them into toads,' she grinned.

'I am super excited to be here in a proper castle with real life witches and I can't wait for lessons to begin.'

'Me next,' Alice chimed in, as soon as Gerty had finished talking. 'I am Alice Smithers, from the world famous Smithers family. You all would have heard of my family as we're well known in the magical world,' she stuck her nose into the air.

'Mommy and Daddy believe that I am extremely powerful so that's why I am here. Of course they will miss me terribly, but I owe it to the Academy to show all of you lower rung girls how to behave like a lady.'

There were snorts and giggles from the other girls after Alice had finished talking.

'I'm Stephanie Jolly, Stef for short.'

'Jolly certainly doesn't suit your personality.' Alice really didn't have any tact.

Charlotte grabbed one of the pillows off her bed and threw it across the room at her, hitting her on the head.

'I can't believe you just did that,' Alice dropped the pillow by her side. 'I shall be keeping that pillow.'

'Give it a rest will you,' Stef grabbed a pillow off her bed and also threw it over at Alice, who only just ducked in time.

Soon everyone was holding a pillow and tossing them around, hitting each other. Laughter erupted and even Alice joined in, as she clashed her pillow against Stef's.

Gerty squealed as a pillow went flying past her head, before she picked one off her bed and flung it over at Charlotte who caught it and threw it straight back. Charlotte then grabbed one of her own pillows and joined in the pillow fight with Stef and Alice. Gerty picked up a pillow and joined in too.

'Settle down girls, you are definitely not showing refinement and you don't want to be caught for your first code of conduct,' a girl blocking the doorway said, her arms folded, another girl standing slightly behind her.

The four girls collapsed on their beds and the floor and let out bursts of uncontrollable laughter. Gerty was the first to recover from her laughing fit and walked over to the girls.

'Hi, are you both new here too?' she asked and the girl with the folded arms nodded. 'My name's Gerty, nice to meet you. What are your names?'

'I'm Margaret Montgomery and my friend is Demi Taylor, we are in the room next door and we couldn't concentrate due to the awful hullabaloo you were making,' she stared at the girls but that just made Stef laugh even more.

'We're going back to our room now, try to keep the noise down and act like grown-ups,' she flicked her hair behind her, before she left the room, Demi following along behind.

'Act like grown-ups,' Stef mimicked the girl's voice, before she flicked her own hair. Charlotte picked up a pillow and threw it at Stef and they all burst into laughter again.

'I must do something adult-like, such as reading an educational book before dinner is served,' Stef said.

'Or get rid of the creases in the sheets,' Gerty laughed.

'Or sit here in silence and be a picture of decorum,' Charlotte sat down on her bed and crossed her legs and pouted her lips.

'Oh how lovely and adult-like you are,' Stef laughed.

Alice couldn't hide her smile as she shook her head and picked up a pillow. 'You should be picking up all my pillows and pumping them up, seeing as you're the ones who threw them at me.'

'No chance,' Stef grinned. 'Hey, it could be worse. You could be sharing a room with Margaret Montgomery and her minion.'

'Shush, she'll hear you,' Charlotte giggled.

'You must act like a grown-up Charlotte,' Stef laughed, as she again flicked back both sides of her hair.

'Does anyone know what time dinner is, I'm so hungry,' Gerty said, putting her hand to her stomach.

'I don't know,' Stef shrugged and Charlotte shook her head.

'At home we have servants who prepare all our food and a butler who calls us into the dining hall when it's ready. The food is always exceptional, especially the caviar canapés and the baked Alaska.

'I'm happy with fries and a burger,' Stef said.

'Me too,' Charlotte said. 'With lots of mayo.'

'Marshmallow ice cream with extra chocolate sauce,' Gerty said licking her lips. 'Ah, now I'm even hungrier.'

'I don't eat burgers,' Alice said, a worried look on her face. 'I hope they have upper class food here or I will waste away. I don't eat common food, like burgers.'

'I'm sure you'll be fine,' Stef smirked.

A bell rang loudly and they all hopped up and looked at each other excitedly, before they headed for the door. 'All witches must proceed to the meeting room,' Molly said, as she flew past their room on her purple flickered broomstick. 'All witches must proceed to the meeting room.'

Stef led the way along the hallway and down the staircase into the meeting room, which now had long tables in it, with long red and black tablecloths on them. The room was already filling up quickly with the other girls. Stef walked over to the end of an empty table and Charlotte and Gerty followed.

Alice saw that Margaret and Demi sat in the middle of one of the tables where no one else was sitting. She walked over to them and sat down next to Margaret.

'Excuse me, but you can't sit there. Don't you dare ever sit there again,' she glared at her.

'Yeah, you're too ugly and no way near cool enough to ever associate with us,' Demi smirked.

Alice fought back tears as she stood up and quickly made her way over to the spare seat next to Charlotte. No one else heard what had happened but even so, the seats next to Margaret and Demi remained empty.

The room fell silent as the Witchress and the other teachers all flew in on their broomsticks and over to the platform, that now had a long table on it. The dragon seat was placed centrally behind the table and looked even grander next to the ordinary bronze framed chairs.

Charlotte looked up at the line of seated staff, noticing how they all looked beautiful. She wondered if she'd be a teacher one day or if she'd marry an ordinary like her mom had and hide the fact that she was a witch. She didn't know the answers to these questions…but she did know that now she knew about the witching world she was curious to learn more and couldn't imagine ever going back to living as an ordinary.

'Welcome to the first dinner of this academic year, we shall start as we always do by saying the witches' creed,' Miss Moffat said.

As she began to speak, the other witches joined in:

'Witches old and witches young
owls and bats and black cats too.
Come together in this castle
to bring out the best in you.

With perfect love and perfect trust
we learn the spells and witches' rules.
Acting for the good of all
now let's eat in this great hall.'

Charlotte looked at Stef and they exchanged awkward glances because everyone else around them seemed to know the words to the creed, including Gerty and even Alice, although she only joined in on the last few sentences.

Charlotte knew that she'd need to learn it for next time so that she didn't stand out, and reminded herself to ask Gerty to teach it to her and Stef later.

As soon as the witches creed had finished the bats flew into the room carrying bowls of broth and baskets of bread rolls. They went to the teacher's table first before they brought in food for the girls.

Charlotte watched and she was incredibly impressed as two bats quickly but precisely placed the bowl of orangey red broth down in front of her. On seeing Stef begin to eat and Gerty grab a roll out of the basket in front of them, she also took a roll and then placed her spoon into her broth. Picking up the silver goblet in front of her, she saw that it was now full of cranberry juice, even though she was sure it had been empty when she'd first sat down.

The main course was a selection of steamed meats and freshly cooked vegetables and dessert was an array of fruits and mini cakes that the bats brought in on three tiered stands. The food was so delicious that even Alice hadn't complained once, although when Charlotte thought about it, she realized that Alice hadn't said anything since she'd sat down.

When everyone had finished eating Molly stood up and said 'luculentam' as she waved her wand. All the dirty dishes, goblets and cutlery immediately vanished and the tables were perfectly tidy.

'I so need to learn that spell,' Stef said, and Charlotte and Gerty nodded in agreement.

'Now that dinner is over it is your free time to do as you wish, may you use it wisely. I request the new students to stay behind and Molly will give you a tour of the Academy. As for the rest of you, you're now free to leave,' Miss Moffat said. She got onto the broomstick that was floating behind her chair and led the rest of the teachers and older students out of the room.

Charlotte watched as the room became quieter. Then she followed the others over to where Molly was standing in front of the platform, her blonde-hair now tied into bunches.

'I don't see why I need a tour, I know where my room is and the meeting hall is easy to find. Surely servants should be on call to show me the remaining rooms as and when I need to see them,' Alice said, breaking her short bout of silence.

'This castle is huge and I'm excited to see more of it,' Charlotte whispered to Gerty.

'Me too.'

'Welcome to Miss Moffat's Academy, I think I've already met the majority of you but for those of you who don't already know me, I am Molly McDonald, head prefect. If you have any questions or problems then my room is on the third floor, it says head prefect on the door so you can't miss it. I'm happy to help you all out-'

'You get you own room?' Alice rudely interrupted.

'Yes I do but I had to share a room when I was your age. If you are insistent on having your own room, then study hard and maybe when you're in your final year here, you too will become a prefect.'

'Fat chance,' Margaret whispered snidely which caused Demi to giggle.

'This castle is a labyrinth of hallways and staircases so it is important to get your bearings. Although if you find yourself lost and alone then simply call out to the bats and they will come and help you. There is much to see so let's begin,' she stepped forwards and the girls that had been surrounding her stepped aside, creating a pathway for her to walk through.

They followed Molly out of the meeting hall and into the depths of the castle.

Chapter Six

The first room they were taken to was the huge laundry room, full of loud, spinning washing machines. Charlotte was surprised that this room looked quite normal and that the clothes didn't magically wash themselves.

'This room is only for your uniforms and ordinary clothes, your formal capes and witch's hats will be collected and washed by the Academy staff after each formal occasion and returned the following morning,' Molly said.

'Excuse me but where are the dryers?' Alice asked.

'Erm, the sun,' Molly pointed out of the window at several long clotheslines.

'What, we have to carry our wet clothes all the way out there and hang them up ourselves?'

'Yes you do.'

'That's an outrage, I am from the famous Smithers family, I can't be expected to do such a thing. I insist that the servants do my washing for me and carry it outside.'

Molly waved her wand in the air and pointed it at Alice as she said, 'Strideo!' Alice immediately shrunk down and her clothes fell into a pile on the floor. A squeaking sound came from within the pile of clothes and a white mouse with brown patches on it scurried out by Stef's feet, causing her to let out a shriek and jump back.

'I probably shouldn't have done that but she was driving me crazy,' Molly shrugged and all the other girls looked at her...shocked.

Charlotte bent down and picked up Alice, cupping her in her hands.

'That will shut her up for a while,' Margaret said to Demi and they both sniggered.

'It's probably best you keep hold of her so she doesn't get trampled,' Molly said, as she walked towards the door.

Gerty bent down and bundled up Alice's clothes, before she followed the others.

'We shall visit the common room next,' Molly said, after she stopped in front of one of the restrooms. 'But first things first,' she took the bundle of clothes out of Gerty's hands and threw them into the rest room before she carefully took Alice out of Charlotte's hands and peered down at her.

'Alice, your whining attitude has to change. If it doesn't I'll turn you into a slug next time.' She stepped into the rest room and lowered Alice onto the ground, before she waved her wand and said, 'Exero,' and then closed the rest room door.

About a minute later a sheepish looking Alice appeared out of the rest room, readjusting her dress.

'Right then, the common room it is,' Molly said, before she continued up the hallway.

The common room was as large as the meeting hall and just as impressive with its marbled floor and high ivory white ceilings. It was full of girls playing various games and Molly walked them over to a table-tennis table. Instead of bats, the girls used their wands and instead of a ball, there was a large, fuzzy bumblebee. When the girls playing hit it, it buzzed loudly and their wands flashed.

Charlotte didn't care much for bees, she'd stepped on a dozing one once and it had caused her foot to swell. On learning that the bee would have died after stinging her, she'd found herself feeling guilty, even though her foot hurt for about a week afterwards.

Molly paused in front of some girls playing limbo under a trail of hairy stinging caterpillars. A short haired girl didn't lower herself enough and brushed her arm against one of the caterpillars. The part of her arm that had touched the caterpillars began to turn green and her hair floated straight up. The girl looked mortified, before rushing off to the rest room.

There was laughter from new girls but the older ones went back to playing limbo with little reaction at all.

'Will she be okay?' Charlotte asked.

'I've told Hetty a hundred times to bend lower, she'll be fine in twenty-minutes,' Molly replied.

Charlotte nodded but made a mental note never to play that version of limbo.

There was laughter coming from the other side of the room, so Molly led them over to it. There was a large picture of a fierce looking green dragon.

'They are playing put the pin on the dragon's tail,' Molly said.

A tall, slim girl placed a blindfold over her eyes and the girl by her spun her around before she reached out her hands and cautiously moved closer to the painting, then stuck a pin into the dragon's tummy.

The painting let out a loud roar that startled the new girls. The girl who was having a turn, was given the pin back. After being spun around once more, she had another attempt, but this time she placed the pin on the dragon's neck. Once again, the painting roared.

'Last chance,' one of the girls said and the others giggled.

Taking more care, the girl hesitated and then placed the pin on the dragon's leg. There was no roar at all and the girl took off the blindfold to see how accurate she'd been. Immediately the dragon came to life and became 3D as it stepped out of the painting and spat fire at her, causing her to jump back as the other girls laughed.

'Sorry.' The girl patted the dragon on its head, which it shook before it went back over to the painting and stepped back into it.

All the new girls behind Molly had moved quickly back, startled by what had taken place. Charlotte was both fascinated and terrified at the same time and wondered what she would stumble upon next.

'I won't be playing that game,' Gerty announced.

'I don't want my hair to be singed,' another girl with long curly red hair said.

'As you can see, you only get three chances and if you miss all three, well then you should be prepared,' Molly grinned. 'These may seem like games but this is where you can practice and refine your skills.'

'I thought games were meant to be fun,' Stef whispered to Charlotte.

'You're a chicken, cluck, cluck,' Margaret sniggered.

Stef looked annoyed but she ignored Margaret and instead focused on Molly.

'Enough of this room, next on the tour is the grand library,' Molly beckoned them to follow her. She walked across the room with the sound of the dragon roaring behind them.

The library was crammed to the high ceilings with row-upon-row of books and a musty old book smell filled the room. To Charlotte it resembled a Victorian library and stepping into it was like going back in time.

There wasn't a computer or any sign of modern technology in sight and even the large oak tables looked aged and worn.

'The Mistress of the Books is busy so we have to wait here,' Molly whispered, as she gestured with her eyes over to where two attractive women were standing in conversation with each other.

Feeling impatient and not understanding why they needed the librarian to talk to them about reading books, Stef walked over to one of the shelves and picked a book up.

A face appeared on the cover of the book and said, '*How to Use Herbs in Potions* by Roberta Mayfield.'

'Shi...vers,' Stef shouted out, dropping the book.

Before she could fully comprehend what was going on she was lifted off her feet up into the air and then turned upside down so that yet again her holey knickers were on display to everyone.

All the girls giggled, even Charlotte who tried to disguise her laughter under her hand.

'Young lady, never drop any of my books again. This is my kingdom and I am a ruthless leader. These books are mostly hundreds of years old and they will be treated with respect,' a woman with long mahogany colored hair said, her stern voice seeming too severe for her youthful appearance.

Stef's face turned a beetroot shade of red from a mixture of the blood pooling to her head as well as her embarrassment. She tried holding her dress over her knickers but it wasn't an easy thing to do as she was feeling dizzy and nauseous.

'S-sorr-.'

'Just don't do it again,' she waved her wand and Stef turned the right way round and landed back on her feet, holding her pounding head and trying to ignore the large smirks on Margaret's and Demi's faces.

'My name is Mistress of the Books and this is my library. I am not here to be your friend, but I am here to assist you with your book choosing if you should need it. This library is a place of great learning and knowledge and you will treat everything in here with the utmost of respect,' she straightened her velvet black hooded cape.

'There will be NO misbehavior in MY library. If you make too much noise or are disobedient in here, then I shall have no hesitation in turning you into a toad. Do it again and I will send a needle and cotton to sew up your mouth. I know every single one of these books from cover-to-cover and I will make sure that they are all respected. I am always watching and I see everything that goes on in this library...everything!' she said, staring at Stef.

'The books have no words or pictures on the cover and they are all very old and all surrounding different aspects of witchcraft. When a book is picked up a face appears on it and the book announces its title, as you already know,' she shot Stef another stern look, causing Stef to look at the floor and hope that she wouldn't be lifted upside-down again.'

'Some pages have words but many of them have images that come to life and talk to the reader. There are two sections in this library, the common section that you can all access,' she gestured around her. 'And the restricted section,' she pointed to further down the room where a section of shelves was roped off. 'You are NEVER to go into the restricted area,' her eyes darkened. 'That section is only for staff and for students in their final year.'

'Choose which book you want out of these drawers,' she led them over to a wall of wooden drawers, all with various categories labeling them.

The highest drawers had an image of a skull on them. 'NEVER go near the restricted drawers, told apart by the skull on them. There will be dire consequences if these are ever tampered with.'

'Look up what you want to read about and choose a card,' she opened a drawer with 'common pets for witches' written on it and pulled out a card.
'The book will come to you,' a book wedged itself off a nearby shelf and flew over to her, landing in her hand.

'*How to Train Your Toad* by Cassandra Jemina Woodley,' a voice said, after a face had appeared on the book cover.

'When you've finished with the book put it down on this shelf on your way out,' she gestured to an empty shelf that was close to the door. 'Books must NEVER leave the library and you must sit down at a table to read them. They are fragile and very old so treat them with the care they deserve.'

Then she narrowed her eyes and stared at all the girls, 'Remember, even if you can't see me I'll be watching you. And no loud noises in the library are tolerated, witches are here to learn.'

Her face turned even darker and she bent down towards them. 'At the far end of the library hall there is a huge wooden door with a dragon handle,' her tone was low and serious. 'Nobody except for Miss Moffat and myself are allowed to enter through this door. The Book of the Dragons is behind it, a book so dangerous that the door is protected by a powerful spell. You must never go anywhere near this door as it would put your life in great jeopardy!'

'That will be all, I best get back to my books. I shall no doubt see you all shortly,' she said, before she walked away from them.

'Right, let's continue the tour,' Molly whispered.

All the girls remained silent until they had left the library, even Alice who after having seen what the Mistress of the Books had done to Stef knew better than to test her.

'She was terrifying,' Stef whispered to the girls, as she rubbed her head. 'I wonder what her real name is. Miss Mean Mistress?'

'Mistress of Misery,' another girl chimed in.

'Mistress Miserable,' Gerty chuckled.

'I'd advise you all to be quiet,' Molly said.

'But we aren't in the library anymore,' Stef said.

'I suggest you always do the right thing, unless you want to be turned into a toad for the day.'

Some of the girls looked over their shoulders and back at the library entrance. No more was said about the Mistress of the Books, but Charlotte couldn't stop thinking about the library. She liked books, always had, but she was worried about going back in there. What if she accidentally dropped a book or what if a restricted book card was in the wrong drawer and she accidentally pulled it out? It was definitely the scariest library she'd ever been into.

'Last up is the flying arena,' Molly said, as she stopped by two large bronze doors that were on the ground floor.

They followed her out into a large courtyard, overlooked by vine-covered walls.

'Here you will be taught by Miss Firmfeather, one of the most accomplished flying instructors in the world.'

'When do we get our broomsticks?' Alice asked.

'Miss Firmfeather will meet with you tomorrow and tell you all about the flying program. As for your broomsticks, you'll be getting them tomorrow but whether you can fly on them or not will be up to Miss Firmfeather.'

There were excited murmurs between the girls at the prospect of soon being able to fly.

'Excuse me but won't we be hurt if we fall off?' Charlotte asked, as she stared at the hard looking ground.

Molly smiled as she jumped up into the air then landed back down on the ground which became bouncy beneath her feet.

'I don't need a soft surface to land on because I've had lessons from my father, so I will simply blitz through the flying lessons,' Margaret said loudly.

Molly gently shook her head but didn't respond, a faint smile on her face.

Charlotte was definitely more excited about flying than she was about going back into the library. Especially now that she knew she would bounce off the ground if she fell off.

'You've all had a huge day today but tomorrow will be even more exciting, so you all need to go back to your rooms and get ready for bed,' Molly said, as she walked towards the doors.

Charlotte took one last look at the flying arena and wondered what it would be like to soar around it on her very own broomstick, before following the group back into the castle.

Back in their room they were excitedly discussing the tour, and how they couldn't wait for flying lessons and how they'd help each other out when doing laundry. Charlotte and Gerty knew better than to mention Stef being turned upside-down or Alice being turned into a mouse, and instead they tried to keep the conversation bright.

'This can't be correct,' Alice shouted from the bathroom. 'Why is there only one? I can't be expected to share a bathroom, I need my own.'

'Seriously, at home I have to share a bathroom with my two older brothers, my little sister and my parents so I don't know what you're whining about,' Stef said.

'I shouldn't be expected to share a bathroom with common girls.'

Stef looked at Charlotte and Gerty and winked and they smiled back before Stef grabbed Alice, followed by the others, who lifted her up into the bathtub.

'Let me go this instance,' Alice squealed out, as she swatted her hands against them.

Stef turned the cold tap on, soaking Alice.

'It's okay Alice, we're at your service,' she giggled.

'You wait till my parents here about this,' she grunted.

'Would you like some more water madam,' Stef laughed.

'No I would not,' Alice snapped, before she splashed at them.

73

Soon they were all laughing, even Alice.

'This bathroom's pretty big,' Stef looked around her. 'We could all use it at the same time if we wanted too,' she grinned.

'There is no chance of us doing that,' Alice said and Stef laughed.

They all dried themselves off and got ready for bed. When Stef turned the bedroom light off she had to stumble her way over to her bed, all the while moaning about the need for a wand so she could turn the light off magically.

Charlotte pulled the covers up to her face and closed her eyes. That's when she heard sniffling sounds and a smothered cry. She crept out of bed and tried to navigate herself over to where the sounds were coming from…Gerty's bed.

'Are you okay?' she whispered, as she gently pulled the covers off Gerty's face.

'Yes,' she sobbed. 'I'm just missing my mom and dad.'

'Come over to my bed and have a cuddle,' Charlotte said, and Gerty nodded before she followed Charlotte and got under the covers.

A few minutes later Gerty was asleep and breathing softly, so Charlotte quietly got out of her bed and tip-toed over to Gerty's.

She thought about the day she'd had. It had been an intense one, but it had opened her eyes to a whole new world, one that brought with it much excitement. She was eager to start lessons and learn more about this Academy. But most of all she was glad that she'd made new friends, even Alice with her annoying snobbish ways. She liked all her roommates and she liked it here.

Her last thought before she fell asleep was that it was going to be all right in this place. She was a witch and this was where she felt she belonged.

Chapter Seven

There was a loud hooting sound and at first Charlotte pulled the covers over her head and carried on dreaming. The hooting continued and realization of where she was became apparent. She kicked the covers off and rubbed her eyes, before pulling herself up in bed and seeing a brown owl perched on the window ledge, it's head cocked in her direction.

'An owl as an alarm, I've never heard of anything so stupid,' Alice said, as she pulled her fingers through her knotty hair.

'Fitness training in thirty-minutes,' the owl hooted, as it moved from one leg to the other.

'What about breakfast?' Stef asked.

'Fitness training first. Breakfast will be served after that. Head for the grassy area through the common room in thirty-minutes.' The owl hooted once more before flying off out the window.

'Wait, come back,' Alice jumped out of bed and rushed over to the open window, peering out at the clear sky. 'This is an outrage, I am here to learn witch skills, not to win a triathlon.'

'I like sport,' Gerty said, as she scrummaged through one of the drawers under her bed and pulled out her jogging pants. 'I play tennis with my dad sometimes,' her face suddenly fell. 'Oh no, you don't think this fitness lesson will involve bumblebees as balls do you?'

'Only one way to find out,' Stef grinned, noticing that Alice had moved towards the bathroom. She raced forwards and barged past her, locking the bathroom door behind her.

'I will be sure to report you for this,' Alice bashed on the door.

Charlotte tried to hide her smile by looking down into one of her drawers. She contemplated what to wear, deciding on a plain grey t-shirt and a pair of black shorts.

'I'm sure it'll be fine Gerty,' she said.

'I hope there's a giant bee, bigger than this room and it stings Stef on her bottom,' Alice grunted.

'I heard that,' Stef opened the door. 'Anyway, the bathroom's free,' she smirked.

'At home every bedroom has a large en-suite and my bath is bigger than this entire bathroom.'

'Well, us common folk are used to sharing,' Stef grinned.

Alice huffed, before she stepped into the enclosure.

Charlotte was curious about what the fitness lesson would be like, she was curious about everything that came with this Academy. This whole world was new to her but at the same time it was more exciting than she could ever have imagined.

After everyone had used the bathroom, she grabbed a black zip-up jacket, and followed the others out the door and down the hallway, turning to see that Alice who was wearing an expensive looking velour tracksuit, was hurrying along behind them.

They walked through the common room and out onto the large grassy area where a group of first years were standing around a slight woman in a plain dark leotard. She was standing perfectly balanced on one leg, her long light brown hair covering most of her face, her oak broomstick laid out in front of her.

Margaret and Demi stood at the far side and sniggered when they saw Charlotte and the others join the group. Charlotte looked away from them and focused on the large object situated behind the teacher, which was a very realistic model of a fierce looking dragon.

'I hope it doesn't breathe fire like the other one did,' Stef whispered.

Charlotte was about to say that of course it would not because it wasn't real, but then she saw it move its tail. She jolted back which caused Margaret and Demi to snigger once again.

The last of the students arrived and the teacher beckoned them forwards.

'Come on girls,' her tone assertive.

They hurried forwards and joined the row of students. There were curious looks in the direction of the dragon but no one seemed excited at the prospect of a fitness lesson, especially not Alice who was standing with her arms folded and a miserable expression on her face.

'Welcome to your first fitness lesson, I am Miss Dread and I am your fitness teacher here at the Academy. I can see by the looks on some of your faces that fitness may not be your favorite activity but that will change,' she looked at Alice. 'One day you will be in a situation where your fitness will need to kick in when your luck runs out.'

Stef stood on the tips of her toes as she rose her arm into the air.

'Yes darling?' Miss Dread asked, as she looked towards her.

'Then couldn't we just use magic?' she asked.

'Not always. Say for instance your wand broke or you were drastically outnumbered, it's always best to be prepared and being physically fit is important for all witches.'

Charlotte glanced at Alice and hoped that her own face did not look as opposed to fitness class as Alice's face did. Charlotte had always been average when it came to sport and worried if "average" would suffice with Miss Dread. She found herself hoping that their teacher was not as severe as her name suggested.

Finally bringing her leg down from her flamingo pose, Miss Dread gestured them to follow her over to the dragon.

All the girls made sure there was a large space between them, and the fierce looking creature, which was staring at them with one eye opened.

'This is Dexter, the Academy's trampoline. Rest assured you won't hurt him and he won't hurt you.'

'We can't be expected to bounce on that,' Alice said.

'It is very easy and rather fun. Here, I shall show you, she climbed up the stepladder positioned by the dragon and began to jump in the middle of the belly area. 'If you feel yourself falling off don't panic as he will catch you with his tail, tongue or claws and safely put you back onto his belly.'

She purposely jumped forwards so it looked like she was going to fall in a heap on the ground but before she could Dexter flicked out his long pink tongue and tossed her safely back up.

Miss Dread stopped bouncing and climbed down the steps, her hair falling perfectly back into place.

'Who's next?' she asked and most of the girls took a step backwards and proceeded to stare at the ground.

'Miss, I will,' Margaret stepped forward.

'Bravo darling,' she took Margaret's arm and led her over to the stepladder. 'Please refrain from bouncing on this end of Dexter,' she pointed to the lower part of his belly.

'Why?' Margaret asked, as she confidently climbed the ladder and stepped onto the center area.

'Just follow my instructions,' said Miss Dread.

Margaret didn't hesitate in jumping as high as she could but it wasn't long before curiosity took hold and she began to jump on the southern part of the dragon's belly. Before Miss Dread had time to warn Margaret to move, Dexter let out a huge fart that caused all the other girls to laugh and swat the air in front of them as they covered their faces with their hands and sleeves. Margaret propelled high into the air and out of the dragon's grasp.

Miss Dread grabbed her broomstick and flew over to Margaret, catching her before she fell and pulling her onto the back of the broom behind her.

'What did I tell you about following the rules?' Miss Dread asked sternly, as she landed the broomstick and glared at Margaret.

'S-sorry,' Margaret muttered sheepishly, the usual smug look disappearing from her face.

'Don't do it again or you'll be in Miss Moffat's office before you can say beetle bubble broth. That goes to all of you,' she looked over at the rest of the girls. 'Right, who's next?'

Alice immediately put her hands to her stomach and feigned a pained look.

'You,' Miss Dread pointed at her.

'I have a stomach ache, I think I need to go back to my room,' Alice cried.

'Nonsense, come on, I'll help you up,' she held her hand out to Alice.

'I really don't feel well,' she stared at Miss Dread's hand, not taking it.

'Nonsense,' Miss Dread grabbed Alice's hand and led her over to the dragon, stopping by the stepladder. She bent over and whispered to Alice, 'I know that you're scared. Trust yourself; I know you can do this.'

Alice nodded but didn't move. Miss Dread stepped in front of her and walked up the ladder. 'Follow me,' she held out her hand, which Alice promptly took, and they both stepped onto the dragon's belly together.

Leading Alice towards the center of Dexter's belly, Miss Dread grasped both her hands and they jumped, gradually going higher and higher until Alice's shrieks turned into giggles and her frown turned into a smile.

'Darling, I knew you could do it,' she gave Alice a congratulatory grin, as she helped her down off the ladder. 'Now my darlings, who is next?' Miss Dread looked warmly at the girls.

All the girls had a turn and they were all forced to admit that it was the funniest and most enjoyable fitness lesson they had ever had.

A few days earlier, Charlotte would never have believed that using a dragon's belly as a trampoline was possible, but now she knew differently. This Academy had opened a door into a new world, one where anything seemed possible, and Charlotte was excited to see what would happen next.

'Darlings, darlings, fantastic, you were all fantastic!' Miss Dread pulled out her wand and made a gold medallion with a long white ribbon appear. 'I give medals out to those I feel deserve them the most and today I have a certain girl in mind,' she looked directly at Alice. 'You darling, you have shown us all that it's okay to be scared and that overlooking fear is a triumph that should be awarded.' She held the medal out to her.

Alice was unable to hide her smile as she stepped forwards and took the medal. She pulled the ribbon over her head and held the medal up so she could study it.

'Thank you girls, you're free to go. I'll see you tomorrow morning bright and early for your next fitness lesson.'

All the girls dispersed and headed back to their rooms.

'This medal suits me, don't you think!' Alice exclaimed, after they had walked into their room.

'You deserved it,' Charlotte smiled.

'You were really brave Alice,' Gerty said, as she fell back onto her bed. 'I've never bounced on a dragon before, it was definitely better than the bouncy castle I had for my seventh birthday. It got a puncture and the whole thing collapsed inwards on us all.'

'I'm sure that I'll get plenty more medals.' Alice took the medal off and laid it out proudly on her bed. 'I'm leaving it here because I don't want it to get damaged.'

'And because we have class after breakfast and the teacher might be distracted by its shininess,' Stef grinned.

'I wonder what we'll do in fitness tomorrow?'

'Dunno,' Gerty shrugged.

'I can't wait, I'm sure whatever it is, it'll be the best lesson by far,' Alice said cheerily.

'It's intriguing how you only have to give a girl a medallion and she does a total back-flip,' Stef smirked.

'You're just jealous because you didn't get one,' Alice replied.

'Yeah,' she snorted, as she searched through her drawer and pulled out her uniform.

'My mother says we should pity those who are jealous of us because it's not their fault they were born less fortunate than ourselves.'

'You just wait until I have my wand, then the next time you make a comment like that one, I will turn you into a slug,' Stef sounded serious.

'You would get expelled for doing that,' Alice could not hide her worried look.

'It'd be worth it,' Stef grinned.

Charlotte looked down at the uniform she had laid out on her bed. It consisted of a black pleated skirt, a white blouse and a black, green trimmed cardigan with a crest that included the letters MMA written above two crossing broomsticks. It was the nicest uniform that she had ever owned and she was eager to put it on.

They all changed their clothes as they chatted about the fitness lesson and the Academy, at the same time, wondering what they'd be given for breakfast.

The bell rang to signal that the meal was ready, and they left their room dressed in their new uniforms, with excited smiles on their faces and as they headed down the hallway.

Chapter Eight

The girls walked over to the same table that they had sat at for dinner the night before and stared confused at the three flowerless plants that were set out centrally along the middle of the table.

'Do they seriously expect us to eat that?' Alice said snobbishly.

Charlotte could not hide her smile at the thought of Alice eating a plant. She looked over at Margaret and Demi who were sitting where they had last time. There was a group of older girls at the end of the table but the spaces next to Margaret and Demi remained empty.

All the staff including Miss Moffat were already sitting at the top table, each of them with the strange plants in front of them as well. The bats flew through the windows holding bowls and placing them down in front of the teachers, then more bats came in and placed bowls down in front of each of the girls. The bats flew off and soon reappeared, dropping pieces of corn into each dish.

'How can they call this a breakfast?' Stef asked.

'There's no way that I'm eating that,' Alice added.

Charlotte looked curiously down into her bowl and that was when the corn began to pop up into her face. All the girls squealed with delight and Gerty in particular, was so surprised that she almost knocked her bowl over.

The bats flew above them with jugs full of milk while the girls shrieked loudly and covered their heads with their arms as the bats tipped the jugs. The milk flowed into their bowls like water from a tap, none of it spilling. The plants in front of them began to shake, as fresh strawberries, raspberries and blueberries grew on each.

Everyone reached out excitedly and ripped off the fruit, placing it on top of their cereal. Stef and Alice both picked up their spoons and began to eat. The room filled with clanging sounds as the spoons hit the porcelain bowls, echoing across the hall.

'Ahem,' Miss Moffat said, as she rose up from her dragon chair, her eyes fixed firmly on Stef and Alice before she led the rest of the girls into saying the witches' creed.

'Witches old and witches young
owls and bats and black cats too.
Come together in this castle
to bring out the best in you.

With perfect love and perfect trust
we learn the spells and witches' rules.
Acting for the good of all
now let's eat in this great hall.'

All eyes were on Stef and Alice who had finally realized what was going on. Both girls tried to quietly put their spoons down and swallow their food as quickly as possible.

Stef began to choke and attempted to stifle the sound, reaching out for a sip of pineapple juice, the golden liquid that had magically appeared in each of the goblets. She tried to take a sip but had begun choking so much that she couldn't manage to drink any, and her face turned into a light shade of purple.

'Open your mouth,' Molly said, as she appeared by Stef's side.

Stef opened it the best she could as Molly called over a bat, and with a wave of her wand she caused it to shrink until it was the size of a small coin. Stef looked on in horror as it flew into her mouth and down her throat, appearing a few seconds later gripping the stuck piece of cereal.

The rest of the girls cheered and Stef looked sheepish, annoyed with herself for causing drama again and bringing negative attention to herself.

'Are you okay?' Charlotte whispered to her and Stef nodded back.

Breakfast was by far the tastiest one that Charlotte had ever had. She'd never tasted fruit as delicious before and looked on in awe as the goblets continued to refill with pineapple juice.

When the meal was finished and the staff departed, Molly, whose hair was in a side braid, addressed the girls.

'I'd like all the new girls to stay behind please, so I can take you to get kitted out with wands and broomsticks.'

Each girl smiled excitedly at the mention of the equipment they'd all be receiving. They knew that once they were in possession of such magical items, they would be well on their way to becoming experienced witches.

Following Molly into a section of the castle that they hadn't previously seen, they passed classrooms where bubbling sounds and explosions came from within. All the doors were shut so the interior of each room was hidden, which only made them all the more curious.
'What's happening in there?' Margaret asked.

'I don't know, maybe someone messed up their potion or something. Standard class antics really,' Molly grinned.

They headed along a quiet corridor until Molly paused by a lone door and chanted some spells, while giving a wave of her wand. The door clicked open and she gestured for them all to follow her. On entry they found a dim-lit, low-ceilinged room, with grey stoned walls and row-upon-row of boxed up wands.

'You must pick the right wand for your potential powers. If the wrong one is sought it will ensure that you cannot claim it,' Molly explained.

Charlotte wondered how they were supposed to find the right wand when each one was packaged and out of sight, but Molly simply smirked at the girls bewildered expressions. Then, with a flick of her own wand, dozens of wands burst from their boxes and floated in the room around them.

'When you've found the right one it will light up in your hand.' Molly gestured for the girls to go ahead.

Each of the girls went wild, chuckling as they chased after a wand. Demi was the first to find hers and Molly gave her an impressed look that caused Margaret to scowl.

Stef was trying to catch a long black and gold trimmed wand but it kept shooting out of her reach. Gerty was trying to grasp for any wand that she could, giggling when each one shot away from her.

Charlotte did not attempt to take any of the wands; she concentrated on studying them, wondering which one would accept her. Her eyes then fell upon a plain oak wand that was floating alongside her. No else seemed interested in it but Charlotte stood on tiptoes and reached out for it, half expecting it to fly away. Instead, however, it remained in place. Her hand firmly gripped it and immediately it glowed. She studied it carefully, noticing that close up it had orange patterns intricately carved into the wood; it wasn't plain at all.

'Great, we have two more,' Molly said, as she looked from Charlotte to Margaret who was also holding a glowing wand.

Realizing that Charlotte had found hers at around the same time, Margaret gave her a stern look then walked over and stood next to Demi.

Gerty was the next to find her wand, followed by Stef. Last up was Alice who was still chasing an elegant looking silver wand even though it kept whizzing away from her.

'That wand clearly does not want you!' Margaret exclaimed, and Demi and a few of the other girls giggled.

'Alice, some wands just aren't right for the person, regardless of their appearance,' Molly continued.

Begrudgingly Alice stopped chasing the silver wand and reached out for the one that was closest, a straight mahogany one. It glowed as she touched it and her face lit with a huge smile.

'Right then, that's your wands sorted. It is of the greatest importance that you look after your wand. Never misplace it or put it in a situation where it may break. A wand is a witch's most important item and each of you must remember that. Also it should go without saying that you are not to use these to perform harmful or distressing spells on each other, unless you want to face your first warning or worse, be expelled.'

Charlotte looked down at the wand in her hand. It had stopped glowing and this made its intricate patterning appear more discreet.

She found herself wondering how something so small could be so powerful. Her mom must have had a wand at some point and she wondered if she still had it, hidden away somewhere so that her dad would never find it.

'Next up are broomsticks,' Molly led them to the back of the room where there was an arched door. She waved her wand to unlock the door and the girls followed Molly inside. Like the other room, it had grey stoned walls but this one was slightly larger and its ceilings much higher. There were hundreds of broomsticks whizzing around and Stef only just ducked her head in time as one flew directly towards her.

'Broomsticks also have the power to reject you, so beware,' Molly said. As she gestured for them to find their broomstick.

Margaret instantly reached out and grabbed one but it wriggled free of her grip and slapped her in the face before flying over to Stef, who grinned at Margaret as she gripped hold of it. Margaret scowled before looking around for another one.

A pale oak broom with flecks of green on the handle flew over to Charlotte and floated in front of her until she grabbed hold of it. Smiling widely, she held tightly onto it, feeling more and more like a witch. The broomsticks were easier to find than the wands, as they were more willing to track their owner. A plain brown broomstick floated over to Alice and she took hold of it with a huge grin.

When all the girls each had a broomstick, Molly beckoned them into the next room where a hat for every girl floated overhead.

'Uniforms must be worn for all classes but hats and capes are only for formal occasions. Please remain still as your hats will find you,' Molly looked up at the hats and then instructed them firmly. 'Find your owner.'

All the hats swirled around before swooping down and landing on each of the girl's heads. They all let out excited gasps and squeals as they reached up and felt their hats.

'Nearly there,' Molly grinned, before she clapped her hands and the bats flew through the window. Each one carried a black cape and placed it gently on the girl's shoulders.

'You all look like little witches now but remember that you haven't been properly trained yet, so no using your wands or broomsticks until you've been taught how.'

As they followed Molly out of the room, Charlotte and Gerty smiled at each other and then looked excitedly at the wands and broomsticks that each was carrying.

Margaret and Demi hung back and were the last ones out of the room.

'This is ridiculous, I don't need lessons. I've been using a wand and flying for as long as I can remember,' she whispered to Demi, before double-checking that Molly couldn't hear her. 'Those rules are clearly for the other girls, not for us,' she smirked.

Margaret flicked her hair behind her back and straightened her hat before she followed Molly and the others along the corridors. She briefly looked down at her wand and broomstick and gave a sly smile.

Chapter Nine

They all had enough time to go back to their rooms and put away their new capes, hats and broomsticks before their first lesson.

'Where do you think we should put them, they might become creased in our drawers?' Stef asked, as she held out her cape and hat and looked around the room.

The wardrobe doors flung open and all the girls immediately jumped back, worried that they'd be sucked into it.

'Who opened that?' Alice asked, as she stared at Stef.

'Don't look at me,' Stef said, 'I was nowhere near it. '

'You could have opened it with magic,' she gestured to the wand in Stef's hand.

'Well I didn't,' she stared at the wardrobe. 'Have you all noticed how it isn't trying to suck anything in?'

The wardrobe shook and all the girl's capes, hats and broomsticks flew up into the air, whizzing towards it. Gerty's hat whipped into the air, directly from her head and Stef tried to grab onto her cape as it flew forwards. Every item disappeared into the wardrobe and it slammed its doors shut.

'Was that meant to happen?' Charlotte asked.

'I hope so. If not, we're all in trouble,' Stef replied.
'How will I be in trouble, I didn't do anything? Alice said.

'Let's worry about it later,' Stef shrugged.

Charlotte nodded, although she found herself worrying that she may never see her hat and cape again and thought of the trouble she would be in if that were the case.

'Are you girl's ready for your first lesson?' Sonya asked, as she and Silvia appeared in the doorway. 'Quickly grab your wands out of the magical wardrobe.'

The girls hesitated, unsure of the wardrobe and its mysterious powers. Silvia laughed and told the girls not to worry. 'Just make sure you only put your magical gear inside that wardrobe, you don't want to insult it with things from the ordinary world.'

They all nodded and tentatively grabbed their wands before joining the other new girls who were waiting in the corridor. They followed Sonya and Silvia and waited as they collected the rest of the girls and then led them all to their lesson.

Charlotte thought about what the lesson would involve and what the teacher would be like. The fitness lesson had been both exciting and terrifying and Charlotte wondered if all the lessons would be like that one.

Sonya and Silvia stopped outside of a classroom, the words 'Brewing Room' written on the door in black font.

'This will be your first lesson with Miss Maker,' Sonya explained. 'Lunch will be after this. Remember, if any of you get lost, call for the bats.

The two prefects stood aside and gestured for the girls to step through the doorway. Margaret and Demi pushed past the others and barged into the room first. They sat in the back row and sniggered at the other girls as they headed towards the remaining seats.

'Hello girls, come in, come in and find a spot,' an attractive young woman in a black corset and cape said. Her dark hair was tinged purple and she wore her witch's hat slightly wonky on her head.

Charlotte followed Gerty and Stef over to free seats in one of the middle rows and Alice sat down next to her. There was a small, black cauldron placed down in front of each of the seats.

'Hello girls and welcome to your first brewing lesson. I am Miss Maker, the Mistress of Brewing. I always get excited when new girls start here, as I love teaching fresh minds who are so enthralled to be here,' she smiled, as she looked around at all the girls.

'I will tell you a bit about me, I have been working here at the Academy for the past seventy-five-years, teaching young witches like yourselves how to brew potions.'

'She doesn't look that old,' Gerty whispered to Charlotte.

Miss Maker's eyes fell upon Gerty and she smiled.

Gerty looked startled, not understanding how Miss Maker
had heard her. She wanted to tell the others that she must
have bionic hearing but she knew better than to say
this…until they were out of the classroom.

'Beauty is skin deep, real beauty comes from within,' she said.

'So does that mean that if we are beautiful witches inside, then we will grow up to look as pretty as you?' Alice chimed in.

Miss Maker let out a gentle laugh as she looked over at Alice.

The ordinaries have their ways but of course, they aren't as effective as ours. They have their creams and lotions and their Botox and surgeries. As a witch we don't need these painful youth makers, we can simply brew potion.'

Gerty exchanged an impressed look with the others. The thought of being as beautiful as Miss Maker for her whole life was an exciting one and she couldn't wait until she was older and had mastered the youth spell.

'So you're saying that we'll be able to stay beautiful for hundreds of years?' Demi asked.

'Well Demi, remember that I said beauty comes from within to begin with. The potion will retain your appearance…BUT if goodness is absent from your soul and heart then there is no potion that is strong enough to save you from ageing into an old hag. Perhaps you need to carefully consider this,' she gave Demi a gentle smile.

Demi looked shocked and diverted her gaze down at her table. All the girls smirked including Margaret, who didn't even try to hide this from her friend.

'Some witchcraft is bad and you should never practice it, not ever. We don't teach those spells at the Academy, they are banned and for good reason. You are here to become strong, independent and capable witches and I am here to teach you how to use your powers for good.'

When you are in your senior year, I will teach you about some of these dark spells, not so you can carry them out, but so that you can try to stop them and reverse them. They are too powerful for you girls to know about. This is why you must NEVER go into the restricted area in the library, at least not until your senior year, and only then with the Mistress of the Books assisting you.'

'Miss, my mother attended this school and she told me about the door at the end of library with the dragon handle,' Margaret quipped.

'You are prohibited from going anywhere near that door, it is totally off limits and protected by a strong spell,' she glared at Margaret, her tone suddenly very icy.

'What is behind that door, Miss?' Alice asked the question they were all thinking but than none of the others dared to ask.

'I am often asked this question by new girls,' she sighed, a concerned look on her face. 'I understand your curiosity but I shall tell you this only once. Hundreds of years ago, when the Academy first started, a witch called Dragina lived here. She was beautiful with long white hair and skin like silk.

Dragina was obsessed with dragons, they were all she liked to talk about and her free time involved ongoing research. She travelled the world looking for dragon eggs, eventually finding some and bringing them back to the Academy.' Miss Maker held onto the table in front of her, a fearful expression on her face.

'It is a long story and not one that I want to go into but the dragons grew very large and caused mayhem. Miss Moffat, being the powerful witch that she is, thankfully brought the situation under control. The secrets to this terrible time are forever locked away in that room and that is why you must NEVER go near it.'

The girls exchanged shocked glances between each other. Charlotte wondered about the mysterious door, and was curious to know what lay beyond it.

Miss Maker shook her head and instantly the dark mood that had covered the room dispelled.

'Today we are going to brew a potion to make you stronger,' she smiled, as she leaned in closer to them. 'Now, you must pay careful attention to my demonstration as you don't want to be too strong,' she chuckled.

'Right, let's begin. You'll find all the ingredients you need laid out in front of you and I shall guide you through what to do.'

Charlotte looked down at the neatly laid out items, not knowing what half of them were. She was overwhelmed and hoped that she wouldn't mess it up.

'Firstly take a pinch of agarwood,' she picked up a small glass bowl that had what looked like shredded wood in it and she took out a pinch and added it to her cauldron. 'Two bay leaves, three hawthorn berries, which I agree are delicious but are also a very useful ingredient for potions.'

Charlotte looked from Miss Maker to Stef and then Gerty to check that she was doing it right, before she dropped the berries into her cauldron.'
'Half a long pepper and lastly a teaspoon of troll fat.'

'Yuck,' Stef said, as she looked down at the small bowl of fat.

'Yes, it is a bit gross but it's very effective,' Miss Maker said, as she walked over to the front row and paused by a cauldron that belonged to a girl with red hair. 'That looks fantastic, Patricia.'

'How does she know all our names?' Gerty whispered to Charlotte, forgetting that Miss Maker could hear them.

'Gerty, Charlotte, how are you getting on?' she smiled over at them.

'Erm, okay,' Gerty muttered quietly.

Yeah, okay I think,' Charlotte added.

'Great!' Miss Maker walked back to the front of the room. 'Now take your spoons and place them into the cauldron, careful not to splash any of the potion. Turn it in a clockwise direction twenty times, like this,' she began to turn her spoon, counting the turns aloud. 'When you've done that, carefully remove your spoon.'

'Now take your wand out and say 'strength potion make me strong,' then add one cup of cranberry juice and stir another ten times in a clockwise direction. Pour a glass and drink up girls. This spell will only last for three hours and then your body's strength will return to normal.'

Stef was the first to drink her potion, followed by Margaret and then Demi. Charlotte and Gerty exchanged looks before they picked up their glasses and drank the liquid.

Charlotte looked down to see her arms begin to bulk up under her cardigan, until large muscles were visible.

'Look, look,' Gerty lifted her blouse up, revealing a six-pack of muscles on her tummy.

'Woah,' Charlotte said, as she looked down at her own stomach and legs and saw that they were changing too.

'My thighs are huge,' Alice said disgustedly, clutching a hold of her muscled leg.

'I feel so strong,' Gerty giggled, as she reached out and lifted Charlotte up with one hand and balanced her above her head, spinning her around like a spinning top.

'I feel weaker Miss Maker, what's happening?' Stef asked, as she stumbled and gripped onto the table for support before looking down at herself. Her arms and legs had become much smaller and she looked skinny and haggard.

There were gasps at Stef's appearance as the other girls gathered around her.

'Can you show me what direction is clockwise?' Miss Maker passed Stef a spoon.

Stef nodded as she put the spoon into the cauldron and stirred to her left.

'Oh dear,' Miss Maker shook her head. 'That is anti-clockwise, you're lucky the spell is only for three hours.'

She led Stef over to the comfy chair that was behind her desk and then addressed the other girls.

'This is a perfect example of how careful you must be when brewing potions and a great lesson for us all. Now, we have tidying up to do. Please be careful when cleaning up the cauldrons and glasses, don't forget your new strength.'

'Have you seen Demi's muscles? They're huge!' a girl with black hair pointed to Demi's arms.

Demi had taken off her cardigan as her arms had almost torn through it, revealing muscles much larger than anyone else had.

'You look like the Hulk,' Alice giggled and the other girls laughed, including Margaret.

Demi burst into tears and snorted as she tried to wipe the tears away with her fingers.

Miss Maker walked over to her and felt her muscles.

'Did you add a little too much troll fat, Demi?' she asked, which caused the other girls to laugh even more.

'It's okay, you are all new here and mistakes are expected. You will all be back to your old selves in a couple of hours.'

After the girls had tidied their area, they sat back down in their seats, still excited at their first lesson as well as their super strength.

'Miss, when will we learn a beauty potion?' Gerty asked.

'It seems that I am always asked this question. Girls, you will soon go the ball with the boys from the Wizard's Academy. I'm sure many of you already know that their Academy resides across the mountain range.' The girls began to giggle at the mention of boys. 'I am sure that you'll all want to look your best for that. And young Stef and Demi, I'm sure that you two will follow my instructions carefully for that potion.'

Both Stef and Demi looked sheepish and all the other girls glanced from one of them to the other.

'Off with you now, back to your dorms,' Miss Maker instructed. Smiling as she pretended to shoo them with her hands.

'I wonder what the boys will be like,' Gerty said, after they'd left the classroom.

'Cute, hopefully,' Stef responded with a grin. She still looked frail but the potion was beginning to wear off.

'I hope they will be nice,' Charlotte added.

'And good looking,' Gerty giggled. 'What do you think we'll look like after we use the beauty potion?'

'I hope it gets rid of the frizz in my hair.' Charlotte grabbed hold of one of her curls and tugged on it with disgust.

'Mine too,' Gerty agreed.

'And mine,' Stef added.

'I hope it dulls down my freckles,' Alice said hopefully.

'I can't wait,' Gerty said, the excitement bubbling through her veins.

'Me neither,' Stef replied.

'Or me,' Charlotte said smiling.

'Or me,' said Alice.

'Do you think there's a potion to make time hurry up?' Gerty asked, the curiosity filling her features.

'There might be,' Stef responded confidently. It seemed to her that there must be a potion for just about everything.

'Miss Maker said the ball was soon, so we shouldn't have to wait long,' Charlotte looked thoughtfully at the others, all the while imagining the excitement that lay ahead.

Deep in conversation, they walked back to their room, each girl in good spirits at the prospect of a school ball where there would be boys, music and possibly even dancing.

***

On hearing that their next lesson was flying, the girls had felt anxious about how to get their broomsticks out of the wardrobe without the prefects there to watch over them. To their surprise as soon as they had entered the room, the wardrobe spat their broomsticks out at them.

After lunch, Miss Firmfeather greeted her new students by whizzing around the flying arena on her broomstick.

They watched in awe as she did loop-the-loops and then stood-up and balanced on it.

'That was amazing,' Gerty said to the others, as she clung tightly onto her broomstick.

'Hello girls,' Miss Firmfeather smiled, as she balanced on her broom in front of them, her arms casually folded. 'I am Miss Firmfeather and I shall be teaching you how to fly your broomsticks. Flying has always been my favorite part of being a witch and I hope that it will be yours too.

'I see that you all have your brooms and I know that you'll be eager to get started but first I need to tell you the rules.' There were moans from some of the girls. 'Rules are important and must be carried out so that everyone remains safe. Firstly, there will be no flying unless I have instructed you to do so. If I tell you to stop flying, then you will do so immediately. If you fall off, don't panic as the ground is enchanted and you will bounce off it. I want you all to enjoy these lessons but also to take your flying lessons seriously. Controlling a broomstick may look easy but that only comes with plenty of practice.'

'Miss,' Margaret shot her hand into the air and Miss Firmfeather looked at her. 'I've been flying for years, so I think I may be too advanced for this class.'

'You will have to start at the beginning just like all the other girls,' Miss Firmfeather said, sitting down crossed-legged on her broomstick. 'Flying is the gateway to new experiences and to seeing the world. I've flown to faraway lands on my broomstick and have floated above places that ordinaries have only ever read about in books.'

'There is a correct way to fly a broomstick and a safe way and I shall teach you these,' she looked at all the girls, pausing for a moment longer at Margaret.

Standing with her broom in-between her legs, Miss Firmfeather's hands gripped the broomstick in front of her and she told the girls to copy her pose.

'Great, now lean slightly forwards and then take your feet off the ground.' Miss Firmfeather took her feet off the ground and hovered on the spot.

Margaret was the first to lift her feet, looking bored as she watched the other girls nervously take their feet from the ground and grip onto their broomstick tightly as they flew up into the air.

'That's great girls, now we're going to practice going up and down,' instructed Miss Firmfeather. She demonstrated flying up and then down in a swift movement.
Most of the girls seemed to master this fairly quickly, except for a petite girl called Fiona, who kept flying higher and higher and seemed unable to figure out how to fly down.

'Wait here and keep practicing girls,' Miss Firmfeather said, before she flew up to rescue Fiona.

Margaret waited until Miss Firmfeather had flown away before she stopped flying in an up and down direction, then swooped above the other girls.

'You're not supposed to be doing that,' Stef said, as she wobbled on her broom.

'I am far more advanced at flying than you babies, she took her hands off her broom as she flew at Stef, who half-ducked, half fell onto her broom, only just managing to hang on.

'I'd say come and catch me…but as if that's ever going to happen,' Margaret smirked.

Charlotte had never been on a broomstick before, yet she was managing to fly up and down with ease. At least that was until Margaret flew into her and caused her to tumble off her broomstick and onto the ground. Thankfully, though, she bounced off.

Margaret smirked again as she flew back over to Demi and went back to flying up and down. Charlotte's arm hurt from where Margaret had flown into her and she rubbed it as she picked up her broomstick.

'Tumbles are expected,' Miss Firmfeather said as she looked at Charlotte, one of her hands holding onto Fiona's broom as she guided her down. 'With practice and determination you'll soon master this skill,' she smiled.

Charlotte felt annoyed, she hadn't struggled with flying at all and she'd only fallen off because of Margaret. She wondered what the girl's problem was and if she would ever stop being so mean to everyone. Surely bullying was against the Academy's code of conduct.

At the end of the lesson, Miss Firmfeather flew into the air and waved at them, before she flicked out her wand and turned her broomstick into a huge rhinoceros, which she glided through the sky above the castle.

'I want to be able to do that,' Gerty said. 'Well maybe not a rhinoceros, I'd prefer a unicorn, with a shiny pink mane and a dazzling white horn.'

Charlotte nodded, thinking that all she wanted was to be able to fly without Margaret making things difficult for her.

Chapter Ten

It was the next morning and the girls were waiting outside for their fitness lesson. Alice had been going on and on about how good she was at fitness. But the others were more apprehensive about what Miss Dread might have in store for them.

When they arrived to find Miss Dread standing on her hands with her legs twisted around her head and a pile of hedgehogs to the side of her, they found themselves feeling even more concerned.

'Good morning darlings, today you shall be indulging in a game of hedgehog dodge ball,' Miss Dread said, before she untwisted herself and stood up on her feet.

'We're throwing those?' Stef pointed to the hedgehogs and Miss Dread nodded. 'But they're so prickly.'
'A little prickle won't hurt and I find that it makes you work far harder than if it was just a normal, boring ball like the ordinaries use.'

'What do you think about this, Alice?' Stef asked, expecting her to moan.

'I think it sounds like fun,' she replied, which caused Stef to roll her eyes.

'Right girls, we'll have two teams, you darling, can be one team captain,' she pointed at Charlotte. 'And you, darling, can be the other,' she pointed to Margaret.

'You can pick first,' she gestured to Margaret.

'Demi.'

'Erm, Gerty,' Charlotte said, hoping that she hadn't offended Stef or Alice by not choosing them first.

'Stef,' Margaret smirked.

'Not the toads!' Stef shouted, which caused Miss Dread to glare at her. Reluctantly she walked over and stood beside Margaret.

'Alice,' Charlotte indicated her friend.

'Melody,' Margaret said and a girl with chin length brown hair walked over and stood by her.

'Patricia.' Charlotte nodded.

They continued to choose until their teams were full and then they began the game.
'Begin on my clap and remember darlings, if you're hit then you're out. If one of the spikey little creatures is coming towards you, you must catch it,' Miss Dread said, before she clapped her hands together.

Margaret was the first to throw her hedgehog, hitting Patricia on the arm and causing her to squeal loudly. Charlotte picked up the hedgehog and threw it back at Margaret but she ducked and Demi caught it in her hands.

Charlotte managed to throw one at Stef, prickling her on her leg before she caught it. Another girl on the team threw one back but it scratched Charlotte's arm and then dropped to the ground. Charlotte was out of the game.

Alice seemed very good at dodging the hedgehogs but not so skilled at throwing them. Although she didn't complain, not once. Not even when Margaret finally managed to hit her on her side.

Stef seemed super competitive, regardless of whose team she was on, and she chucked a hedgehog at Gerty, which prickled her on her bottom.

'Ow, ow, ow,' Gerty squealed out, as she hobbled her way over to the sideline and stood next to Charlotte.

'Stef is ruthless when you get her in a team, I think you should have picked her first,' Gerty said.

'I'll remember that next time,' Charlotte grinned.

Margaret and Stef were the last girls left, so Margaret's team were declared the winners and Miss Dread handed them all a color changing sweet.

'That's it for now darlings, go and get ready for breakfast,' Miss Dread said, as she waved them all off.

'Sorry,' Stef said to Gerty, as she walked up alongside her.

'That's okay, although I never want to be on the opposite team as yours again.'

'Bleurgh,' she almost choked and Gerty looked at her oddly.

'The sweet changed to blackcurrant flavor, yuck. It's okay, because now it's changed to strawberry.'

'I hope it goes back to blackcurrant,' Gerty grinned.

'Sore loser,' Stef chuckled, emphasizing the word - *sore*.

***

After breakfast, Molly escorted them to their next lesson and they entered the classroom to see a stunningly beautiful woman with chestnut hair pinned elegantly back.

They all took their seats (which Gerty found difficult, thanks to Stef and the hedgehog) and looked at the woman in awe.

'She's like a fairy princess,' Gerty whispered to Charlotte.

When all the girls had taken their seats, the woman gently rose to her feet and studied each of them.

'I am Miss Scarlet, the teacher of spells. I'm sure that the majority of you have heard about the *Book of Spells*. This book contains most of the spells that exist, everything from basic spells such as lifting an object to the more advanced ones such as changing an object's appearance. During your time at the Academy we will work through this book and teach you many spells,' she was well spoken, her tone refined.

'Miss,' Stef shot her hand up and Miss Scarlet looked at her. 'Is the *Book of Spells* kept at this school?'
'Where or where not it lays, is not of importance to you. The spells that you will be studying are in the text book you will find in front of you,' she picked up a leather bound book.

'We will be doing a spell today but first I must warn you, spell making isn't an exact science and things can go wrong. You must take my classes seriously and with the utmost respect. I know that young witches like to experiment, but you must remember the Academy's code of conduct at all times.'

'Please can you all turn to page four in your books,' she opened her textbook and held it up for them to see. 'Today you are going to learn how to use your wands with a simple throw and return spell. Your partner will be the girl closest to you,' Stef turned to look at Gerty and Charlotte to Alice.

'One of you will say 'cup go' as you throw a cup at your partner,' she held up a glass cup. 'The other will flick their wand out in front of them, like this,' she tightly held onto her wand as she gave it a stern flick in front of her. 'Whilst you are doing this, you need to focus on how you want the cup to stop. View your wand as a barricade that's there to protect you.'

'You,' she pointed at a worried looking girl in the front row. 'Please throw your cup at me whilst saying 'cup go.''

The girl nodded, she stood up and said the words 'cup go,' as the cup flew towards the teacher.

Miss Scarlet flicked her wand out swiftly in front of her and the cup stopped abruptly and fell to the ground, where it bounced off the hard floor and flew back to the thrower. 'That's how it's done. Now it's your turn. Remember what I said about focusing on your wand. The strongest witches are those who successfully know how to channel their wands. You must think of your wand as an extension of your mind and body.'

Alice shrieked as a cup hit her head but on her third attempt, she managed to stop the cup in front of her, a huge smile on her face.

Stef and Gerty were struggling and neither of them could seem to master this spell. Miss Scarlett went over to them and demonstrated how they needed to flick out their wand.

Charlotte glanced at Margaret, who had stopped the cup every time. She looked bored. Seeing that Miss Scarlet was distracted with Gerty and Stef, Margaret used her wand to fill her cup with dragon's wee.

'Empty yourself over Charlotte's head,' Margaret said to the cup, smirking as she watched it whiz across the room, stop over Charlotte's head and then soak her in the foul yellow liquid.

Charlotte shrieked out and watched as the cup flew back to Margaret who stood there smirking.

'Oops,' she feigned an apologetic look.

'What is going on?' Miss Scarlet asked sternly.

'It was an accident,' Margaret replied innocently.

'You can escort Charlotte back to her room so that she can change her clothes.'

'It was only a bit of liquid, it's not like it has hurt her. Besides, I want to be here for the lesson.'
'This is not up for discussion and may I suggest that you use this time to think about your behavior as I can assure you that I shall not tolerate disobedience,' Miss Scarlet glared, the annoyance evident on her face.

Charlotte and Margaret did not say a word to each other as they walked towards Charlotte's room. Charlotte was upset as she was just getting the hang of the cup spell and now she had to waste the lesson time. She was there to learn, not fall victim to Margaret's bullying games. She found herself worried that Margaret would always try to ruin things for her, and result in her falling behind in her lessons.

After changing out of her wet smelly clothes and taking a quick shower, Charlotte left her room to see that Margaret was still standing outside, her arms folded. She immediately began to walk off and Charlotte followed her.

As they passed the library, Margaret unfolded her arms and forced a smile.

'Can we stop here for a bit? There's a book I want to find out about.'

Charlotte nodded, she wanted to get back to class and thought that Margaret could look for this book afterwards, but she also did not want to get on the wrong side of her. As they walked nearer to the entrance, Margaret stopped and turned to Charlotte.

'I need to be able to trust you with a secret,' Margaret said and Charlotte nodded. 'In this library is a very powerful and special book called *Salem Secrets* and it contains spells that very few witches know about. My mother told me about it and I just know that I need to find it and read it. Promise me that you won't tell anyone Charlotte, you want to be my friend don't you? You have to help me because if you tell anyone, then we'll be enemies forever.'

'I guess I could help you,' Charlotte said reluctantly, feeling trapped and nervous.

'Great,' Margaret grinned. 'You can distract Mistress of the Books whilst I find it.'

Charlotte had a bad feeling but knew that if she didn't go along with Margaret then the rift between them would only grow worse.

After seeing that the Mistress of the Books was sitting behind her desk reading a book, Charlotte walked over to her, trying to calm herself as she stopped in front of the desk and coughed to clear her throat.

'Ex-excuse me,' she squeaked and the Mistress of the Books looked up.

'I was wondering if you could help me, you see my dad is an ordinary and I have no idea on even the most basic skills of witchcraft.'

The Mistress of the Books looked impressed at Charlotte's diligence and desire to learn. Standing, she walked around the desk and smiled.

'Of course, follow me,' she led Charlotte over to the beginners' section of the library and pulled out a book.

'*Newbies Guide to Witchcraft* by Gloria Arlington,' the book boomed.

'Now this book has everything you need to get you started. It also explains magic to you in a non-confusing way and I highly recommend it,' she held it out to Charlotte. 'Follow me, there are plenty more books I can find for you.'

Whilst this was happening Margaret entered the library and sneaked across the room before she crawled her way over to the restricted area. She grabbed a worn looking black leather book. '*The Darkest of Spirits* by Garrent Worthington,' it announced. She looked over her shoulder before she put it back and grabbed another one. '*Desiree's Dark Magic*, by Desiree Penelope Fancroft.'

Margaret felt frustrated, she didn't have much time and she couldn't find the book she was looking for. She held her wand out in front of her and looked at it.

'*Salem Secrets* come to me, quickly now so I can see.'

Flames appeared, engulfing a whole section of books in a heat of embers and scarlet flames.

Whilst the Mistress of the Books was pulling out a book, Charlotte looked over her shoulder to see the back of Margaret hurriedly leaving the library. She looked over to the restricted area and saw a shadow of smoke appearing. Rushing quickly over there, she was horrified to see that flames were burning some of the ancient books. She tried to put out the fire, wafting the flames with her hands...but this only seemed to make them worse.

The Mistress of the Books looked up and saw what was happening. Aiming her wand at the flames, she chanted a spell. The flames disappeared and the books appeared undamaged.

'You,' the Mistress of the Books glared at Charlotte accusingly.

'I didn't do it,' her voice was timid.

'To the head witchress' Office NOW!'

***

Charlotte had spent the last few hours stuck in a dark, windowless room. It contained a hard looking bed and an old wooden chair, which she sat on, hoping that she wouldn't be in there long enough to need use of the bed. Tapping her fingers against its frame, she wondered what would happen to her.

Charlotte knew that she'd been stupid, of course. Margaret would not have stayed around to take the blame. Now Charlotte was in serious trouble whilst Margaret was no doubt carrying on without a care for the mess she'd caused. Charlotte should have refused to distract the Mistress of the Books. Instead, she should have simply returned to class. She didn't need Margaret as a friend, she'd always known that, which made what she had done even more foolish.

If they expelled her for this, then what? Would she end up at Witchery College or would she have to go back to an ordinary school? She did not want to leave the Academy and her new friends, she liked it there and she wanted to stay. But she also didn't want to tell on Margaret.

The door creaked open and a woman wearing a smart black fitted suit appeared.

'Charlotte, Miss Moffat is ready to see you now,' she pressed her finger to the thin black framed glasses that were perched on the edge of her nose. Charlotte presumed that they were more for fashion than for practicality, as she'd seen no other staff member wearing glasses.
Charlotte nodded, before following her out of the room, blinking her eyes to adjust to the light. The woman led her over to Miss Moffat's office and held the door open for her, gesturing for her to step inside.

Miss Moffat sat in a large black leather armchair behind an extravagant looking mahogany desk.

Molly and the Mistress of the Books were sitting on a small couch at the far side of the room, and on a chair in front of the desk was Charlotte's mom.

'Charlotte, take a seat,' Miss Moffat gestured to the empty chair, and Charlotte moved towards the seat alongside her mother.

Her mom looked at her but Charlotte glanced away, feeling embarrassed. She could not look her mom in the eye and see how ashamed she was.

'It is important you know that lies will not be tolerated in my office,' Miss Moffat said sternly and Charlotte nodded. 'Now tell me, Charlotte, what happened?'

'Erm, I don't know,' Charlotte muttered.

Her nose instantly grew half an inch longer and Charlotte was horrified to find that when she glanced down, she could easily see the sudden extension.

'I'll ask again Charlotte. Remember, lies are unacceptable and will not be tolerated. So tell me. What happened?'

'I'm really not sure, Miss Moffat,' she said and her nose instantly grew longer.

'I will give you one more chance to tell the truth,' she leaned in closer to Charlotte, the anger alive in her eyes. 'If your nose grows again then you shall be expelled from my Academy.'

'Go on Charlotte, tell us what happened,' her mom encouraged, a pleading smile on her face.

Charlotte did not want to anger Margaret, but she also did not want to face expulsion. She had begun to love the Academy and she was desperate to stay.

'I think, no I'm pretty sure that Margaret did it.'

'Do you mean Margaret Montgomery?' Miss Moffat asked.

'Yes,' Charlotte lowered her head and her nose reduced by half.

'Why was she in the restricted area?' the Mistress of the Books jumped in, a concerned look on her face.

'Remember that you have no more chances,' Miss Moffat added.

'She was looking for a book in the restricted area,' she blushed and her nose returned to normal. She reached up and touched it, relieved that it had gone back to its regular size.

'And what was your involvement, Charlotte?' Molly asked.

'I was supposed to distract the Mistress of the Books whilst Margaret looked for the book.'

Mistress of the Books was standing there staring at Charlotte, holding one of the books from the reserved section. 'You mean to tell me that your story of being behind all the others in witchcraft, and wanting some extra help, wasn't true?' Her tone tasted of outrage. 'You were using me young lady and I'm very, very, very cross with you!' Immediately her hand erupted into a ball of flame.

'I'm so s-sorry,' Charlotte burst into tears, terrified. 'I shouldn't have done it, I'm really sorry.'

Miss Moffat used her wand to extinguish the flame in the librarian's hand. 'Why did you do it Charlotte?' It doesn't seem like you to deceive someone.'

'Margaret asked me to. She said that if I didn't, we'd always be enemies. I was scared of getting on her bad side. I find her intimidating and we are in every class together.'

Miss Moffat let out a sigh, before she turned to Molly.

'Please can you take Charlotte back to her room? She shall remain there for the rest of the day.'

Molly stood and waited by the door as Charlotte scraped her chair back and got to her feet. Her mom gave her an unhappy look but still pulled her into an embrace and kissed her on the top of her head.

'This is out of character for my daughter,' she tried to explain.

'Don't worry too much. It seems to me like a case of peer pressure. It seems as though she has learned a lesson the hard way.'

Charlotte's mom let go of her and she walked over to Molly, giving her mom one last apologetic glance and receiving a smile back, before she left the room.

***

For the rest of the day Charlotte lay face down on her bed and sobbed into her pillow. She pretended to be asleep when the other girls returned from their last class for the day. She didn't want to have to explain what had happened.

She thought that they'd be gossiping about it all, but instead she overheard them say between themselves that they hoped she was okay. Even Alice didn't have anything horrible to say, which made Charlotte quietly sob even more.
These girls were her true friends, not Margaret.

'Charlotte, I have a message for you,' an owl hooted, as it perched on the windowsill.

Charlotte rolled onto her side and pulled herself up into a sitting position, her legs hanging over her bed as she rubbed her sore, bloodshot eyes before looking towards the owl.

'You're allowed to leave the room for dinner.'

'It's okay, I don't feel much like eating.'

'You will want to come, there's a very special announcement that you won't want to miss.' It gave her one last look before it flew off.

'Come on Charlotte, you need to eat.' Gerty said, walking over to Charlotte and putting her arms around her.

'But everyone will be staring at me.'

'If they do, I'll turn them into a toad,' Stef grinned, pulling her wand out and pretending to cast a spell.

'Then you'd get into trouble,' Gerty giggled.

'Well, we'll protect you some other way, after all we are your best friends.'

At that moment, Stef could never have realized how those words had touched Charlotte's heart.

'Okay,' Charlotte gave a slight smile. 'I'll come.'

'Great, then let's get going, I'm hungry,' Alice responded, as she hurried towards the door.

'The bell hasn't rung yet,' Gerty said, but as soon as she'd finished speaking the bell began to ring.

'About time, we never had to wait like this at home,' Alice complained, before stepping out of the room, followed by everyone else.
When Charlotte entered the dining hall, some of the other girls were staring at her and gossiping. She looked at the ground and tried to block them out.

'They'll have something else to talk about soon,' Gerty said.

'Yeah, besides, they're more concerned with what has happened to Margaret,' Stef added.

'I heard she's been expelled,' Alice piped up.

'I heard they sent her to the bad witches' school,' Gerty said, excitedly.

'No, she's been turned into a toad and put into the school's lily pond,' Stef grinned, and Charlotte couldn't help but chuckle.

They took their seats in the grand hall and Charlotte looked over at where Demi was…sitting alone, depressed and vulnerable. Margaret was nowhere in sight. Her absence only making the gossip about Charlotte increase.

The room fell silent as Miss Moffat flew in on her broomstick. Instead of going over to her usual place on the platform, she stood in front of the top table and faced the students.

'I need to talk to you girls. Today, I am shocked and saddened to say that one of our new students, Margaret Montgomery broke our Code of Conduct in the worst possible way. I will not go into her misdemeanor but I will say that what she did was completely unacceptable. I could hear you all gossiping on my way to the great hall and no, she is not a toad. Ladies, it is time to stop gossiping and spreading stories.'

They said the witches' creed and then hundreds of plates flew through the windows and landed on each of the tables. There were shrieks and squeals as dozens of red spotted spiders appeared on the ceiling above each table and began to weave spaghetti onto each of the plates. Charlotte shuddered but didn't say anything, she'd never been keen on spiders.

A leprechaun in a baseball shirt and cap appeared in the corner of the room and hit meatballs onto everyone's plates with lightning speed, before he did a little jig and then vanished.

Just when the new girls thought that things could not get crazier the bats flew in through the windows carrying jugs of tomato sauce and poured it onto each of the girl's bowls.

'Do you get your food delivered to you like this?' Stef asked Alice, before she put a whole meatball into her mouth.

'Of course not,' Alice said snobbishly, as she cut a meatball in half and waved it mid-air. 'Although I do have to admit that this dining hall is much more fun than being served by servants at home.'

Charlotte looked around her at all the chatting, laughing girls. No one was looking at her anymore, each girl was too preoccupied with her food and how it was being served. This place was magical and she never wanted to leave.

As soon as the girls left the room Stef began to gossip about Margaret, only her words came out in an unrecognizable language. She tried again but once more, her words made no sense.

When some of the other students tried to talk about Margaret their words also sounded gibberish and the corridors were filled with what sounded like a bizarre version of Chinese whispers.

'I give up, Miss Moffat must have put a spell over us all or something,' Stef sighed. 'Oh well, I'm sick of hearing about Margaret anyway.'

Charlotte didn't say anything but she was secretly glad as she didn't want to think about Margaret or where she was and the fact that no one was able to talk about her made this easier. Miss Moffat had given her another chance and she had to make the most of it, not dwell on the past. She was a witch and this Academy was where she was meant to be. There was no more room for errors or foolishness, from now on Charlotte was determined to study hard and prove that she deserved to be there.

***

The next week carried on as normal. The girls settled into their daily routines, they learned new spells, and their friendships grew closer. Demi continued to act lost without Margaret, sitting by herself at meal times. Although she had begun to talk to the other girls a bit, Stef and Alice didn't have much to say to her and Demi ignored Charlotte as she blamed her for Margaret's disappearance. Gerty, with her huge heart, felt sorry for her and spoke to her in passing.

Breakfast had just finished and Charlotte realized that she'd left her wand in her room, so she hurried back to get it. She grabbed it from the wardrobe and was about to leave when she turned to see Margaret standing in front of her, her arms folded and a fierce look on her face.

Charlotte tried to step past her to escape through the door. The door slammed shut. She reluctantly turned back to look at Margaret, knowing that she had no choice except to see what Margaret wanted. She was far more advanced with spells than Charlotte was.

'We need to talk,' Margaret glared, uncrossing her arms and revealing the wand that she grasped tightly in her right hand.

Charlotte looked at the door, rummaging desperately through her brain for any sort of spell that would help her.

'No one's coming to rescue you, it's just you and me,' Margaret smirked, as she took a step closer towards her.

Book 2

Miss Moffat's Academy
for
Refined Young Witches

Chapter One

It was clear from the stern look on Margaret's face that she was set on revenge. It was just the two of them alone in Charlotte's room and she only had to glance at Margaret to know that she wasn't in a forgiving mood.

'Margaret, I didn't know you were coming back?' Charlotte looked at the ground, before she chewed on the side of her lip.

Charlotte gripped her wand tighter in her hand and tried to think of a spell, any spell.

'You won't be needing that,' Margaret flicked her wand in Charlotte's direction, causing her wand to fly out of her hand and hurtle across the room, landing on the carpeted floor.

'I'm s-sorry Margaret, I didn't want to get you into trouble, I really didn't but I would have been expelled if I hadn't told Miss Moffat what had really happened.'

'You're nothing but a tell-tale.'

'I couldn't get expelled for something you did. You ran off and left me to take the blame and I didn't tell, not until I had to.'

'If there's one thing I can't stand, it's a tell-tale,' she flicked her wand as she said the word 'Blattam.'

Before Charlotte could ask her what spell she'd just cast she began to shrink until she found herself covered in a pile of clothes; her clothes. She could see two long antennae wriggling out in front of her and she took a step backwards to get away from them. The antennae moved with her and her legs, she no longer just had two, instead she had six.

Charlotte wasn't human any more, instead she had been turned into a cockroach. She crawled out from under the clothes and looked up at the giant smirking Margaret.

'My mom says that roaches are the worst kind of vermin so it seemed kinda fitting for you. See ya around, that's if you manage not to get squashed first,' she sniggered as she peered down at her.

Charlotte watched as Margaret strutted out of the room, she was left there wondering what to do now. Her teacher at her old school had told her once how cockroaches had been around for millions of years and that they could survive nuclear explosions. She hoped that this was true, as she didn't want to end up a crumpled mess on the bottom of someone's shoe. She worried if this spell would last forever unless she somehow managed to explain what'd happened to someone and get them to change her back.

Charlotte scurried across the room and flew up onto her bed. Her wings were weak but she managed to get them to work a bit.

She wondered if Margaret had been let back into the Academy or if she'd just snuck in to get revenge? Charlotte hoped that she wasn't back as she didn't want to look at her smug face every lesson if she managed to survive this.

The door swung open and Stef, Gerty and Alice entered the room and walked over to their beds.

'I wonder where Charlotte is?' Gerty asked, as she dropped down onto her bed.

'Dunno, hope she's not in any more trouble,' Stef replied.

'I don't see why she would be, she's not one for rule breaking.'

'True, although I hope she's not in any more trouble over the Margaret thing.'

'I hope not,' Gerty gave a worried look.

'I wonder where Margaret is?' Alice asked.

'I hope she's at the bad witches' school with no friends and rat soup for her lunch,' Stef said.

'Ew,' Gerty chuckled.

'If they try to serve us rat soup here my parents will be hearing about it,' Alice stuck her nose in the air.

Charlotte knew that she needed to get their attention...so she fluttered her flimsy wings and managed to find enough power to fly over to Gerty. She landed on her arm and tried getting her attention.

'Gerty, Gerty, it's me Charlotte,' she crawled up her arm.

Gerty looked down and saw the bug on her arm, she let out a shriek and tried swatting it away as she jumped up onto her feet.

'What is it?' Stef rushed over to her.

'C-c-cockroach,' she frantically flicked out her arm even though Charlotte had now fallen onto the floor.

Alice squealed and jumped up onto her bed, swiping away at the air.

'I'll find it,' Stef said, as she stomped her feet on the ground.

Charlotte darted out of the way and scurried under Alice's bed, which made her scream even louder.

'This is an outrage, wait until my parents hear about this,' Alice shrieked.

'Please, it's me,' Charlotte pleaded but no one could hear her words.

Stef continued to stomp her feet across the floor and Charlotte raced past her and managed to fly over to the open window and throw herself out of it. She half-flew, half-fell down and landed in a bush outside.

She wanted to cry, only she didn't think that cockroaches could. Her own friends had been terrified of her and had tried to squash her and now she was outside somewhere in the surroundings of the Academy not knowing what to do next.

She decided to keep on scurrying forwards, eventually she found herself in the flying area where a group of older students were being instructed by Miss Firmfeather as they whizzed around the arena.

A girl with long black hair landed her broomstick and Charlotte immediately began to climb it.

'Please, I'm a student here. I need help,' she said; only her voice came out as a buzzing sound.

'Yuck,' the girl said, as she flicked Charlotte off her broom and onto the ground.

'Please, I'm not a real cockroach,' Charlotte pleaded, as she scurried up another broomstick.

The broomstick began to shake and Charlotte tumbled onto the ground. Soon broomsticks were smashing against the ground and multiple feet were trying to stand on her. She weaved in-between them all before she hurried away.

She stayed out of sight and watched as the lesson finished and the girls left the flying arena.

Suddenly she smelt something and her antennae frantically moved in front of her. Before she could stop herself she was letting them lead her, until she found herself by the black trashcans at the back of the Academy.

One of the bins had been knocked over and garbage had spilled out onto the ground. She didn't want to go near it...yet she found herself with an overpowering craving to find food within the dirty, putrid trash.

She crawled over to it and rooted through it until she found a mouldy old sandwich. Before she could stop herself she was nibbling at it, enjoying the vulgar taste.

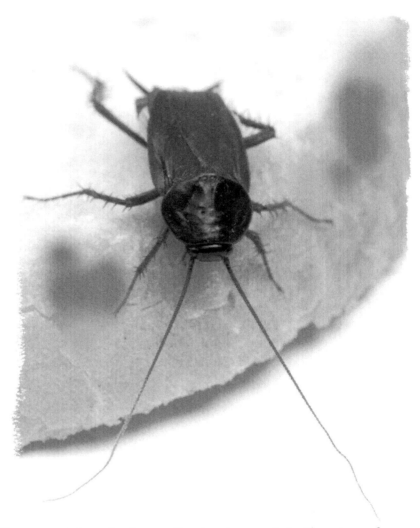

The next thing she knew the trash rose into the air and dropped into the now upright trash can, only Charlotte was still on the ground, and she wasn't a cockroach any more, instead she was back to being human. A piece of the mouldy sandwich was still in her mouth and she spat it out, a nauseous feeling rising inside of her as she wiped her mouth onto the back of her arm.

'What are you doing in the garbage?' a woman in a black apron said, as she stared at Charlotte. Her arms folded and a frown creased on her forehead.

Charlotte quickly wrapped her arms around her legs, aware that she had no clothes on. Her cheeks flushed redder than the beetroot her mom used in soup and she could still taste the mouldy sandwich on her lips.

'Wait here,' the woman said, she disappeared through a door and returned with an oversized jumper and a pair of baggy white trousers. 'The best I can do,' she threw then over at Charlotte.

'Thanks,' she replied, as she hurriedly got dressed.

She knew that she looked ridiculous as the trousers were at least two sizes too big on her and she had to hold them at the side so that they didn't fall down. However she definitely favored these clothes over no clothes at all and was grateful to the woman for helping her.

'You're not coming through my kitchen. You're filthy. You're have to walk the long way round,' the woman said, before she turned her back on Charlotte and walked off.

'Okay,' Charlotte nodded.

She turned her head and gave a piece of advice, 'I advise you to keep a wide berth from whoever decided to turn you into a cockroach.'

'I plan to,' Charlotte muttered.

Luckily classes were taking place so Charlotte managed to walk through the castle without being seen, at least that was until she got to the corridor that led to her room.
'Charlotte Smyth, why are you wearing that and why do you have bits of old food all over your face?'

Charlotte turned to face a very unimpressed looking Molly, her blonde hair tied into two pigtails that flowed down the front of her fitted school blouse.

'Erm I, erm it was. I'm sorry, it won't happen again,' she spluttered out, not wanting to mention Margaret in fear of more revenge attacks.

Margaret hadn't hesitated in turning her into a cockroach, so she dreaded to think what spell she'd cast on her next time. Charlotte felt as though she would never be able to compete with Margaret when it came to spells because Margaret had experience with spells whereas she didn't.

'We have standards at this school, don't let me see you like this again.'

Charlotte nodded, before she hurried over to her bedroom. She jumped into the shower but failed to fully get rid of the smell of garbage, as if it had embedded itself in her nose.

She changed into her uniform and used her wand to cast the hair-drying spell that Gerty had taught her. Afterwards she left her room to go and find the others, luckily it was currently a study lesson and she knew that they'd be in the library. She knew that the Mistress of the Books would probably give her a stern look, but as long as she didn't talk she shouldn't be in too much trouble.

She was not going to be defeated by Margaret Montgomery, even if that meant she had to spend the rest of her morning searching the library for anti-cockroach spells.

Charlotte knew that she belonged at this school and she wasn't going to let Margaret sabotage this.

Chapter Two

It was lunchtime and Charlotte was staring into her bowl of yellowy-colored soup that the bats had just placed in front of them all. Seeing food brought back memories of the mouldy sandwich and she had to force herself not to heave.

'Are you okay Charlotte, you look pale?' Gerty asked, as she grabbed a slice from the enormous baguette that spanned the entire length of the table.

'Yeah, fine,' she swallowed, as she brought her hand up to her mouth

'Where were you all morning? You're lucky that the Mistress of the Books only gave you a filthy look when you you eventually arrived,' Stef said.

'I don't really want to talk about it.'

'You're not in trouble again are you?' Gerty asked.

'I hope not,' Alice said, before she dipped a piece of bread in her soup. 'I can't be seen sharing a room with a troublemaker, it looks bad on my character.'

Stef tore a piece off her bread and chucked it at Alice, hitting her in the face. She gave Stef an annoyed look, before she went back to sipping her soup.

I had an unpleasant distraction,' she mumbled.

'Are you going to explain to us what you mean or are we supposed to guess? Stef asked.

'I think that we need some sort of code in future, so that if one of us gets turned into something we can alert each other.'

'Okay, you're going to have to explain what you're on about because now I'm confused,' Stef said.

'It's just been one of those mornings,' Charlotte pushed her barely touched bowl of soup away.

'Are you not eating that?' Stef asked, as she stared at Charlotte's bowl.

Charlotte shook her head, so Stef grabbed the bowl and transferred her spoon into it.

'Say if one of us got turned into a rat against our will, how could we signal this to the rest of us?'

'Squeak three times,' Gerty giggled.

'Bite Stef on the ankle,' Alice said, which caused Stef to glare at her.

'What if we couldn't squeak or bite? What if we were a slug or a snail?' Charlotte enquired.

'Leave a slime trail saying help,' Stef chuckled.

I was thinking more like we mark a spot on the floor in our room with chalk and then we can use our wands on any creature that stays put on it.'

'Has something happened?' Gerty looked at Charlotte.
'I was just thinking about the time Alice was turned into a mouse, that's all,' she lied.

Charlotte thought about telling them about what had happened with Margaret but she didn't want them to feel sorry for her or think that she was a weak witch. She just hoped that they'd remember what the mark she was going to chalk in their bedroom would be for and that none of them would ever have to use it.

***

'So girls,' Miss Maker said, as she twirled a strand of her purple tinged dark hair around her finger. 'What potion would you like to make today?'

'Really, we get to choose?' Gerty asked.

'Yes, we will make the most popular suggestion.'

There were excited murmurs between the girls at the prospect of this but Miss Maker looked unfazed as she awaited their suggestions.
'How about a potion that makes us super fast, then we'd be amazing at our next fitness lesson?' Gerty said.

'Miss Dread would not appreciate that being used during her lessons,' Alice said.

'No, I don't suppose she would,' Miss Maker chuckled.

Charlotte wanted to suggest that they make a potion to prevent spells from being cast upon them but she couldn't get the words out.

'An extra-time potion, so that we don't have to get up so early?' Stef suggested.

'That's stupid, I want one that makes all my clothes fold themselves,' Alice said.

'Boring,' Stef rolled her eyes. 'Besides, there's bound to be a spell for that.'

'How about a potion to talk to animals?' Gerty asked.

'Too complicated,' Miss Maker said.

'A potion to change our hair color,' Patricia said, as she flicked out a strand of her red hair.

'I don't want to change my hair color,' Demi sneered. 'I wouldn't mind a beauty potion to make me look my best for the ball. It's only two weeks away and I want to look as gorgeous as possible.'

'That's a marvellous idea Demi,' Miss Maker smiled, as she readjusted her witch's hat slightly so that it remained somewhat wonky.
She turned around and began to pull items out of the labelled compartments that lined the wall behind her.

The ball would be the first time that they met the boys that attended the nearby wizard's school and they all wanted to look their best for it.

'I was going to suggest making a beauty potion but Demi beat me too it,' Stef huffed.

'It doesn't matter,' Charlotte smiled, trying to appease Stef.

'I hope it works,' Gerty said excitedly. 'I want to look older and for my hair to be extra shiny and to be taller. I'm fed-up with looking like I'm the youngest.'

'But you are the youngest,' Alice said.

'That doesn't mean I want to look like I am.'

Miss Maker caused a large pile of ingredients to float in front of her before she made sections from each separate with her wand. They floated over to each girl and landed on the board in front of their mini cauldrons.

'Right girls, make sure to listen carefully to this carefully or else the results could be catastrophic,' she looked over at their worried faces. 'Now, let's get started,' she winked.

'Firstly you will need a sprig of lavender,' she held up her sprig, before she placed it into her cauldron.

The rest of the girls carefully placed their lavender into their cauldron and eagerly awaited their next instructions. Charlotte tried to remain focused on Miss Maker, as she didn't want to become distracted and mess up her potion. 'Next you'll need a pinch of chestnut powder,' she picked up a small amount of the beige looking dust.

'How can we be sure we've measured it right?' Stef asked.

'If it fits between your thumb and forefinger then you should be fine.'

Stef picked up the chestnut powder three times before she settled on an amount and sprinkled it into her cauldron.

'Now take one cherry,' she picked it up by the stem. 'And throw it all in.'

Miss Maker hummed quietly to herself and waited until all the girls had finished.

'Now, take your essence of peppermint,' she lifted up a small bottle. 'And apply two teaspoons,' she poured it onto the spoon before she brought it up to her nose. 'Peppermint is such a delightful smell, it reminds me of the mints my grandmother makes at Christmas.'

'Now, I see you're all ready so let's continue,' she looked around the room. 'Now, stir once clockwise. Once anti-clockwise and then twice more clockwise Now, pick up your blossom tree petal,' she lifted a pinkish-white petal. 'And crumple it under your fingers and then sprinkle it in.'

'I hope I'm doing this right?' Gerty whispered to Charlotte. She smiled but didn't reply, as she was concentrating.

'Now stir your potion three times anti-clockwise and you're done,' she took her spoon out of her potion. 'Demi, you only stirred twice.'

'No, I'm sure I stirred three times.'

'I can assure you that it was only twice,' Stef gave a sly smile.

Demi shrugged before she stirred her potion one more time anti-clockwise.

'Looks like you're all done, now all that's left to do is to wait for the potions to settle and then sip it down.'

'How does this potion work?' Stef asked, as she peered down at her smoking cauldron.

'I can't know for sure, as potions vary.'

'It will be good results though won't it?' Alice asked.

Miss Maker smiled, 'Of course, why do you think all your teachers look so young and beautiful? I think that your potions would have settled by now, so go ahead.'

Demi was the first girl to pour the potion into her glass but she waited until she saw that other girls had drunk theirs before she took a sip from it. Gerty and Charlotte exchanged looks before they both emptied their glasses.

'Do I look any different?' Stef said, her arm on her waist.

'No,' Charlotte shook her head.

'This potion doesn't work,' Demi sighed.

'I suggest that you give it time to bloom,' the teacher chuckled.

The girls glanced around at each other as they tried to spot signs that the spell was working. They were beginning to think that the spell was a dud and that nothing would happen, that was until Stef gave Gerty a double-look.

'Gerty, you look different,' Stef said, as she stared at her. 'You look younger.'

'Younger! How can I look younger?' she looked horrified, as she touched her face.

'You look slightly shorter too,' Alice chimed in.

'No I don't,' Gerty fought back tears.

'You look fine Gerty,' Charlotte said, as she looked down at her arms, noticing how her cardigan had become baggier on her.

'They've gone, where did they go?' Demi shouted, as she looked down at her chest. 'I want them back right now.'

Stef began to laugh as she looked over at Demi's hysterics. Demi was the only girl in their class who needed a bra and this potion had made her as flat chested as the rest of them.

You're as flat as an iron,' Stef snorted.

'Shush,' Charlotte said to Stef, followed by a wink.

'Miss Maker, this spell was supposed to make us look good, yet we all look like little kids. You must reverse the spell immediately!' Demi insisted.

'Nonsense, you all look beautiful,' Miss Maker smiled.

'I look stupid, I need to be back to normal,' Demi grasped her arms across her chest.

'You'll have to wait until the spell wears off.'

'What! But the ball is next week,' Stef said.

'You'll be back to normal in a few weeks.'

On hearing this, the room was filled with groans and disgruntled looks from the girls.

'Are you saying that we could be stuck looking like this at the ball?' Demi said.

'It's hard to know with magic. None of you need to worry, you all look glowing.'

'I don't want to look glowing, I want to look my age,' Demi growled.

'That's it for today, now clear up your cauldrons and then you can go,' Miss Maker addressed the girls. Begrudgingly the girls did as Miss Maker said, including Demi, although she took the longest to tidy up as she refused to move one of her arms away from her chest. Once they'd all tidied up Miss Maker dismissed them and they headed for the door.

'Bye girls,' Miss Maker said cheerily.

'Bye,' Charlotte said, forcing a smile. She was annoyed at the effects of the potion, but Miss Maker was still her favorite teacher and she didn't want to appear anything but polite towards her.

'This sucks,' Stef said, when they were out of earshot of Miss Maker.

it's not fair!
We look like 8 year olds!!!

'It's not so bad,' Gerty jumped on the spot. 'I have some lip-gloss and baby pink eyeshadow we can use at the ball.'

'Great,' Stef rolled her eyes. 'Not only will I look like a little kid, I will also look like Barbie doll.'

'Stef,' Charlotte glared at her.

'Sorry Gerty,' Stef sighed. 'I just really wanted to look good for the ball.'

'You always look good,' Gerty smiled.

'All that matters is that we're all be together at the ball, forget the boys,' Charlotte said.

'You're right, I can't wait,' Gerty squealed.

'My mother has a room full of make-up at home, I'd ask her to send some of it over to me, but it's very expensive,' Alice said.

'It doesn't matter Alice, I'm sure Gerty's lip-gloss will be just fine,' Charlotte smiled.

'Who needs boys anyway? Stef said.

'Yeah, they like dirt and find stupid jokes funny,' Gerty said.

'Yeah, we don't need them,' Stef put her arms around Gerty and Charlotte's shoulders. 'Girl's rule and boys drool.'

'Ew,' laughed Gerty.

'You could try asking your mom about the make-up Alice, if you tell her that you look about eight she might take pity on you,' Stef grinned.

'I do not look eight,' she gave an indignant look.

'Just messing,' chuckled Stef.

'Not funny,' Alice smiled.

They all continued up the corridor, the thought of the ball and the prospect of meeting the boys from the Wizard's School at the forefront of their minds.

Chapter Three

For the last week the main topic echoing through the corridors was about the school ball. The new students were talking about what refreshments would be served, what songs would be played and most importantly what the boys from the Wizard's School would be like. Whilst the older girls were discussing the boys by name, what outfit they'd be wearing and any potions that could improve their image, dancing and what they should say to boys. The Academy was at one with excitement and the mood was electric.

It was only an hour until they left for the Wizard's College and Charlotte and the others were getting ready.

'Whose taken my sparkly red ballet pumps?' Alice said, as she looked from girl-to-girl accusingly.

'I haven't seen them,' Gerty replied.

'My aunt brought them for me from a boutique in Paris and they aren't where I left them.'

'Nope, not seen them,' Stef shrugged, as she held up two dresses. 'Blue or green?'

'I like the blue one,' Charlotte said.

'Yeah, me too,' Gerty said.

'Both would clash terribly with my shoes, so give them back.'

'I don't have your stupid shoes,' Stef groaned, as she put the green dress down on her bed and hung onto the blue one.

There was a knock at the door and all the girls turned to look at it.

'Come in,' Gerty said.

The door opened and in walked Sonya and Silvia, both of them looking stunning in strappy knee-length dresses, Sonya's in baby blue and Silvia's in magenta.

'Who put this there,' Sonya said, as she tripped over a red shoe that was by the door, managing to grab onto the doorframe to steady her balance.

'Erm, that's mine,' Alice rushed over and picked up the shoe, a sheepish look on her face.

'You both look great,' Charlotte said.

'Thanks,' they replied in unison.

'You both look beautiful and I still look like a little kid,' Gerty bounced down onto her bed.

'No you don't Gerty, you look good,' Sonya said, as she took in Gerty's pretty pink floral dress.

'You know the potion has worn off, thank goodness,' Stef said, as she tied the sash on her dress.

'I know but I still look younger than the rest of you.'

'Well you are younger,' Stef said.

'You look great,' Charlotte smiled. 'And I love your dress.'

'It's cute isn't it?'

'Very.'

'We're just checking by from room to room to see how everyone's getting on?' Sonya said.

'We're nearly done,' Stef said.

'What are the boys like?' Gerty asked.

'The same as any other boys really. Some are cute, some make your skin cruel,' Silvia said.

'Do you remember that boy from the last ball, the one with the manically crazy hair that wouldn't stop following you around?' Sonya looked at her sister.

'Don't remind me,' she shook her shoulders. 'I had to hide under the refreshment table at one point just to get away from him.'

'Will there be boys from established wizard families there as I can't be seen dancing with just anyone,' Alice said, as she patted down the material of her cream dress.

'What makes you think they'd want to dance with you anyway?' Stef said.

'Alice, I have no idea. You'll just have to ask them when you're there,' said Sonya.

'I shouldn't have to ask them anything, a boy from an established family should come over to me and begin the conversation.'

'I don't think they'll be walking around with neon lights on them saying where they're from, not unless you try a spell,' Stef chuckled.

'Alice, we suggest you go to the ball intent on having a good time and if you find a boy, established or not, then so be it,' Sonya said.

'What boy could resist those shoes,' Gerty pointed down at Alice's feet, she'd found the other shoe under her bed and now had both of them on.

'They are Dorothy shoes, I like them when I'm not tripping over them,' Sonya said.

'My grandmother got them for me from Paris, from a very expensive shop,' Alice moved to the side to show them off better.

'We had better go check on the other girls. When you're ready head down to the great hall, Molly will be waiting there for you,' Silvia gave a wave as she headed out of the door, her sister following her.

'Let's go,' said Stef, as she grabbed her wand off her bed and threaded it through the sash on her dress.

'Are you sure I look okay?' Gerty said, as she did a spin that caused her dress to flow out like an upside-down umbrella.

'You look great, now let's go and dance,' Charlotte grabbed Gerty's arm and led her over to the door.

'Come on Dorothy,' Stef looked back over at Alice who was rummaging through the pile of clothes on her bed. 'You can't be late for the Emerald City.'

Alice's Dorothy Shoes
—no comment—

Alice grabbed her wand off her bed and hurried over to the others.

***

Molly was stood in front of the staff table on the platform in the grand hall. She was wearing a corseted black-netted dress and she wore a black heart shaped clip in the side of her hair.

'Right everyone, a few rules before we head off to the wizard's college. No spiking the punch bowl with magic, no using love spells on the boys and remember that you are representing the Academy, therefore you must be on your best behavior at all times.

Right, follow me in an orderly fashion outside,' she walked down off the stage and then gestured for them to follow her out of the side door.

'I'm so excited,' Gerty said to Charlotte, as they followed the crowd of students towards the door.

'Me too,' replied Charlotte, as she managed to move her foot just in time before a girl in high heels stood on it.

They squashed through the doorway and out into the yard where a circular gold and black carriage was waiting for them. Harnessed to it were eight white wooden carousel horses, their manes painted on in golds and pinks and there were black-feathered headdresses attached to their halter.

'Wow,' Gerty said, as she grabbed Charlotte's arm in excitement. 'I used to love riding on the carousel horses when I was little.'

'How are those horses meant to get us anywhere, they aren't real?' Stef said.

Just then one of the horses near the front neighed loudly and moved its front leg that caused Stef to jolt backwards.

'Okay but I still don't know how we are all meant to fit in that, it's tiny,' Stef remarked, as she watched as some of the other girls climbed up the steps and into the carriage.

'Let's find out,' Charlotte pulled Stef forwards.

'I don't mind if you go first,' Stef said, as she let Charlotte pass her.

Charlotte nodded, before she walked up the steps and into the carriage. Inside was at least the same size as the grand hall and it was full of circular glass tables surrounded by gold and red padded chairs.

'Double wow,' Gerty said open-mouthed, as she walked in behind Charlotte.

Alice came in next, she was pulling on Stef's arm. They both stopped still when they saw inside the carriage, which caused the girl coming in behind them to walk straight into the back of Stef.

'Move it,' she growled.

'Sorry,' Stef muttered, as she and Alice walked over to Charlotte and Gerty, who were now sitting at one of the tables.

'This is cool,' Stef said.

'You weren't thinking that a minute ago when you were making excuses not to come in here,' Alice said.

'I was not, I just thought I'd forgotten my wand, that's all,' Stef blushed.

'At my old school we had this rickety old bus to take us on school trips. It constantly smelt of vomit and the springs from the seats dug into my back. This is definitely an improvement,' Charlotte said.

'I've never been on a bus, they sound awful,' Alice shuddered.

'They weren't so bad, well, apart from that school trip bus, that was terrible. Nothing like this though, this is amazing,' Charlotte said.

'My parents have a private chauffeur so I'm used to transport that isn't overcrowded,' she looked around her at all the dressed-up girls sitting in the carriage. 'I suppose that this is passable.'

'Well I think it's amazing,' Charlotte said.

'Me too,' Gerty giggled. 'I can't wait, I've never been to a ball before.'

The carriage began to move and there were shouts of excitement between all the girls. The ball they had been anticipating since the beginning of term had finally arrived.

***

The Wizard's School was over the mountain range, disguised by a thick array of oak trees. The carriage passed under an arched gateway saying *Alexander's College*, and the magnificent brick castle came into view. Most of the girls jumped out of their seats and crowded around the windows, trying to get a glimpse of the castle.

The carriage came to a stop and Molly appeared by the door, her wand gripped firmly in her hand so that Charlotte thought she resembled a Gothic fairy.

'So, as you've all no doubt figured out, we're here. No pushing or shoving when getting off the carriage and if people near the front get off first that will make things easier. When you get outside wait in the yard with Sonya and Silvia for me and we shall lead you into the college.

Remember that just because you're out of the Academy doesn't mean that the code of conduct doesn't apply. If anyone rule breaks here it will be taken more seriously than it would be back at the Academy because you are representing it. This doesn't mean that you can't have a good time, just remember who you are and where you are,' Molly nodded to Sonya and Silvia and they stepped outside.

'Jasmine, you can start the line,' she pointed to a dark-haired girl in a black and white floral dress.

Ignoring what Molly had said some of the girls from the back tried to shove through the crowds, so that they could get out of the carriage before them.

'Watch it,' Stef said, as she got elbowed in the ribs.

Alice seemed to get pushed further back into the carriage, until she was almost at the back of it and then someone stood on the back of her shoe, causing her to lose her footing and step out of it. She had to wait until all the girls had passed her before she could put it back on.

'What's the rush?' Molly said, as she waved her wand and said the word 'Remitto.'

Instantly all the girls left in the carriage found that they could only move in slow motion.

'Now, those of you at the front go first,' Molly said.

The girls at the front slowly moved their way to the door, unable to move their arms and legs quickly.

'M-m-o-l-y,' a girl said as she passed her but on realizing that her words came out slowly too, she decided not to say anything else.

As soon as the girls stepped out of the carriage they went back to walking at a normal speed.

'Where's Alice?' Charlotte asked Gerty and Stef, as they stood outside. They'd managed to get off the carriage fairly quickly without getting shoved too much.

'Maybe she decided that the carriage is too common for her and she's waiting for her own personal chauffeur to collect her and drive her right up to the door,' Stef smirked.

'Stef,' Charlotte stared at her but failed to hide her smile.

'I was only messing.'

'There she is?' Gerty pointed over to a red faced Alice who stumbled her way down the steps of the carriage, followed by Molly. 'What happened to you?'

Alice went even redder, almost matching her shoes. She didn't reply to Gerty, instead she looked down at her feet.

'Do my shoes look okay?'

'Yes,' Stef rolled her eyes. 'If you like over-the-top sparkles, then they look great.'

'I meant they don't look damaged do they?'

'No,' Gerty crouched down and inspected them. 'They look perfect.'

'Follow me,' Molly shouted, as she walked past the girls.

The high ceilings and brick-walled corridors carried a medieval feel to them. There was a knight-of-armor by one of the walls and colorful eagle-crested banners, shields and crossing swords decorating the walls.

'It's like a fortress,' Gerty whispered to Charlotte. 'Do you think they had proper battles here back in the olden days.'

'Probably,' Charlotte replied.
Molly led them into a large hall, with disco lights and music playing. There were chairs lining the sides of the room and a large table filled with snacks, cups and a punch bowl. Also in the room were boys, some were dancing, some were at the refreshment table and some were sitting on the chairs...but all of them stopped what they were doing and stared over at the girls as they entered.

Some of the older girls rushed over to certain boys and greeted them with hugs and smiles. There was a boy by the refreshment table, with floppy dark hair that was swiped across his forehead who winked over at Molly. She failed to hide her smile as she coyly looked back at him before looking away.

'Welcome, welcome to Alexander's,' a tall man in a black waistcoat and pinstriped trousers said as he took wide strides across the room.

'Ah Molly, I presume Miss Moffat is well?' he slightly lowered his head to her so that he wasn't towering over her as much.

'Alexander, yes she is very well and sends her regards.' Molly sounded so formal and grown up!

'It has been too long since I saw her last, we are so near yet it seems so far away. Running a school is very time-consuming.'

'Yes, I imagine it is.'

'Now, now, don't just stand there,' he turned to face the new girls who were still lingering in the doorway. 'Go and dance.'

'Let's get a drink and go and sit down somewhere,' Charlotte said to the others.

They made their way over to the drinks table and Gerty used the large punch bowl spoon to fill up four cups. With their drinks in hand they walked over to a row of empty seats and sat there awkwardly.

Some of the older girls were dancing with the boys, while most of the new girls and boys sat on opposite sides of the room, not knowing how to approach each other.

Demi seemed immune from first dance nerves, even without Margaret for company. She was already on the dance floor with a few girls from the year above, twirling in her leopard print skirt.

Charlotte looked across the room at the sitting boys, her gaze falling upon a brown-haired boy, with wide eyes and golden skin. He noticed her looking at him and she quickly lowered her gaze, her heart increasing in pace.

'We're at a dance, so we need to actually dance,' Gerty stood-up and pulled at Alice and Stef's arms. 'You too Charlotte, you're not getting out of it just because I'm out of arms.'

'Okay, okay,' Stef groaned, as she got to her feet.

Gerty led them over to the dance floor and began to sway in tune to the music. Stef swung out her arms and legs and Demi sniggered over at her.

'*Bonum saltator,*' Gerty flicked her wand out in front of Stef.

'What did you do to me?' Stef glared at Gerty.

'Try dancing now,' she smiled.

Stef began to dance and soon realized that she was in rhythm to the music, moving as a skilled dancer would.

'Go Stef!' Gerty wolf-whistled, as Stef danced around the dance floor.

A group of boys and girls saw Stef and began to clap and one boy with spiked dark hair walked over to her and began to dance with her. Demi stopped dancing and glared over at Stef, an annoyed look on her face.

'There's no way that Stef could dance like that without some help, what spell did you use?' Demi said, after she had marched over to Gerty, Charlotte and Alice.

'I don't know what you're talking about,' Gerty grinned.

'I don't believe you. It doesn't matter anyway because I'm far more advanced at casting spells than you are, you're just a kid,' she huffed, as she aimed her wand at herself and said '*Peritus saltator.*'

She smirked before she cartwheeled across the floor and then spun on the spot like a spinning wheel. When she came out of the spin she did a row of back-flips before she began doing some fancy dance moves across the room.

'Talk about overdoing it,' Gerty giggled.

'She's making me dizzy just watching her,' Charlotte said.

'The dance floor at home is far larger than this one, we throw a grand ball every summer. I suppose you can all come to the next one,' Alice said.
'Will there be cute boys there?' Gerty asked.

'There are a few boys our age that are invited with their parents that I suppose are okay.'

'It doesn't matter about the boys, we'd love to come,' Gerty smiled.

'That sounds great,' Charlotte said.

'That spell you used was good, look at Stef go,' Charlotte said to Gerty, as she pointed over at her still dancing with the boy on the dance floor.

It was then that Charlotte noticed three really great looking boys...standing there and smiling at her group. She looked down, feeling a little embarrassed.

When she looked up again, the cute browned-haired boy wasn't standing with his friends any more, instead he was walking across the room, his friends following him.

At first she thought that they were going to the refreshment table but instead they kept on walking across the room towards her. Her pulse was thudding in her head and her hands started to sweat.

'Do you want to dance?' the shortest boy said to Alice. She blushed as she nervously nodded and followed him onto the dance floor.

The cute boy looked at Charlotte and gave her an awkward smile, he was just about to ask her to dance when Demi grabbed his arm as she danced past him.

'Dance with me,' she said, not giving him much of a chance.

The third boy stammered, 'Hi,' and then walked off, blushing.

'He was clearly about to ask you to dance,' Gerty sighed. 'That girl should find her own boy and not kidnap other peoples. She has ruined everything!'

'It was hardly kidnapping and he might not have wanted to dance, he might have wanted to ask me something else,' she looked over at the boy who was swaying uncomfortably next to Demi's exaggerated dance moves.

'He didn't go by choice, you should go over there and get him back.'

'No way,' she shook her head, before she looked over at him and saw that he was looking back at her.

Demi continued her wild dancing, her face looked exhausted but her body seemed unable to tire. She flayed her arms around and that's when she whacked the boy in the head with her elbow. He dropped to the ground with a thud and Charlotte raced over to him and bent down by his side. His eyes were shut and he wasn't moving.

'I didn't mean to hurt him,' Demi said worriedly, as she danced around the boy, unable to stop.

'I know Demi, just go and dance over there and give him some room,' Charlotte said, as she pointed across to the other end of the dance floor.

'Please, wake-up,' she whispered to him. 'You're too cute not to be okay.'

'Thanks,' the boy said, as he winked at her, before he pulled himself up into a sitting position.

Charlotte blushed and looked down at him awkwardly. They both smiled at each other and soon their smiles turned into laughter.

'Are you okay?' Alexander rushed over.

'Yes sir, a rogue elbow can't keep me down,' the boy replied.

'I'm glad to hear it,' he stretched out his arm and helped the boy up. 'I suggest you watch out for elbows and other limbs if you're considering asking this young lady to dance,' he looked over at Charlotte.

'I think I've had enough of dancing for one night,' he blushed. 'Any chance you want to sit down and talk for a bit?' he looked at Charlotte with his beautiful eyes and dazzling smile.

'Yes. Erm, I mean, yeah, that'd be great,' she spluttered out.

They walked side-by-side over to the chairs and sat down next to each other.

For a few minutes they sat in silence passing smiles between each other.

'I'm Charlie.'

Charlie...So Handsome!

'Charlotte.'

'It's good to meet you Charlotte,' he smiled.

'You too.'

The music stopped playing and a loud horn sounded. All eyes fell on Molly who was standing by the refreshment table.

'Thank you to Alexander's College for hosting what I'm sure you'll all agree was a magnificent night?' there were cheers of agreement from the girls and some of the boys. 'All girls are to follow me outside to return back to the Academy. Make sure you've got all of your belongings, especially your wands,' she glanced a look at the dark-haired boy who'd winked at her earlier, before she led the girls out of the hall.

'I better go,' Charlotte said.

'I'll see you at the next dance,' he smiled.

'I'd like that.'

She stood-up and looked over at Gerty and the others who were waiting for her. She gave one last smile to Charlie, hoping that the next ball wouldn't be too long away.

'For the record, I think you're cute too,' he said.

Charlotte couldn't hide her grin, as she gave him a wave and joined the others. They all began following the other girls out of the hall.

'He's very cute,' Gerty giggled.

'He is, isn't he?' Charlotte smiled. She felt like she was walking on a cloud and butterflies were flying around her stomach.

'He's alright but Benjamin was cuter,' Alice said.

'Did Demi ever stop dancing?' Charlotte peered back at the empty dance floor.

'Who cares,' Stef said.

'Maybe she danced herself back to the Academy,' Gerty laughed.

'More like she got expelled for crimes against dancing,' Stef snorted.

'He had such lovely eyes,' Alice gave a thoughtful sigh. 'Like dark blue jewels, but not the cheap kind. They were as blue as the sapphire engagement ring my mother has.'

'You're see him again soon enough,' Gerty put her arm around Alice's shoulders.

'How could anyone resist those shoes,' Stef grinned.

'Do you think that's the only reason he liked me? I can't possibly wear the same pair twice,' Alice looked worried.

'He liked you for you, regardless of your sparkly shoes,' Charlotte said.

'Yes, you'll right,' Alice smiled.

'What was your boy like?' Charlotte asked Stef.

'He was okay,' she smiled.

'Just okay?' Gerty asked.

'Not, just okay, but okay,' she grinned.

'At the next dance I'll ask Charlie if he has a friend for you,' Charlotte looked at Gerty.

'Really?' Gerty said excitedly.

'Yep.'

'I can't wait,' she did a jig on the spot.

'Nobody ask Miss Maker for a beauty spell before the next ball,' Stef said.

'If she makes us do one, I'm not drinking it,' Gerty said.

'We don't need to ask her for dancing spells as Gerty has that one covered,' Charlotte grinned.

'Yeah, that spell was great and it really showed Demi up which is always a bonus.'

'Demi managed that all by herself,' Gerty said.

'I hope she's still dancing on the journey back, that'd make Molly so annoyed she'd probably turn her into a mouse,' Stef laughed.

'Home time,' Gerty sighed, as she looked over at the carousel horses and carriage.

Charlotte turned back and took in one last look at the castle, before she turned around and followed the others onto the carriage. It had been a magical night, one that she was sure she would remember forever.

Chapter Four

It was breakfast time and the grand hall was full of students, all talking amongst themselves as they grabbed fruit off the plants in front of them. Large black and white birds flew through the windows and dropped hard-boiled eggs into each of the eggcups in front of the girls.

Alice and Gerty placed their arms over their heads, worried that the eggs would hit them instead, but the birds didn't miss, nor did the eggs break.

'What shall we do today?' Gerty asked, as she cracked the top of her egg with her spoon.

It was Saturday so they didn't have lessons today, which meant an entire day of free time.

'It has to be inside the castle, no way am I going out in this weather,' Stef gestured to the window, drops of fierce rain were splatting against it.

'We could go to the games room,' Gerty said.

'I'm not playing bumblebee table tennis, my arm still hurts from where that thing stung me last time,' Stef said.

'You said that you were good at table tennis,' Gerty chuckled.

'Yeah, well I'd never played it with bumblebees for balls before.'

'I need to go to the library to study. If one of you could come with me that'd be great, as the Mistress of the Books always gives me funny looks since the Margaret thing. I don't like being in there alone,' Charlotte said.

'I'm not spending my free day in the library,' Alice remarked.

'I'll come with you,' Gerty said cheerfully.

'Who's that girl sitting with Demi,' Stef pointed over to the table near the door.

A pretty girl with shoulder length black hair was sitting opposite Demi.

'I've not seen her before, have you?' Gerty asked.

'No,' Stef said and both Charlotte and Alice shook their heads.

'She looks slightly older, maybe she's from the year above,' Charlotte said.

'Possibly, although I recognize most people in this place and I don't recall her at all,' Gerty said.

'It was only a matter of time before Demi replaced Margaret,' Stef shrugged.

'I guess, I just hope that she's nicer than Margaret,' Charlotte said.

'Everybody's nicer than Margaret,' Gerty grinned. 'Imagine someone meaner than Margaret, it doesn't bear thinking about.'

'Do you think Margaret's at the bad witch school?' Alice asked.

'I doubt even they would have her,' Stef snorted.

'I just hope she doesn't come back here,' Charlotte looked down at the remnants of her egg, recalling what it was like being a cockroach. 'Let's get out of here,' she pushed her chair back.

'Hang on,' Stef grabbed a few more pieces of fruit off the plant and popped them into her mouth. Then she grabbed a couple more and put them into her cardigan pocket, causing Gerty to give her a look.

'What, they're for later,' Stef replied.

They all glanced at Demi and the new girl as they walked past them. They were chatting to each other as if they'd known each other for years and they didn't seem to notice that anyone was looking at them. Charlotte found herself hoping that this girl was nothing like Margaret because they definitely didn't need a new one of those around.

***

Charlotte had spent the last few hours in the library with Gerty. The Mistress of the Books hadn't taken her eyes off her since they'd arrived, but that was to be expected.

Charlotte didn't want to cause trouble, she just wanted to study and she hoped that the Mistress of the Books would eventually realize that.

Charlotte loved being at the Academy but she felt like she was miles behind everyone else because she hadn't grown up surrounded by magic. She kept up with the spells and potions in class but out of class she didn't know anywhere near as many spells as Gerty or Margaret did. That's why she was using her weekend to learn some spells and Gerty was a great help.

'This is a good spell,' Gerty whispered, as she moved the open book over to Charlotte.

'Spell blocker,' the book spoke quietly, so that Charlotte had to lean in closer to it to hear it. 'Aim your wand at the person who is casting a spell on you and as soon as they begin casting it flick out your wand and clearly say the word *'Prohibere.'* This will block their spell.'

'Prohibere,' Charlotte said under her breath, before she wrote the word down in her notebook. *'Prohibere.'*

'Shush,' the Mistress of the Books said, as she glared over at her.

Charlotte closed the spell book and sighed. She wanted to be able to learn spells without the fear of being turned into a toad or having her mouth sewn-up.

She continued to communicate with Gerty via hand signals, not daring to utter a word.

When they were finished in the library they put their books on the shelf by the door and were about to walk through it when Demi appeared with the girl from breakfast.

'Charlotte, Gerty, this is Destiny, she's new here and she'll be in our class,' Demi said.

Hey,' Gerty smiled.

'Hi,' Charlotte said.

'Shush,' the Mistress of the Books said to them.

'Demi's just showing me around, this place is so massive,' Destiny whispered.

'Shush,' the Mistress of the Books said again.

'We better go, it was nice to meet you,' Charlotte quietly replied.

The next thing she knew the Mistress of the Books had flicked her wand and Charlotte had shrunk down into a pale brown mouse.

'There is to be no sound in my library,' The Mistress of the Books said sternly.

Gerty bent down and rummaged around the pile of clothes and pulled out Charlotte, cupping her in her hands.

'Ew, get it away from me,' Demi squealed, as she jumped back.

Gerty held Charlotte in one hand and picked the pile of clothes up in her free hand and walked over to a table.

Eventually the Mistress of the Books strode over to the table and flicked her wand, causing Charlotte to change back into a human. She quickly reached for her clothes, as Gerty stood in front of her and tried to cover her from view of the other girls in the library.

'No more talking in my library,' she said sharply.

Both girls hurried out of the library and out of earshot of the Mistress of the Books.

'So much for that blocking spell.' Charlotte sighed and whispered, 'She will never like me.'

'I don't think using that spell on the Mistress of Mean would have been a good idea, she probably would have turned you into a slug for the entire weekend if you'd used that on her,' Gerty said.

'I know, it's just that I'm trying to learn new spells. It's hard to do that when I'm a mouse.' Charlotte smiled.

'I thought she said she turned people into toads?'

'Maybe she's turned so many people into toads she fancied a change,' Charlotte shrugged. Having to deal with an aggressive librarian was starting to get to her.

'Anyway, we'll have to develop sign language for when we're in the library,' Charlotte made exaggerated gestures with her hands.

'That might be a good idea,' Gerty chuckled.

'Come on,' Gerty grabbed Charlotte's arm. 'Let's go and find the others and tell them about Destiny.'

*****

'It seems a strange time to start at a school, are you sure she wasn't just looking around?' Stef said, kicking her legs out behind her as she lay out on her bed.

'No, Demi definitely said that she was new here and in our class,' Charlotte said.

'If Demi said it, then it must be true,' Stef said sarcastically.

'I don't see why she'd lie about this, she introduced Destiny to us,' Charlotte said.

'Yeah and Charlotte got turned into a mouse by the Mistress of Mean for talking,' Gerty laughed.

'Really!' Alice said, as she peered up from the book she was reading.

'Yes, really,' Charlotte groaned.

'It was unfair, seeing as Charlotte hardly did any talking, it was mainly Demi.'

'It's my own fault that the Mistress of the Books doesn't like me, I shall just refrain from talking in the library again.'

'That's probably for the best, I prefer you human,' Stef grinned.

'I suppose there was an opening at the Academy now that Margaret's gone,' Alice said.

'We don't need a new Margaret though,' Stef said.

'She seemed nice,' Gerty said.

'She's friends with Demi, so she can't be that nice,' Stef replied.

'I suppose we'll find out soon enough,' Charlotte said, believing that no one could possibly ever be as bad as Margaret.

***

The weekend came to an end and a new week began. Destiny was at breakfast wearing her school uniform and chatting away to Demi. It seemed as though she was an official student at the school and the girls weren't sure what to think about this.

They were on their way to their class with the Mistress of Spells when Stef walked up alongside Destiny and Demi.

'What is she doing?' Alice asked Charlotte and Gerty.

'Being Stef,' Charlotte replied, as she walked over to Stef.

'Hi, I'm Stef, I see that you're new here?' she grinned at Destiny.

'I'm Destiny, Destiny Catslove, although I've already met some of you,' she smirked over at Charlotte.

'Squeak, squeak,' Demi giggled.

'It's a strange time for you to start here?' Stef enquired.

'I got expelled from my last school,' she shrugged.

'Really! What did you do?' Gerty asked.

'I was only messing around with a spell, they went wayyy overboard on their punishment,' she rolled back her eyes. 'My parents were furious, for the whole of the journey back they went on and on about the family name and how I needed to think about my actions, blah, blah, blah.'

'I'm Alice Smithers, from the well-known Smither's family. No doubt you've heard of us?' Alice said.

'No, I haven't. It's not my fault that school took itself too seriously. I wanted to go to Witchery College but my mom said, 'no respectable witch goes there,' she mimicked in a high-pitched tone.

'Why would you want to go there, they practice black magic?' Stef asked.

'Exactly, it's so frustrating being a witch and not being able to learn the spells I want to. Anyway, I'm stuck in this place now and I can't get expelled again as it's not worth the aggravation from my parents.'

'You're tall, how old are you?' Stef asked.

'Twelve, it was my birthday last week. Looks like that makes me the oldest, she looked down on the other girls, stopping on Gerty. 'And you're definitely the youngest,' she smirked.

'I was moved up a year,' Gerty said coyly.

'Gerty's a talented witch, she deserved to be moved up a year,' Charlotte said.

'Yeah, sure,' Destiny rolled her eyes. 'Anyway, see you in class,' she turned her back on the girls, grabbed Demi's arm and hurried her up the corridor.

'Why did you do that? Charlotte turned to Stef.

'What?'

'Go over and talk to her?'

'Why not?' she shrugged.

'Because she might be as mean as Margaret and she's already seen me be turned into a mouse.'

'She seems okay to me,' Gerty smiled.

'I suppose so,' Charlotte said under her breath, unable to trust her own words.

'I've never heard of her family before, so they obviously aren't as well-known as my family are,' Alice said.

'Come on, we have a class to get to,' Stef gave Alice a gentle prod in the back.

'I was already walking at an adequate speed, there's no need to prod me,' she struck out her arm to prod Stef back but she dodged out of the way.

'Can't catch me,' she grinned.

'Tribus *digitorum ictu*,' Alice flicked her wand at Stef.

'Ow!' Stef said, as she jumped forwards. 'Who did that?'

'Did what?' Alice smirked.

'Prodded me in the back. Ow, it happened again,' she glared at Alice.

'I don't know what you're on about,' Alice feigned concern as she hid her wand down by her side.

Gerty placed her hand over her mouth to try and disguise the fact she was giggling and Charlotte bit down on the side of her lip. There weren't many times when Alice got one back on Stef, so this was a rare occasion.

'Ah, make it stop,' Stef moaned, as an invisible force jabbed her arm. 'You guys suck,' she rubbed her arm and looked at Gerty and Charlotte who were still struggling to hide their laughter.

'I don't see anything,' Alice said, keeping her composure.

'I'll get you back for this Alice Smithers, just you wait and see,' Stef grinned, before she began to laugh too.

They walked into class in good spirits and sat down at their seats. Miss Scarlet was sitting behind her desk, her hair as usual was elegantly pinned back.

'Quickly girls,' she said to the room and the rest of the girls hurried to their seats.

'I see we have a new girl in our class,' she smiled over at Destiny.

'So I shall briefly go over what I've told you before, no doubt some of you will benefit from the reminder. As you all know the *Book of Spells* is an ancient, extremely powerful book. Only I am allowed to touch it, but that doesn't mean that you won't be learning from it. You all have copies of the book but only I have the original, kept away where only I can see it.'

'Miss, how did you come to own it?' Stef asked.

'It was a matter of timing and having a pure heart. I like to think that the book was looking for me as much as I was for it.'

'Surely other witches and wizards want it too?' Demi asked.

'Indeed they do but they will have to make do with their copies. There are plenty of other spell books, most of them were written hundreds of years ago. I have some in here,' she gestured over to the large bookshelf at the far side of the room. 'And plenty more in my quarters. Collecting these books is a great pleasure of mine. We should all have pleasures and hobbies in life as they strive us onwards.'

Demi and Destiny giggled loudly and Miss Scarlet glared at them.

'I think Mistress of the Book's hobby is turning students into mice,' Charlotte whispered to Gerty.

'Some would say her main passion is books,' Miss Scarlet said and Charlotte blushed. 'Please refrain from talking in my class.'

Charlotte mouthed, 'sorry miss,' as she lowered her head.

'Passion is what drives us forwards and causes us to thrive. Without passion succeeding becomes ever more difficult. One should never lose their passion. Now, all turn to page one-hundred-and-one in your books. Today we shall we practising a simple color-changing spell. As you can see there is an apple in front of each of you. With this spell you should be able to turn it from green to blue.'

'What's the point in a blue apple?' Alice said.

'It is merely a tool for you to practice with. Maybe if you put more thought into your spells instead of questioning instructions you would be more advanced at spells.'

Alice looked sheepish and Demi and Destiny continued to giggle.

'Will both of you please be quiet and concentrate on the spell at hand,' she stared at them.

They both stopped giggling and smiled at each other. Destiny waved her wand around in exaggerated movements that caused Demi to start giggling again.

Miss Scarlet flicked out her wand and a wart appeared on both of Demi and Destiny's noses. They both let out shrieks and covered their faces.

'Now make sure that you speak clearly when casting the spell,' she stood up and looked at the apple on her desk. '*Recensere azureus.*'

The apple immediately changed into a sky blue color.

'Cool,' a girl in the front row said.

'Can you eat it?' Patricia asked.

Miss Scarlet reached over and picked up the apple, bringing it up to her mouth and taking a moderate sized bite out of it.

'Delicious,' she gave a sly smile. 'The apple is still an apple, it is only the color that has changed,' she placed the apple back on her desk.

'It's important that you pronounce the spell clearly. Place your wands down on the table and repeat after me,' all the girls did as she asked, including Demi and Destiny who were still covering their faces. '*Re-cen-sere.*'

'*Re-cen-sere,*' the girls repeated in unison.

'*Az-u-re-us.*'

'*Az-u-re-us,*' they repeated.

'Good, good, one last time but this time we shall combine the words together. Re-cen-sere az-u-re-us.'

'*Re-cen-sere az-u-re-us,*' the class said.

'Wonderful, now let your passion show in your skills and turn that apple blue. There will be a prize for the person who excels the most.'

Miss Scarlet had made the spell look simple but it turned out to be more difficult than it looked.

A girl near the back of the room managed to set her apple on fire and Destiny turned hers black instead of blue.

'*Recenere azueou*s,' Stef said confidently. Her apple shook before it vanished. Huh, where's it gone?' Stef peered around for it. 'Who stole my apple? Demi, give it back.'

'It's not my fault you suck at magic, so I suggest you shift the blame back on yourself,' Demi sniggered, one arm still covering her face.

'It appears you said the spell wrong. Making an object disappear is no mean feat but it's not the spell we are practising. No doubt your apple will pop up somewhere in the Academy. I suggest you work on your pronunciation further.'

Charlotte had tried the spell twice already but nothing had happened. She looked over at the other girls' apples, noticing how Alice's hadn't changed and Gerty's was now a deep shade of purple, a fact she seemed proud of.

'*Recensere azureus,*' Charlotte said, as she flicked her wand out in front of the apple and watched with delight as it immediately turned to a sky blue colour.
'Brilliant work Charlotte,' Miss Scarlet said.

'Thanks,' Charlotte blushed.

Spell practice finished and all the girls sat back down in their seats and chatted amongst themselves.

'Silence,' Miss Scarlet said and the class fell quiet. 'Good effort was made by you all. To those of you who managed to master the spell, well done. To the others, keep on practicing and remember that clear pronunciation and saying the words with a determined force is important. You may think that all a witch needs to do is flick their wand around and utter a few choice words but I can assure you that spell casting is an art-form that requires practice and attention to detail. You must never give-up, nor must you ever take what we do for granted.

For successfully completing the spell first...the prize goes to Charlotte,' Gerty and Stef cheered and some of the other girls clapped. 'This is your reward,' she passed her a small vial full of a glittery silver substance.

'What is it?' asked Stef.

'Fairy dust, sprinkle it when you need some guidance and it will help you make your decision.'

'Cool,' Charlotte said under her breath, as she held the vial up to her face and studied it.

'It is of great importance that you only use it sparingly.'

'Thank you and I will,' Charlotte smiled, as she placed the vial down on the table.

'Miss, I was wondering, could you tell us more about *The Book of Dragons?*' Stef asked.

At first Miss Scarlet gave her an icy glare and Stef sank further down into her chair, worried that she was going to be turned into a toad.

'*The Book of Dragons* is strictly prohibited for young witches such as yourselves. It is dangerous to even the most powerful of witches and in the past has caused many problems. I advise you to keep away from this subject and to forget about this book,' she said firmly, her stern gaze seeming to fix on all of the girls at the same time.

'Right girls, first things first,' her tone was cheery as she waved her wand over at Demi and Destiny and the warts on their noses vanished. 'You better get off to your next lesson and remember a true witch never stops learning.'

Charlotte grabbed her books and her vial of fairy dust. She gave Miss Scarlet a smile and followed the others out of the door.

'I didn't know fairy dust was an actual thing,' Gerty said, as they left the room and walked up the corridor.

'You didn't know that fairies existed?' Stef snorted.

'Of course I did, I just didn't know that fairy dust was a thing, that's all.'

Charlotte didn't say anything, she didn't want to admit to them that until today she'd had no idea that fairies were real. When she was little she used to go down to the bottom of her garden where the plants bloomed in violets and yellows and she pretended that fairies lived amongst them. There was so much in the world that she hadn't known about and she felt like a novice.

'I've never seen fairy dust before,' Alice said and Charlotte held the vial up for her to see.

'What! You don't have a room full of it at home,' Stef grinned.

'No, we don't. As I just informed you, I've never seen it before.'

'Come on Stef, it's not like she baths in it or anything, Gerty giggled.

'I think Miss Scarlet would class bathing in it as using too much,' Alice replied.

'You'd end up looking like a glitter bomb,' Stef laughed.

'Maybe you should try that look at the next school dance,' Alice grinned.

'Perhaps,' Stef smirked.

They arrived back at their room and changed their books. Charlotte tried to think of a safe place to put the vial and decided to hide it in the draw under her bed, wrapped up amongst her clothes.

'When are you going to use the fairy dust?' Gerty asked.

'I don't know, I'm not really sure how it works.'

'I'm sure you'll just know when to use it, you're smart,' Gerty said.
'Thanks,' she smiled, deciding that she was going to save it until the time came when she knew that she'd really need it.

'It's a shame she didn't leave the warts on Demi and Destiny's faces,' Stef said, as she walked towards the door.

'They'd be walking around everywhere like this,' Gerty covered her face with her arms and paced up and down the room.

The other girls burst into laughter as they watched Gerty.

'Stop it, I can't breathe,' Charlotte said in-between laughter, as she clutched her stomach.

'What's so funny about this,' Gerty's muffled voice said through her arm, which caused them to laugh even more.

It was a full five-minutes before they eventually stopped laughing enough to compose themselves and leave for their next class, knowing that they'd have to walk extra quickly to get there on time.

Charlotte had arrived at this Academy clueless about magic and not knowing anyone. Now she had a vial of fairy dust in her draw and some of the best friends she could ask for. Better still Margaret had gone and hopefully they'd be no more surprise visits from her.

She knew that Miss Scarlet only awarded those she truly believed deserved it, which meant that Charlotte was improving at spells. She was a witch, it ran through her blood and she was going to keep on learning to be the best that she possibly could be.

Chapter Five

The girls trudged their way across the yard over to Miss Dread, who was balancing on her two hands, her legs bent over her shoulders.

'I hope she doesn't expect us to copy that position?' Gerty whispered to Charlotte and Alice, as she gripped her broomstick tighter. Miss Dread had told them at the end of their last lesson to bring their broomsticks today, but she wouldn't tell them why.

'Same, although it'd be funny to watch people try it,' Charlotte replied.

'I'm sure it's not that difficult,' Alice stopped walking and balanced on one leg. 'See, easy,' she said, before she began to wobble and grabbed onto Charlotte's shoulder to steady herself.

'I reckon you should keep on practicing,' Gerty giggled.

'Come on girls, stop dawdling,' Miss Dread shouted over to them.

They quickened up their pace and walked over to Stef, who was talking to Melody about what pets they were going to get when they were older.

'I want a fluffy cat and I'd put a spell on it so that it didn't malt all over my furniture,' Melody said.

'I want something more unique, like a bat. I'd call it Shade and let it live in my attic,' Stef replied.

'A bat, how ridiculous,' Alice snorted.

'Darlings, gather round,' Miss Dread said, as she flipped her legs over her head and landed on her feet on the ground. She stood-up, and turned around to face the girls.

'I've got an exciting lesson in store for you today. Come, come,' she gestured for them to follow her. She led them across the yard and over to a grassy hexagonal area that had a basket in each of its corners.

'I hope we finally get to play Save the Princess,' Gerty said excitedly.

'I hope so, I'm great at it,' Stef said.

'You haven't started playing it yet?' Destiny sniggered. 'At my last school we started learning it on the first day of term.'

Charlotte looked from Destiny to the hexagonal field with a perplexed look on her face. She had no idea what Save the Princess was but she didn't want the others to know this, so she remained quiet as she focused her gaze on Miss Dread.

'Darlings, the time has come for you to learn how to play Save the Princess.'

'Yes!' Gerty jumped on the spot and everyone turned and stared at her. 'Sorry, I've just never played it before,' she replied coyly.

'It's good to have an interest in something darling, you need to channel that into the game,' Miss Dread looked at Gerty, before she turned her gaze across the rest of the girls. 'For those of you that aren't familiar with Save the Princess, it is to witches what hockey or football is to ordinaries. As you can see the game is played on a hexagonal base and on each of the six corners is a basket.

You shall be split into two teams and your aim is to fly on your broomsticks and get a ball into each of the six baskets, whilst at the same time you need to try and block the other team from getting the ball in before you.

You shall start with the first basket,' she cartwheeled over to the first basket and put her hand against it. 'The first team to get their ball into this basket will be rewarded with a spell. A ghost shall appear and tell you what you've won.'

'A ghost?' Alice worriedly said.

'Yes darling, a ghost. It shall tell you a spell, it is wise to think carefully about when to use it as it can only be used once and it shall only last for five-seconds. When all the corners have been fought over then a tower shall rise in the middle,' she jumped into the middle of the hexagonal and gestured to the space before she darted out of it.

'Princeps *turrim*,' Miss Dread said, as she directed her wand towards the middle of the hexagonal.

The ground began to shake and Gerty grabbed onto Charlotte's arm. A large bricked tower rose out of the ground and kept on rising higher and higher. When it stopped, the top was only just visible.

'Your aim is to get this doll,' she pulled a princess rag doll from behind her back, 'to the top of the tower before the other team get their princess doll up there.'

'This is the part where the spells you won earlier become useful, although as I said before, you can only use them once so use them wisely.'

'If one player falls from the tower, then their whole team must return to the start line before their climber must restart their climb up the tower. Be warned that it is not as straightforward as it looks, as the tower will not make things easy for you.'

'It looks easy to me,' Stef whispered to Charlotte.

They saw a shape in the sky nearing them that soon came close enough for them to realize that it was Miss Firmfeather. She flew across the yard on her broom and landed down by Miss Dread.

'Hi girls,' Miss Firmfeather waved.

'Miss Firmfeather is here to assist me with assessing you all,' Miss Dread said.

'Assessing?' Demi asked.

'All we want is for you all to try your best,' Miss Firmfeather smiled, as she put her broomstick down and picked up an ancient looking telescope. Surely she wasn't going to watch up that closely!

'Darlings, let's begin,' Miss Dread looked over to the girls. 'Red team,' she pointed at Destiny. 'Black team,' she pointed to Demi. 'Red, black, red, black, red, black, red,' she pointed at the rest of the girls in turn as she gave them a team color.

'Prepare to be beaten,' Stef said to Charlotte and Alice, who'd been put into the opposite team to her and Gerty.

'I doubt it,' Alice replied.

'Come on darlings, you can do this,' Miss Dread clapped her hands.

The girls split into their teams, Miss Dread cast a spell to lower the castle and then the game began. The girls whizzed around the court, throwing the ball without much persuasion. Charlotte lowered her head just in time as Destiny lunged the ball at her.

'You were meant to catch it,' Destiny growled.

'Sorry,' Charlotte blushed.

The only sports Charlotte was used to were tennis and hockey, so this was new to her. She had only just learned how to fly a broomstick and now she had been put into a fast paced and skilled game. She wanted to give it her best, but she felt like a penguin out in the desert.

'Come on girls, focus,' Miss Firmfeather said, as Miss Dread jotted notes down in her notebook.

'Alice,' Patricia shouted, as she threw the ball at her. She looked up just in time and caught it, throwing it into the first basket before Stef had time to intercept her.

A transparent ghost of a man dressed in armor appeared in front of Alice and caused her to fly backwards until she was pressed against the basket.

'The spell you've won will send an icy chill down the opponent you choose to freeze at will, *duratus*,' the ghost said, before it vanished into the air.

'Good job Alice,' Miss Dread said, which caused Alice to smile widely.

'Beginners luck,' Stef quietly snorted.

Demi scored next, getting the ball in the second basket and then one into the third basket. When it came to this game she was fast on her broomstick and ruthless, flying straight at the opposite team with force until they had no choice but to move out of the way.

'Come on, that's not fair,' Melody said after Demi had shoved into her and snatched the ball out of her hands.

'That's the name of the game,' Miss Dread shouted. 'Darling, you must hold tightly onto the ball before you throw it.'

Destiny tried to get the ball off Demi but she threw it over to a blonde girl named Victoria before Destiny could grab it. Victoria leaned back to try and catch it and ended up bashing into Charlotte who lost her balance and fell off her broomstick. She bounced onto the field and sighed, before she lifted herself off and picked up her broom.

'Come on Charlotte, stop sitting around,' Alice shouted to her, after she'd thrown the ball over to another girl.

Charlotte brushed herself off before she got back onto her broomstick and tried to regain her balance as she flew her way back around the court.

By the time the red team got their ball into the sixth basket Melody had grazed her knee and Destiny had a huge bruise on her arm from where Demi had shoved into her to get the ball.

The tower rose up from the center of the court and two princess dolls, one with red hair and in a red dress and the other with black hair and in a black dress appeared at the base of it.

'Normally they'd be one climber per team but today you shall take it in turns so that I can assess you,' Miss Dread said, as she appeared up from her notebook. 'Demi and Melody can go first, the rest of you can use the spells but remember to cast them wisely. Also, don't forget that the tower has plenty of surprises in store for you.

Also if you teammate falls then you have to return to your team start-line,' she gestures to a black and red line on the ground in front of the tower. 'And you can't move away or use any of the spells you've won until your climber is up and back on the tower.'

Demi was the first to grab her doll and begin to climb up the tower.

'Go on Melody,' Destiny shoved her forwards.

'That's not fair, Miss Dread hadn't told us to start,' Melody grumbled, before she grabbed the doll and began the ascent up the tower.

'Don't forget about your spells,' Miss Dread shouted over to the girls on the ground, who were both stood in their teams looking clueless.

'Use the ice one, arhh, what was it?' Destiny said to her team.

'I know it,' Charlotte said, as she looked up at Demi, who was about a quarter of the way up the tower. She flicked out her wand in her direction and said '*duratus.*'

Demi instantly froze on the spot, unable to move at all.

'Melody, hurry up and pass her while she's frozen,' Destiny shouted up at her.

Melody nodded and she started to climb up the ladder of the tower as quickly as she could. She placed her hand onto the next rung of the ladder and that's when a pair of large stone hands appeared from either side of the tower and gave Melody a shove. She screamed out as she let go of the ladder and tumbled down onto the bouncy ground.

'Melody is out, Charlotte, you go next,' Miss Firmfeather said.

Charlotte tried to ignore her nerves, as she picked the princess doll off the ground by Alice and began to climb the ladder.

'You need to be quicker than that,' Destiny shouted. 'Demi's almost halfway up,' she pointed over to Demi who was now unfrozen and way out in the lead.

'*Gestat,*' Stef said as she waved her wand at Charlotte.

Charlotte's grip began to slip, as if there was slimy oil on her hands. She tried to grab on the ladder but she couldn't grasp it, then the princess doll slipped out of her hand and she found herself sliding down onto the ground. She landed on her feet, embarrassed at how little progress she had made up the castle.

'That was a good use of a spell darling,' Miss Dread looked over at Stef.

'Thanks a lot,' Charlotte looked at Stef, unable to keep her stern look for long before it turned into a large smile.

'Sorry,' Stef grinned.

Destiny didn't wait for Miss Dread to tell her to climb, she raced forward and picked the doll up.

'I'll show you how it's done,' she said confidently, as she began to climb up the tower.

Demi was closer to the top of the tower than she was to the bottom and she was convinced that she was going to win. She quickly climbed onto the next step and then the next, then the snakes appeared through gaps in the tower wall, slithering around her arms and legs so that she became tied to the ladder.

'Do something,' she screamed down to her team.

'Erm, *dimissus*,' Stef flicked her wand up at the snakes. Her wand immediately flew out of her hand and hit her across the wrist before it flew over to Miss Dread.

'Stef, you can't use spells that you didn't win. You are disqualified so come and stand over here with us,' Miss Firmfeather said.

'Well I didn't know,' Stef muttered, as she glared at the ground.

'I thought you said you were good at this game?' Gerty grinned.

Demi managed to shake the snakes grip off and carry on up the tower.

'*Magna Pila,*' Charlotte shouted, as she waved her wand up at Demi.

She began to expand so that she resembled a ball with legs and arms sticking out of it. She was now too large to hold onto the ladder and she rolled all the way down the tower and landed in a heap on the ground.

'Good one,' Patricia patted Charlotte on the shoulder.

'Victoria, your turn,' Miss Firmfeather said.

Victoria grabbed the princess doll and stepped around the now shrinking, unhappy looking Demi before she began to climb up the ladder.

The tower began to violently shake, Victoria held on tightly to the ladder and leaned in close to the tower whilst Destiny struggled to hold her grip and soon found herself falling onto the ground. The red team let out sighs and groans, as they watched as the tower stopped shaking and Victoria continued her climb.

'I thought you implied that you were the best at this,' Alice snorted.

'Let's see you do better,' Destiny snarled, as she thrust the princess doll into Alice's hands.

'Okay, fine,' she couldn't hide the doubt from her voice, as she headed towards the steps.

'*Cito,*' Demi flicked her wand up at Victoria. She began to hurry up the ladder with super fast speed, becoming too fast for any arms or snakes that tried to grab her.

'Oh no, she's not far from the top,' Charlotte sighed. 'We have one spell left and so do they.'

'Well let's use it then,' Destiny pulled out her wand.

'No, not yet,' Charlotte reached out and lowered Destiny's wand.

Alice was surprising herself and the other girls, she climbed like a squirrel and weaved out of reach of the grabbing arms. She wasn't far behind Victoria and she was convinced that she was going to reach the top first.

'*Multum unguibus,*' Demi said, as she aimed her wand at Alice.

'Look out,' Patricia shouted but Alice was already aware of the spell and managed to dodge out of its way.

'That's not fair,' Demi moaned.

'Looks like you're out of spells,' Destiny smirked, as she goaded the other team.

Lips appeared near the top of the tower and green gooey gunk spewed out from them and covered Alice and Victoria.

They both squealed, Victoria was the first to lose her balance and fall down from the tower, while Alice managed to hold on.

'Yuck,' Alice said, as she stuck the princess doll under her arm and tried flicking the slime off her. 'It better not make my hair green!'

'Keep on going Alice!' Charlotte shouted.

Gerty ran up to Victoria, grabbed the doll off her and raced up the steps. Even though they were now slippery from the slime she still managed to get up them quickly.

'*Paulo genus*' Charlotte said, as she cast a spell at Gerty and hundreds of little spiders appeared and crawled over Gerty's skin.

'Good one,' Destiny said and Charlotte smiled.

'Ah, eek, eurgh,' Gerty shrieked but she kept on moving up the ladder.

Stone arms reached out and wrapped themselves around Alice. She tried to wriggle free from their grip but they were too strong.

'Hurry up Alice, she's about to overtake you,' Destiny shouted.

'You can do it Alice,' Charlotte said.

'Come on Gerty!' Stef shouted from her place over by the teachers.

None of the teams had any spells left so it was just the girls against the tower. Gerty overtook Alice and dodged the snakes that appeared through the tower gaps, as she made her way up to the top. Alice finally managed to escape the stone hands and hurriedly tried to catch up to Gerty.

The lips reappeared and more gloop flowed down the tower and covered the girls. Alice stopped and clung on tightly to the ladder until the slime had finished, but Gerty kept on going.

'Don't just stand there, move,' Destiny shouted up to Alice.

The gunk stopped and Alice continued to climb but she was too far behind Gerty now. Gerty placed the princess doll at the top of the tower and the black team all cheered.
'That's a black team win,' Miss Dread said.

'Great try girls,' Miss Firmfeather smiled.

'Now, the girls that didn't get to climb wait here, whilst the rest of you can go and sit over there,' Miss Dread pointed across the yard.

'Well done Gerty, you were great,' Charlotte said to Gerty, as she walked up alongside her. 'And sorry about the spiders.'

'Thanks and I forgive you. It was the most fun ever, I hope I get to do it again.'

'I had more slime over me than you did, look, you're barely covered,' Alice pointed at Gerty.

'That's not exactly true,' Charlotte said, as she looked at Gerty's slime-drenched arms, hair and clothes. 'Gerty looks like a slug.'

'You can be a slug too,' Gerty giggled, as she tried to wipe some slime off her arm onto Charlotte, who managed to dodge out of the way in time. They both laughed as Gerty chased after her.

'So immature,' Alice said under her breath, before she glanced up longingly at the top of the tower and let out a sigh.

After all the girls had attempted the princess tower they all gathered around Miss Dread and Miss Firmfeather. Miss Moffat and Molly were now also there, which made Charlotte feel extra nervous.

'Well done girls, although you all got off to an interesting start you all showed great promise and greatly improved. We are yet to decide upon a final team but we can announce who the climber will be. Well done Gerty, you shall be the climber,' Miss Dread looked directly at her.

'Me?' she pointed her thumbs inwards to herself, a surprised look on her face.

'Yes, you are the best witch for the job.'

'Thank you!' she squealed, as she excitedly grabbed onto Stef's arm, covering her in slime.

'Gross,' Stef wiped the slime off her arm as she stepped away from Gerty.

'Sorry,' she grinned.

Alice folded her arms and sighed loudly as she looked away from Gerty.

'Alice, you shall be the substitute climber,' Miss Dread kept her gaze down at her notebook as she spoke.

'Well done Alice,' Charlotte said.

'Yeah, well done,' Gerty smiled.

Alice didn't reply, instead she sighed again, although she couldn't hide the faint smile from her face.

'You are all to report here for Save the Princess training on the dot at sunrise,' Miss Dread's words were followed by groans from the girls. 'It's going to be a tough week but practice makes perfect, I know you can all do it. Oh and darlings, don't forget your broomsticks.'
'My Academy has an excellent reputation when it comes to Save the Princess. We have won many trophies and had students go on to play professionally. Of course it is satisfying to win, but it is more important to know that you've tried your best and that you've played fairly and in the spirit of the game,' Miss Moffat said, as she glanced over the girls with her intense dark eyes.

She gave them all a slight smile before she nodded at the teachers and Molly before flew off on her broom.

'Remember darlings, bright and early tomorrow morning,' Miss Dread said cheerfully. And don't be late,' she added sternly, before she gave them all a wave and walked off with Miss Firmfeather.

'Bye girls, remember to fly smoothly and remain in control of your brooms,' Miss Firmfeather turned and said to them.

'Can we go now?' Stef asked Molly.

'First I want you to all gather around me,' she beckoned them forwards, until they were huddled closely together. 'By all means play fairly, but the girls from Witchery College tend to to be a little darker in their approach and may not play nicely,' she whispered. 'Anyway girls I'll catch you all later,' she walked away from the girls and up the yard, her clipped up hair bouncing as she moved.

The girls gave each other confused looks before they dispersed and left the yard to go back to their rooms.

'What did Molly mean?' Stef said to her friends.

'I don't really know,' Charlotte replied.

'It's exciting, although my legs are really sore right now,' Gerty bent down and rubbed her legs.

'Well I'm glad I'm not the climber when we are against Witchery College as they might cask a dark spell on me,' Alice said.

'You can't use spells you didn't win remember,' Charlotte said, shaking her head. Sometimes Alice really got on her nerves with her negative comments.

'I'm sure it'll all be fine and they'll stick to the rules of the game,' Gerty was unable to hide the slight doubt from her voice.

'It'll be fine Gerty, besides you were amazing climbing up that tower. You were like the lizard that I saw run up a building when I was on holiday with my parents once.'

'Gerty the gecko,' Stef chuckled.

'I suppose you were okay,' Alice said.

'Thanks guys,' Gerty smiled.

'And Miss Dread looked at you when she said your name which is a first, usually we just get called *darlings*,' Stef mimicked Miss Dread's voice on the last word.

Alice gave an annoyed look as she looked away from the rest of the girls, recalling to herself how Miss Dread hadn't looked at her when she'd announced her as substitute climber.

'You guys do stink though,' Charlotte said, as she looked from Gerty to Alice. 'You can both have first dibs on the bathroom.'

'I think we need it,' Gerty wiped some slime off her arm and studied her fingers. 'Alice, you can use the bathroom first.'

'I am the one who is covered in the most slime. If this ruins my expensive tracksuit, then I'm sending the Academy the dry-cleaning bill.'

'I wonder if there's a spell for removing slime?' Charlotte asked.

'Probably, there's a spell for most things. It might come in useful to find out what it is as I have a feeling this isn't the last time I'll get covered in it,' Gerty grinned.

The fitness lesson had been tiring, messy and intense but Charlotte decided that compared to tennis and hockey it was by far the best sport there was. The thought of playing it again made her both excited and nervous at the same time.

She hoped that she'd make the team because she enjoyed casting the spells, but she knew that she needed to improve her flying skills for her to stand a chance of making the team.

Chapter Six

The next week bought with it plenty of Save the Princess practice. Not only were they training at sunrise everyday but Miss Dread had decided to increase this to an extra practice before dinner as well. All the girls were tired and their limbs ached but they had also made vast improvements.

It was after their last practice before their match against Witchery College and all the girls were sat in a semi-circle in the yard around Miss Dread and Miss Firmfeather. They only had a morning practice today as Miss Dread wanted them to have time to recuperate before their match tomorrow.

'Darlings, you all did superbly today. Gerty, you're a natural climber,' Miss Dread smiled, as she looked down at her notebook. 'If you don't make the final team then you shall be on the sub-line which is just as important as playing, because you shall remain part of this team. Because of this you all need to keep your fitness levels up and you all must continue to attend practice on time.The team list for your first match is as follows: Gerty as climber.'

Stef and a few of the other girls cheered and Gerty grinned.

'I don't know why you're cheering when we already knew that,' Alice said.

'The rest of the team are Demi, Destiny, Patricia, Stef, Alice, Victoria and Charlotte.'

'We made it,' Stef gave Charlotte a high-five. 'I knew that we would.'

'I knew that I'd be playing, I am the substitute climber after-all. I need to get the feel for a proper game, rather than having my talents wasted sitting on the sub-line,' Alice added.

'Big-headed much,' Stef rolled her eyes.

'You're just jealous because you're not the substitute climber,' Alice huffed, rolling her eyes.

'I know that you can all succeed darlings. You have all trained hard and I am proud of every single one of you girls. Now darlings go and shower then get some breakfast and I'll see you here tomorrow for the match. Remember that we don't give up at this Academy and you all need to trust yourselves darlings, because you can do it. Now go,' she shooed them with her hands. 'Before I make you do extra practice,' she chuckled.

The girls stood up quickly and hurried away, believing that Miss Dread probably would make them do extra practice if they lingered there for too long.

'At least two of our team are good players,' Demi said loudly to Destiny, as they walked past the others.

'Erm, we're all good players else we wouldn't have made the team,' Stef replied.

'If you say so,' Demi said and both her and Destiny sniggered.

'I'm so excited,' Gerty smiled.

'Yeah, me too,' Charlotte chewed on the side of the lip.

Charlotte was pleased that she'd made the team but she was also nervous at the thought of playing against Witchery College. She'd heard so many stories about them, most of which were bad. Worst of all she was afraid that the rumors about Margaret now attending Witchery College were true and that tomorrow she'd be face-to-face with her once again.

***

It was a placid afternoon and the girls were standing in the yard, dressed in team kits that they'd found laid out on their beds after their morning practice. They consisted of a pleated black skirt and a white t-shirt with the crossed wands crest and 'Miss Moffat's Academy' written on the back of them in black font.

Miss Moffat, Miss Dread and Miss Firmfeather were standing next to a broad shouldered woman who wore black shorts and a burgundy top with the word 'referee' written on the front and back of it. As she spoke to the teachers she fiddled with the whistle that was hanging from her neck.

Rows of tiered seats were now placed around the court and most of the seats were filled by the other teachers and students who were chatting excitedly amongst themselves.

'That cloud over there doesn't look good, I hope it doesn't rain as it will frizz up my hair,' Stef pointed at the black cloud that was in the otherwise clear sky, before she continued to stretch her arms behind her back.

'I think it's moving closer,' Gerty said, as she stretched out her legs one at a time.

'Yeah, it definitely is.'

'They better cast a rain-cover spell, or else I'll end up with a cold for the next week,' Alice moaned.

The black cloud seemed to be moving closer towards them, it's speed increasing and with it the sky began to darken. Stef and Demi both placed their hands over their heads in preparation for the rain.

'It's not a cloud,' Destiny sniggered. 'Look,' she pointed up at it.

The black cloud was nearly upon them, only Destiny was right, it wasn't a cloud at all but instead it was a group of witches on brooms surrounded by a fleet of bats.

'Why do you still have your hands over your head?' Alice asked Stef.

'I don't trust them not to turn into an actual rain cloud or something,' she replied, not moving her hands.

A beautiful witch in a long black dress and a shawl made of glossy black feathers was the first to land, closely followed by the students, who were dressed in all black. Charlotte scanned her eyes over the girls in search of Margaret but she couldn't see her there.

'Look, her hair, she's got feathers,' Gerty whispered to Charlotte.

Charlotte looked at the woman and that's when she realized that Gerty was right, her hair was a thick mass of shiny black feathers, just like a ravens.

Most of the girls looked around the same age as the first years, besides a couple of girls who were older. They weren't dressed in the team sports kit like the others but instead wore short black skirts and fitted black blouses with the crest on the right side of it, the words 'Witchery College' written below it.

The older girl with dark skin and braided hair glared over at Molly and Charlotte noticed how Molly clutched tightly onto her wand as she gave her a stern look back.

Miss Moffat walked over and greeted the feather-haired woman with an awkward hug before she led her and her team over to the court.

'Come on darlings,' Miss Dread walked over to them. 'And don't forget to suck it up girls. I know that you can all do this, so don't you dare quit.'

'Why would we quit?' Stef whispered to Gerty, as they followed Miss Dread over to the court.

'Are you okay Charlotte?' Victoria asked Charlotte, on seeing how pale she'd gone.

Charlotte nodded, too nervous to speak. She clutched onto her broom tightly for support and looked over at the Witchery College girls who were sniggering over at them.

Miss Moffat and Mistress walked out into the middle of the court and all eyes fell on them.

'To those of you that don't already know, this is Mistress Ravenshawk, the principle of Witchery College. On behalf of my Academy, I welcome her and her students and hope that their time here is enjoyable,' Miss Moffat addressed the crowd.

'Thank you Miss Moffat,' Mistress Ravenshawk said, her voice soft but still managing to carry with it a strong sense of authority.

'It is an honor to be here for what I'm sure will be a pleasurable game. I'm sure it won't be long before we return the favor and have you back over to our grounds.'

'May the games begin,' Miss Moffat shouted and leprechauns appeared either side of the court and blew their trumpets loudly.

Both teams jogged a lap of the court, whilst the onlookers clapped and cheered. When they'd finished they both gathered in their teams and the referee walked over to the sideline of the court.

'Girls, I'm in no doubt that you can do this,' Miss Firmfeather smiled. 'Remember to stay focused, hold tightly onto your broom and remember how important timing is with the ball, don't let go of it too early or too late.'

Mistress Ravenshawk had her team gathered in tightly around her as she quietly spoke to them, making sure that no one else heard them.

Miss Moffat and Molly appeared in front of them and Miss Firmfeather nodded at the girls before she walked over to the referee.

'Witchery College are a formidable team but I believe in you and I know that you will give it your all. I want you all to do your best and most importantly...enjoy yourselves. It is important that you don't forget that you're representing this Academy, so show team spirit and give it your greatest effort. I'm far too nervous to stand here and say anything else, so I'm going to leave you all with Molly and go and take my seat,' Miss Moffat said, before she quickly walked across the court.

'Good luck girls and you better win or I'll turn you all into toads,' Mistress Ravenshawk winked, as she gave her team a wave as she followed Miss Moffat over to the reserved seats on one of the lower rows.

'I'm so nervous I think I may throw-up,' Gerty muttered.

'You'll be fine, just don't fall,' Destiny patted her on the shoulder, a confident look on her face.

'We'll be fine, those girls look ghastly, look at how ugly they all are,' Demi gave the other team, a large false smile.

Charlotte didn't say anything, instead she kept her gaze directed at the ground and hoped that she didn't look as nervous as she felt. Her arms were shaking and she tried gripping harder onto her broomstick so that no one noticed this.

'Are you okay?' Gerty whispered to her.

'Yeah, just nervous,' she whispered back.

'Miss Moffat's right, we just need to go out there and enjoy ourselves. Whatever happens, we've trained super hard and we just have to do our best,' Gerty smiled.

'Gather in,' Molly gestured them forwards. 'Miss Moffat's words contain a fine sentiment and all...but we are here to win. There's no way that you can lose against Witchery College,' she shuddered. 'My advice would be to play then at their own game,' she winked. 'You have to win or I might do some toad changing myself,' she smirked.

'No pressure then,' Stef rolled her eyes, before she followed Demi and Destiny out onto their starting positions on the court.

Charlotte stood in front of the third post by the side of a scary looking girl from Witchery College. Not only was she a good few inches taller than Charlotte, she also hadn't stopped snarling at her since they'd both taken their positions.

Gerty was standing in the middle of the court next to Witchery College's Climber. She was all smiles as she looked over at Charlotte and gave her a thumbs-up. The referee walked over to them and magicked up a large toad, half of it was orange and the other half was blue.

'Which color do you choose?' the referee said to the climber from Witchery College.

'Blue,' she replied without hesitation.

'Miss Moffat's Academy, you're orange. The side that the toad lands on first gets the ball,' she said, before she threw the toad high up into the air.

Both teams watched as the toad fell down onto the ground, its blue legs touching down onto the ground before it bounced back up.

'Blue it is,' the referee handed the ball to the Witchery College's smirking climber.

'Mount your brooms and wait for the whistle,' the referee watched as all the girls got onto their broomsticks and then she placed the whistle in her mouth.

The whistle blew and both teams flew up into the air and wasted no time in flying around the court. The Witchery College girl with the ball threw it over to the tall girl. Charlotte tried to intercept the girls catch but ended up being elbowed out of the way, only just managing to keep balanced on her broomstick.

Destiny snuck up behind the girl with the ball and snatched it out of her grasp. She flew away from her before she threw the ball over to Demi who then managed to get it past the Witchery College girl and into the basket.

There were loud cheers from the girls and the crowd and snarls and groans from the girls from the opposing team. The ghost appeared and floated in front of Demi and all the girls listened to what spell it was going to give her.

'Kittens are as sweet as honey, apart from their fur-balls as they aren't funny. Fur-ball overload with *fur-pila*.'

Charlotte made a mental note of the spell as she watched the ghost vanish. The game continued and Witchery College whizzed around the court, bashing into the girls brooms and grabbing the ball out of their grasps. Miss Moffat's team took the aggression well, remaining on their brooms and grabbing for the ball when they saw the opportunity.

Although Miss Moffat's team were trying their best Witchery College won the next two baskets, mainly because of the tall girl who kept a firm grip on the ball whilst still managing to swipe her broomstick and her elbow into the opposition.

Stef had the ball but Witchery College were closing in on her and she couldn't fly free.

'Alice,' she shouted, before she threw the ball over to her.

Alice reached out and caught it in one hand and the onlookers cheered excitedly from the side-line. A girl with her hair tied into bunches flew with speed towards Alice, trying to grab at the ball. Alice, ducked out of the way and threw the ball into the air, it spun over to the third basket and bounced against it. Charlotte held her breath as she watched the ball slow down it speeds and wobble from side-to-side before it tipped into the fourth basket.

The crowd cheered loudly and Alice grinned widely.

'As an eight-legged creature, you'll scuttle as you move. Accuracy and speed is what you have to prove, *Stilio crura*,' the ghost announced, before he disappeared.

A girl from Witchery College shoved Demi off her broom to claim the fifth basket.

'That wasn't fair!' Demi said with disgust. 'That basket shouldn't count!' she stared at the referee but got no reaction.

'Go on Miss Moffat's,' someone shouted from the crowd.

'Let's do this,' Stef said, before the referee threw the ball into the air and she charged forwards for it, managing to swerve out of the way of one of the opposing girls with such force that it caused them to topple off their broom.

Stef reached out her hands and grabbed it just before the girl with bunches could. There were more cheers from the crowd, blocking out the disgruntled snarls from the Witchery College girls.

Stef whizzed her way over to the sixth basket, weaving her way around the opponents. Suddenly the grass beneath her rose up like snakes and wrapped itself around Stef's arms, legs and broomstick. She shrieked out as the ball dropped out of her hand and onto the ground. The grass roots let go of her suddenly and she toppled down onto the ground, her broomstick landing on her leg with a thud.

Stef grabbed her broomstick and pulled herself up, but one of the Witchery College girls had already grabbed the ball.

'They used an illegal spell,' Molly shouted over to the referee but she ignored her and stared out at the court...a smiling, dazed look on her face.

Mistress Ravenshawk gave a sly smile as she discreetly lowered her wand. She was adamant on her team winning and fair didn't come into it.

Charlotte saw the girl with the bunches putting away her wand, she knew that she'd cast the illegal spell on Stef and wondered why the referee hadn't disqualified her for it.

The girls tried to get to the ball back but the Witchery College girls were on full defence, swatting away anyone who got in their way. The last basket was scored and groans filled the stands and the court.

'They cheated!' Destiny said, as she flew over to the referee. 'Didn't you see the grass grab at Stef, that last basket should have been ours!'

The referee didn't reply, instead she gave a large smile and rocked her head in time to an unheard tune.

An annoyed Destiny went over to her team, who were being pep-talked by Miss Dread.

'Darlings, I know you can do this. You have won some excellent spells so don't waste them, stay strong as a team, communicate and Gerty, climb as if your life depends on it.'

'What is wrong with the referee?' Stef asked, as she rubbed her bruised leg.

'It seems as though foul play is afoot which gives you girls more reason to beat them. If you win by cheating then you haven't properly won, you have to rise above them and prove that you're the better team. Now drink your pumpkin juice as you must hydrate and remember to suck it up, as I know you can all do it,' she nodded at them, before she back-flipped her way back over to Miss Firmfeather who was attempting to communicate with the referee to no avail.

'It doesn't look like the referee will be of any use,' Charlotte sighed.

'Whoever cast that spell on the referee must have been super powerful,' Gerty said.

'Aren't you worried? If they cast that spell on Stef, imagine what they might cast on you when you're trying to climb that tower,' Alice said.

'Nah, what happens, happens. All I can do is try my best which is what I'm going to do,' Gerty shrugged, as she skipped her way over to the middle of the court where the castle had risen up.

'I hope that I come out of this alive,' Patricia said to Charlotte as she walked past her.

Charlotte bit down on the side of her lip as she walked over to the starting position. This morning she had been terrified that Margaret would show up, but instead she was equally as afraid of the other Witchery College girls. She wasn't about to give up though, if Gerty was willing to climb up that high tower knowing that any number of spells could be cast upon her, then Charlotte knew that she could try her hardest to help her from the court ground.

Miss Firmfeather blew the referee's whistle to signal the start of the tower run and both the tall girl and Gerty raced over to their dolls and began to climb their sides of the tower.

Gerty was ahead of the other climber, dodging and weaving away from the towers grabbing hands as she went higher and higher with no signs of tiring.

'*Tempestatis nubes,*' one of the Witchery College girls cast a spell up at Gerty and a storm cloud appeared over her head and drenched her.

This didn't deter Gerty who continued to climb at a fast speed. Charlotte looked up and saw how close Gerty was to the top of the tower and then she looked over at the opposing climber who wasn't far behind her. She met the eye of Demi and Stef for approval before she flicked out her wand at the Witchery College climber.

'*Fur-pila,*' she shouted and the climber stopped on the spot, bent over and began to cough out large balls of fur.

'Gross,' Stef chuckled.

'Go Gerty,' Charlotte cheered.

'*Arma,*' the girl with the bunches said and Charlotte's wand flew out of her hand and spun over to the stands.

Charlotte rushed after it, dread filling her body at the thought of it breaking. As she neared the stand Molly stood-up and pulled Charlotte's wand from behind her back.

'I told you that they didn't play fair,' Molly whispered.

'Thank you, thank you so much,' Charlotte gave a relieved sigh, as she took her wand off Molly and raced back onto the court.

Gerty had managed to dodge two of the Witchery College spells and was now only a couple of steps from the top. She had her princess doll outstretched and her team was cheering excitedly.

Mistress Ravenshawk twitched her nose and said something under her breath as she subtly pointed up at Gerty.

'Honk, honk,' Gerty said as her hands and feet turned into flippers and she slid all the way to the bottom of the tower, the princess doll landing on her head.

'What happened?' Charlotte rushed over to her.

'How could you let that happen, you were an arm's reach away from winning,' Demi grunted.

'Honk, honk,' Gerty held out one of her flippers.

'They're nothing but a bunch of cheaters, let's beat them,' Stef pulled Gerty up onto her flippers.

The tall girl had almost reached the top of the tower and Molly was not impressed. She took out her wand and muttered out an incantation, smirking to herself as the tall girl instantly blew up so that she resembled a balloon and floated away from the tower, screaming out in a rage as she flew away.

'This is an outrage,' Mistress Ravenshawk stood-up and abruptly strode over to the referee. 'They clearly just used an illegal spell, do something?'

The referee grinned at her before she spun in a circle and then tipped her head from side-to-side. Mistress Ravenshawk huffed before she walked off, her feathered-hair blowing slightly in the breeze.

Mistress Ravenshawk looked over at Gerty whose arms and legs were back to normal and she had picked up the princess doll and was running towards the tower. She struck out her wand in a swift movement and the grass beneath Gerty's feet turned into thick, wet concrete. The faster Gerty tried to run, the further she sank into it.

Gerty was stuck and the concrete continued to move out across the rest of the Miss Moffat's girls until all of them were also stuck.

'What now?' Stef shouted.

'We have one spell left, the spider one,' Charlotte said.

'Then let's use it now,' Demi said, as she readied her wand. She tried hard to pull the spell from her mind but she couldn't remember it.

'*Stilio Crura,*' Charlotte said firmly, as she waved her wand over at Gerty.

Gerty began to shake before eight long furry legs sprouted out of her side, pulling her human legs out of the wet concrete and scuttling across it.

'Go Gerty!' Stef shouted, as she watched Gerty reach the tower and crawl her way up it.

The climber from the opposing team had deflated and was now at a similar point on the tower as Gerty was. Feathers came out of the holes in the tower and tried to tickle Gerty off but she didn't let go of her grip.

One of the tower hands grabbed the opposing climber and nearly swiped her off it. She steadied herself just as gunk poured from the lips that appeared near the top of the tower and covered them both. Gerty had a minor slip but soon recovered whereas the other climber lost her footing and only just rebalanced her grip in time.

'*Velox scanders,*' a short girl with freckle covered cheeks from the opposing team shouted, as she flicked her wand up at her climber.

The spell was meant to make her climb very fast but the girl had cast it wrong, causing their climber to move quickly the wrong way down the tower.

Her team yelled at her and Mistress Ravenshawk appeared at the sideline and once again attempted to argue with the referee.

'Go on Gerty!' Charlotte shouted.

'Keep on going!' Demi screamed.

Charlotte held her breath as Gerty made the last few steps and then stretched out her arms, placing the princess doll safely on top of the tower.

Loud cheers erupted and all the Academy girls hugged each other, including Demi who excitedly grabbed Charlotte into an embrace before awkwardly letting go of her.

'We did it,' Stef cheered, as she patted Alice on the shoulder.

'Of course we did, I'm from the type of family that does not know how to lose!' she replied.

'Foul,' the girl with bunches shouted over at the referee. 'They cheated so we should win.'

'We did not cheat,' Demi marched over to her. 'You're just a sore loser.'

'The game should be rerun!'

'No chance!' Demi replied.

Mistress Ravenshawk looked frustrated as she walked across the court over to the tall girl, her wand at the ready.

Charlotte thought that she was going to turn her into a toad but instead she thrust the girl's broomstick at her and said something that Charlotte couldn't quite hear.

The Witchery College team were either crying or shouting at Miss Moffat's Academy team and spells were flying between the two sides.

The girl with bunches was now clucking and walking about like a chicken, much to Demi's amusement and Patricia had been turned as blue as a blueberry.

Molly was in a heated debate with two of the older girls from the Witchery College and although outnumbered, Molly didn't look in the slightest bit concerned. She managed to turn both of the girls into grey rats before they had a chance to cast a spell on her. Molly grinned as she stepped over them and their pile of clothes as she walked off to join the girls on the court.

The tall girl was glaring at Charlotte, her wand raised. She was about to use the blocking spell that Gerty had found for her when she saw Miss Moffat flick her wand.

Calmness ascended on the girls and all the cast spells reversed. Both the tall girl and Charlotte lowered their wands and walked over to their teams.

Miss Moffat walked into the center of the court where the tower had now been lowered and she coughed loudly to clear her throat. All attention turned to her and the yard fell silent.

'Congratulations Witchery College on your superb effort and thank you for travelling over to our Academy. It was a pleasure to host you and to see you play strongly. Now, my girls, you showed that strong will and exquisite teamwork will pay off. I am very proud of you all and there will be a special celebration for you on the weekend.'

Miss Moffat nodded over at Mistress Ravenshawk who nodded back, the furious look still on her face.

'Come on girls, let's go,' Mistress Ravenshawk clapped her hands loudly and her broomstick appeared by her side.

All of the Witchery College girls flew over to Mistress Ravenshawk, including the two older girls that were now human but were still twitching erratically.

They all glared and growled in the direction at the other girls as they took off up into the air and flew off, a mass of bats surrounding them.

'We did it,' Gerty wrapped her arms around Charlotte and Alice.
'If you've got slime on my clothes then you can wash them,' Alice replied, although she didn't move away.

'But it isn't one of your expensive tracksuits?' Gerty giggled.

'I still don't want it to get dirty.'

'We couldn't have done it without you Gerty, you're a natural climber,' Charlotte said.

'Eek, we won,' Gerty ran on the spot.

'I wonder what the celebration will be?' Charlotte asked.

'I hope there will be cake there,' Stef said.

News of their win had spread and as they walked back to their rooms every student congratulated them.

'I could get used to this, it's like being famous,' Stef said, as she pushed their bedroom door open.

The others followed her into the room and the doors of the large ornate wardrobe immediately opened and sucked their broomsticks out of their hands.

'Mistress Ravenshawk didn't look very happy, do you think she'll turn her girl students into toads?' Gerty chuckled.

'I hope she does, they deserve it after cheating. I would have scored that sixth basket if it wasn't for their illegal move,' Stef said.

'Do you know why her hair is made of feathers?' Charlotte asked and Gerty shook her head.

'I know why, my mother told me,' Alice said.

'Do you really know?' Stef asked.

'Of course I do, my great-grandmother attended school with her.'

'Please tell us Alice,' Charlotte begged.

'Okay then,' Alice sat down on the edge of her bed. 'Many years ago Mistress Ravenshawk attended this Academy, only she wasn't known by the name Ravenshawk then, her name was Celeste. She was a powerful witch but she was disobedient and chose her desire to win at all costs, over loyalty. There was a witch called Roxanne who was also very powerful and Celeste was jealous of her.'

'Was Roxanne your great-grandmother?' Gerty asked.

'Of course not,' Alice said snootily. 'Anyway Celeste was so jealous that she used a spell from the *Book of Dragons* to take away Roxanne's powers. It just so happened that Roxanne's father, a man called Lord Adogold was one of the most powerful wizards in the world. When he found out what Celeste had done to his daughter he was furious. He hunted her down and although she was a strong witch...her powers were no match for him. He turned her into a raven and for many years she flew around the skies unable to turn herself back.

One day Lord Adogold decided that she'd paid the price for her actions and he turned her back into a human. He kept the feathers growing from her scalp so that she would remember never to dare cross him or his family ever again.'

'How do we know you didn't just make that up?' Stef said.
'I did not make it up, look it up if you don't believe me.'

'Maybe you looked it up in the library already and what you said about your great-grandmother going to school with her was nonsense.' Step was trying to push Alice's buttons.

'I'll have you know that Violet Alexandra Pennyford was very much a student here. If you don't believe me I suggest that you consult the Academy records,' Alice huffed.

'We all believe you Alice, Stef's just messing with you,' Charlotte said.

'I find it fascinating, she was a bird for all those years probably thinking that she'd never be human again. Imagine soaring through the skies,' Gerty held her arms out either side of her and pretended to fly around the room.

'Don't you know any wing spells?' Alice asked.

'I tried one once but it didn't go so well,' Gerty stopped pretending to fly and walked back over to her bed.

'Why, what happened?'

'Well, I ended up temporarily turning myself into a penguin.'

'They're a flightless bird,' Stef laughed.

'I know but I did make a very cute penguin. My mom was certainly surprised when she found me waddling around the kitchen trying to open a tin of sardines with my beak,' Gerty chuckled.

'Penguins are my favorite, when I was younger my parents used to take me to the zoo and I would scream if they tried to move me away from the penguins. In the end, they took it in turns to stand with me whilst the other one went off and looked at the other animals,' Charlotte said.

'Charlotte making a scene, who'd have imagined that,' Stef smirked.

'Like I said, I really liked penguins,' she grinned.

'I like penguins too but I'd rather be human. Anyway, I'm going to wash this slime off because I stink,' Gerty held her towel under her arm and headed towards the bathroom.

'That's probably for the best, you do smell pretty bad,' Stef waved her hand in front of her nose before she burst into laughter.

'You don't smell so great either,' Gerty laughed back, before she disappeared into the bathroom.

'Do you know a spell to make the weekend hurry up, I want to see what surprise Miss Moffat has for us?' Charlotte said.

'Nope,' Stef shook her head.'We'll just have to wait it out.'

'You girls are so impatient, it's only a few days away,' Alice said, as she tugged her brush through her hair.

Charlotte and Stef both exchanged knowing looks and tried not to laugh.

'I still can't believe that we won, it's the best feeling ever,' Charlotte smiled, as she fell back onto her bed.

'We're a strong team and we have Gerty for a climber so we were sure to win,' Stef replied.

'Do you think we will face Witchery College again sometime soon?'

'Probably.'

'I hear that it's in a black castle surrounded by a moat of boiling tar, so you better hope that you don't fall off your broomstick when flying over to it,' Alice said.

'Yeah right, I suppose you know that because your great-great-great-aunt was a student?' Stef goaded.

'I come from a very respected wizarding family and none of us have attended Witchery College.' Alice put her nose into the air, how dare any of these lower-class witches make fun of her family.

As the two girls carried on bickering Charlotte closed her eyes and relived the game in her head and a contented smile spread across her face.

Chapter Seven

It was the girls' first lesson with Miss Zara, their fortune-telling teacher and they were all excitedly apprehensive about it.

'I hear that she's strict and that she once turned a second year into a slug for a whole week,' Gerty said, as she walked alongside Charlotte up the hallway.

'Do we have to go to this class, my mother says that fortune-telling is nonsense anyway and that we are in charge of our own fate,' Alice groaned.

'Don't let Miss Zara hear you say that,' Stef said and a worried look appeared on Alice's face.

'She can't be that bad,' Charlotte said, as she pulled on Gerty's arm. 'Come on, let's make sure that we aren't late.'

'And that we get good seats,' Stef added.

They hurried into class and over to the front row, which was the only place where there were four seats together. Miss Zara was sitting behind an intricately carved oak desk, a large glass ball on a stand in front of her. Her long dark hair fell in ringlets down her blue trimmed black dress and she wore a beaded black choker around her neck. She wasn't looking at the girls, instead she was glancing down at the worn-covered book that was in front of her.

The girls exchanged looks between themselves and sat in silence. They didn't dare speak just in case Miss Zara turned out to be as terrifying as she was made out to be.

'I am Miss Zara, fortune telling is what I shall teach you. Unimportant is what you might think this lesson is. You take your spells and your potions, you say they are more useful. I vant you all to understand that my lessons count,' she said in a strong Russian accent.

'Come, come,' she gestured for the girls to gather around her. 'This crystal ball is important, very much so. 'Fortune telling is not alvays correct, because your actions can change your future. However, your futures are all in the crystal ball for this point in time.'

'So you can see what will happen to us in the future?' Demi asked.

'Yes, it is in there. Who will volunteer?'

'Me,' Stef shot her arm into the air.

'Miss, you should choose me to go first, after all I know my future is assured as I do come from a first class witching family,' Alice chimed in and Stef rolled her eyes.
'Yes, Alice Smithers, let's look at your future first,' Miss Zara gave a slight smile as she leaned over the crystal ball.

'The Magic Mirror Company is where you work.'

'Don't you mean I own it?' replied Alice.

'You work the assembly line, installing magical powers into the mirrors.'

'What do you mean by that?' Alice said angrily.

'You know, magic mirror on the wall, I give you the powers to install, yada, yada, yada,' she waved out her hand. 'Don't believe me, see for yourself.'

Alice looked down at the crystal ball and saw a woman with the same mousey brown hair and freckles. It was an older version of herself. She was wearing a long white lab coat with a badge saying 'Magic Mirror Spell Installer,' pinned onto it.

'No, it can't be,' Alice muttered, before she walked back to her seat and sat down in shocked silence.

'Stephanie, your turn,' Miss Zara said. She looked back into the crystal ball. 'Big things vill happen to you Stephanie Jolly.'

'Are they good or bad big things?' Stef asked.

'You are destined to marry the most influential and wealthy wizard in the world. Together you vill rule over a kingdom of magical people and creatures and bring good deeds to your land.'

'Gosh!' Stef exclaimed, her legs beginning to wobble so she leaned against the desk to steady herself.

'Who is he?' Gerty asked.

'You have met him recently.'

'Do you think it's the boy you were dancing with at the dance?' Gerty said.

'I doubt it, he didn't look like he would ever be a powerful wizard,' Destiny said.

'Demi seemed to like him,' Charlotte added.

'I did not,' Demi grunted.

'This is so exciting, make sure you invite us to the wedding,' Gerty clapped her hands.

Stef just stood there speechless before she nodded her head and walked over to her seat, sitting down next to a now even more annoyed looking Alice.

'Gertrude, your turn,' Miss Zara studied the crystal ball. 'Umm, let's see. Ah yes, Gertrude Baggs, you're going to live in the normal world and as a witch you vill be able to help many people around the world. I see you on the world stage as a humanitarian, you are receiving a reward. Let's see, aahh, yes, the Nobel Spell Prize.'

'That's the perfect reading for you Gerty,' Charlotte hugged her friend.

Gerty excitedly jumped on the spot, a huge smile on her face.

'Charlotte Smyth, you are next. Such a big heart you have, full of love and goodness. Charlotte you are going to become a teacher at this Academy. And one day when Miss Moffat retires she shall entrust you to become the principal at this esteemed school.'

The other girls gasped on hearing this and they all looked at Charlotte, who blushed, not knowing what to say.

'Your fellow teachers vill admire your special ability to turn around girls who are on the edge,' she glared over at Demi. 'Into respectful young ladies.'

'That's really great Charlotte, you'll make an amazing teacher,' Gerty wrapped her arms around her dear friend.

'One reading is all I have enough energy left for,' Miss Zara yawned. 'Demi, come closer,' she gestured her forwards. 'It shall be you.'

Demi looked wary as she reluctantly took a step forward.

'Let me see,' Miss Zara fell silent as she concentrated on her crystal ball. 'Demi Taylor, do you like iPhones?' she glanced up at her.

'Erm yes, they're by far the best type of phone.'

'Good, good, because when you leave school you're going to repair shattered iPhone screens in a phone repair factory.'

'What!' Demi shouted.

'It's not all bad Demi,' Miss Zara patted her on the shoulder. 'You are by far the best worker in the entire factory. Every day you will repair hundreds of screens, with a little help from your magic ability.'

Demi stared at her open-mouthed, too startled to show her anger.

'What about my good friend Margaret Montgomery, do you know what her future will be?' Demi enquired, still feeling wounded on hearing about her future.

'Good news, you'll see her every day.'

'Will she be working in the iPhone factory as well?'

'No, but a fast food restaurant is across the road from there, I see her flipping burgers.'

Demi lowered her head, she didn't want to hear anything else Miss Zara had to say about her future as her words were too awful for her to comprehend.

'Remember that the future is always changing, but if you want to change the future...you must change your behavior,' Miss Zara addressed the girls, stopping on Demi.

Demi nodded her head before she looked down at the desk in deep thought.

'Over the coming months I shall teach you how to read the crystal ball without my help. For today this is the end of the lesson,' Miss Zara gave them all a smile before she went back to reading her book.

The girls all left the classroom, chatting excitedly amongst themselves about Miss Zara's future predictions. They found her fascinating and frightening at the same time and they were all curious to learn how to be able to read fortunes by themselves.

Chapter Eight

The weekend arrived and with it came their reward for winning Save the Princess. The yard had been turned into a party paradise, with a large table full of cupcakes and sweets. There was a constantly flowing fountain, one side of it contained red soda and the other chocolate. There was also a color-changing candy-floss stand. The candy-floss was being spun by large grey owls.

'This is the best party ever,' Gerty said, as she dipped her eighth strawberry into the chocolate side of the fountain.

'It's definitely better than the last party I went too,' Charlotte grinned.

'Look,' Alice pointed up to Miss Firmfeather, who had turned her broomstick into a rhino and was flying above them.

'Girls, who wants a ride?' she smiled down at them.

'Me, me,' Gerty squealed, as she waved her arm in the air.

'Do you think flying is a good idea, the amount of chocolate strawberries you've had?' Alice said.

'I once ate a family bag of chocolate buttons and then went on a plane and I was fine,' Gerty replied.

Miss Firmfeather landed the rhino in front of them and beckoned an excited Gerty forwards. She flicked out her wand at Gerty and made her feet lift off the ground and up onto the back of the rhino. They flew a couple of laps around the yard before Miss Firmfeather helped Gerty down with a spell.

Alice went next and Charlotte and Gerty cheered for her as she and Miss Firmfeather flew around the yard. Stef walked over to the candy-floss stand where a group of second-years were holding a stick of color-changing candy-floss.

'That looks so cool,' Stef said to them.

'You have to get some, the flavors change depending on what color it is,' a girl with waist length blonde hair said.

'The pink is watermelon favor,' a wavy-haired, petite girl said.

'A large candy-floss please,' Stef said to the owl and it held the stick in its beak as it spun it around the candy-floss.

Stef was on her way back over to the others when a giant bubble engulfed her and lifted her up into the air.

'What the fudge,' Stef said, as she she looked down at the ground and saw Sonya and Silvia waving back at her. They blew another huge bubble that surrounded another unsuspecting girl.

'Put me down right now,' the girl shouted.

Stef shrugged before she sat down in the bubble and put her feet up against it, rolling herself forwards as she bit off chunks of her candy-floss.

The other girl in the bubble saw what Stef was doing and copied her, her outcries soon turned into shouts of joy as she rolled around the yard. Soon girls were begging Sonya and Silvia to blow bubbles at them and dozens of girls were rolling around in the huge bubbles.

Stef's bubble lowered itself onto the ground before it popped and Stef walked over to her friends. Charlotte and Gerty both pulled chunks off Stef's currently green candy-floss.

'Yum apple,' Gerty said.

A Beyoncé tune began to blare out across the yard and Miss Dread was using the Save the Princess court for a dance floor.

'Come on girls, come and dance,' she gestured them over.

'I love this song,' Gerty grabbed Charlotte and Alice's arms and pulled them forwards and Charlotte called out to Stef to join them.

Stef stood on the side-line as she finished her candy-floss and watched as the other girls joined in on the dance floor and copied Miss Dread's moves.

'And spin,' Miss Dread said, as she spun on the spot and all the girls copied her.

Stef finished her candy-floss and joined the girls on the dance floor.

Five Beyoncé songs later and the girls walked off the dance floor out-of-breath but in full spirits. They stood on the side-line and retrieved their breath before they walked across the yard.

'Got me looking, got me looking so crazy in love,' Gerty sang.

'What now?' Charlotte asked.

'We haven't been on Dexter yet,' Alice pointed over to the far side of the yard where girls were bouncing on the dragon's belly.

Demi and Destiny were already bouncing on Dexter and Alice eagerly joined them, followed by the others. To start with all the girls were being sensible and careful, avoiding bouncing into each other, but then Charlotte misjudged her bounce and accidentally brushed into Demi's arm. Charlotte thought that Demi would shout at her, but instead she giggled and gave her a gentle shove.

Soon all of them were bouncing high on Dexter, holding hands and laughing.

'Higher!' Destiny yelled, as she pulled on Alice and Stef's hands. 'Let's jump higher!'

Destiny pulled on their hands too much and then they all tumbled down onto Dexter's belly, giggling.

'Do you think we'll get a party like this, every time one of our team wins?' Gerty asked.

'I hope so,' Demi replied.

'It's worth it just for the candy-floss, talking of which,' Stef shuffled her way over to the ladder by the side of Dexter.

The rest of the girls stood back up and grabbed each other's hands before they began to bounce again. Charlotte couldn't hide her smile, she didn't like conflict and she was glad that they were getting on with Demi and Destiny. Winning Save the Princess had shown them that they were a team and they succeeded far more when they worked together.

Alice slowed down her jumping and tugged on Charlotte's arm as she gestured for her to look across the yard. Charlotte stopped on the spot and Demi followed Charlotte's gaze.

When she saw what Charlotte was looking at...Demi abruptly stopped, the smile vanishing from her face.

Standing across from them, her blond hair swiped behind her back and a severe look on her pretty face was Margaret Montgomery. The yard fell silent as the rest of the girls noticed her, including Stef who almost dropped her candy-floss.

Charlotte found herself thinking about the vial of fairy dust that was tucked away in the draw under her bed. She regretted the fact that she didn't have it on her...as she could have done with some guidance right now. The girl who'd nearly got her expelled and who'd turned her into a cockroach, leaving her to be squashed, was back at the Academy.

Margaret looked far from happy as she glanced over at the girls who were on Dexter and who had clearly been having a brilliant time without her. She felt betrayed and angry and she clutched her wand tightly as her gaze remained unfaltered.

Book 3

My First True Love

Chapter One

The season was fall and the crisp sunset-shaded leaves surrounded Charlotte like a blanket. She looked down and saw that her feet were bare and with each step the leaves rustled beneath her.

Although she was outside it held the warmth of a summer's day and the floral print sun-dress she wore suited the temperature.

Behind two arched trees up ahead stood Gerty, Stef and Alice, who waved over-excitedly at Charlotte. She waved back before she began to run across to them. A gust of wind flew past her, causing the blue ribbon that was tied in her hair to come loose and flail in front of her. She reached out and grabbed onto it and began to weave it around her wrist, only the fabric kept on coming, until it was now snaked up the majority of her arm.

She looked down at her ribboned arm questioningly and she was about to continue wrapping the ribbon around her wrist, only she realized that there was no more ribbon to thread.

'Charlotte, over here,' Gerty shouted from up ahead, as she waved and jumped up on the spot.

'Coming,' Charlotte shouted back, only her words seemed to get lost in the air.

She looked back down at her arm to see that the ribbon had vanished, only she didn't linger on this fact, as if the ribbon had never existed.

She walked across the leaves, only they didn't crumple beneath her feet any more, instead they popped and crackled like her mouth did after she'd poured an entire bag of Pop Rocks into it.

Charlotte kept on walking forwards, only she didn't seem to be gaining on the others. Again this didn't seem to alarm her, instead she kept on walking until suddenly she stopped abruptly. The leaves blew up from the ground and whirled around her like a mini tornado.

She blinked her eyes and saw that all the leaves had disappeared, revealing the vividly green grass beneath it. She looked up to see that Gerty was standing there, with Stef and Alice just behind her.

'Charlotte, you made it,' Gerty smiled, as she grabbed Charlotte's her hand.

'About time,' Alice huffed.

As Gerty pulled her forwards Stef and Alice stepped aside and a boy with brown hair and wide eyes stepped forwards.

'Charlie,' Charlotte smiled.

'Come on Charlotte, there's not much time left,' he gestured for her to follow him.

'Time left for what?'

Charlie kept on walking, his pace quickening so that Charlotte had to jog to keep up with him. Suddenly the sky darkened and the grass beneath her feet vanished, revealing a black tar like substance that wrapped itself around her feet and tried to pull her down.

'Charlie,' she shouted, as she tried to pull her feet free.

'Come on Charlotte, there's not much time left,' Charlie turned to look at her and gave her a smile, before he turned his head back and then ran off.

'No Charlie, wait. Please wait. Help me,' she shouted, only he kept on running until she could no longer see him.

The black tar had dragged her down into it, so that it now reached her knees. The more she tried to pull herself free the more it seemed to pull her down.

Her wand, she needed her wand. She patted her hands against the sides of her sun-dress, only it didn't have any pockets. She didn't have her wand on her, she was stuck.

A girl with long blonde hair appeared and walked with ease across the tar towards her.

'Please, help me,' Charlotte said, the tar now at her waist.

The girl reached her and peered down at Charlotte, a smirk on her face; it was Margaret.

'It looks like you're in need of this?' she pulled an oak wand from behind her back.

Charlotte reached out and tried to grab her wand but Margaret pulled it away from her.

265

She took a few steps back from Charlotte before she dropped the wand into the tar and watched as the black substance engulfed it.

'Whoops,' Margaret sniggered, before she turned her back on Charlotte and walked away from her.

'Please, come back,' Charlotte shouted, the tar now at her shoulders. 'Margaret!'

The tar crawled up her neck and she took a deep breath in before it covered her mouth.

She was falling in a vat of darkness. She tried to scream but it was met with silence.

She landed with a bump on her feet, the crisp autumn leaves were beneath her and all her friends were stood beneath the two arched trees.

'Are you alright Charlotte?' Gerty said, as she stood in front of her.

'I think so,' Charlotte replied, before she walked alongside Gerty over to the others.

'Hi Charlotte,' Charlie smiled.

'Hi,' Charlotte smiled back.

'Come on girls, let's leave these love-birds to it,' Stef rolled her eyes, before she led a waving Gerty and a sulking Alice away.

'It's just us,' Charlie grinned.

'Yes, it is.'

'Shall we go for a walk?' he held his hand out to her.

'Yes, sure,' she put her hand in his and couldn't hide her smile as they walked hand-in-hand across the meadow of leaves.

The sun grew brighter, far too bright for this time of year. It caused her hair to stick to her forehead and her arms to itch with sweat. She stopped walking and wiped the sweat off her forehead with the back of her arm.

'Is something wrong?' Charlie looked at her worriedly.

'No, no, I'm fine,' she forced a smile.

Charlie's hand slid free of hers as sweat poured from her palms. Charlotte blushed as she wiped her hands against her dress, only the sweat didn't go away, instead it grew worse, streaming out of her pours like a river until soon both her and Charlie were floating in it.

Charlotte opened her mouth to say Charlie's name, only her word was muffled by the sweaty water. She forced her head above the water as she glanced over at Charlie who had drifted further away from her and who she could see was battling with the water. The boy she liked was drowning in a river of her own sweat. This was bad, very, very bad.

The sweat water vanished and she found herself back in Miss Moffat's Academy, in the great hall. She was relieved to see that Charlie was there, along with most of the girls from her class.

'Charlie,' she said, only as she spoke a pink frosted cupcake flew out of her mouth and hurtled over to Alice like a Frisbee, hitting her in the face.

'I'm sorry,' Charlotte said and this time two more cupcakes flew out of her mouth and hit Gerty and Demi. Charlotte quickly placed her hands over her mouth and looked around the room. The others were now circling her, smiles on their faces as they eagerly waited for the game to continue.

She couldn't hold on any more, the pressure was just too strong. She couldn't help but move her hands and her mouth immediately opened, causing dozens of cupcakes to hurtle out of her mouth and fly at people.

Stef and some of the others managed to duck in time whilst others were hit on the arm and the head. Chuckles filled the room, chuckles that were aimed at her expense.

The cupcakes kept on flying out of her mouth and she looked on horrified as a glittery blue frosted cupcake was spinning its way over to Charlie. The cupcake smacked into the side of his head, covering his hair and part of his face.

He looked directly over at Charlotte, the welcoming look on his face had now changed into a look of disgust.

An enormous fart echoed through the room, it was so powerful that it caused the entire room to spin. Charlotte found herself whirling around the room, surrounded by cupcakes...and Charlie, he was there too, looking over at her.

She tried to swat the cupcakes away but the vortex that now surrounded her was too strong. Charlotte let out a loud scream, Charlie looked over at her and soon he was screaming too, so that their shrieks combined together.

It was just her scream left, her single high-pitched scream as she was left alone in this vortex of cupcakes in a place in time that she didn't understand.

'Charlotte, Charlotte,' a far off familiar voice said.
Water, swirling, frosting and the sound of her name being called were all that currently existed.

'Charlotte, wake-up,' the familiar voice said, as gentle hands shook her.

Charlotte blinked open her eyes and three blurry figures leaning over her came into her view.

'W-what? Where am I?' Charlotte looked around her feeling confused.

'You're in your room, it's us,' Gerty said.

'You had one heck of a nightmare, it woke us all up. I'm surprised it didn't wake-up the entire Academy. Whatever you were dreaming about must have been bad,' Stef said.

'Well I'm glad you're awake,' Alice sighed. 'But I need at least eight hours of non-interrupted sleep else it is bad for my complexion and my mind. I refuse to take responsibility if I am late for lessons tomorrow, you can take the blame for it.'

'Shut-up Alice,' Stef grunted. 'It's not like she chose to have a nightmare.'

Alice huffed before she shuffled her way over to her bed.

'You're so sweaty,' Gerty said, as she swiped a strand of Charlotte's hair out of her face.

The word 'sweaty' was all it took for Charlotte to sit up with a start and put her hands to her face. Her forehead was damp with sweat but at least she wasn't swimming in it like she had been in her nightmare.
'Are you okay?' Stef asked.

Charlotte nodded and forced a smile.

'Thanks for waking me up, like you said it was just a silly nightmare. I'm glad it wasn't real though.'

'I'm glad it wasn't either, from your screams it sounded like it was a terrifying one,' Stef grinned.

Gerty perched on the edge of Charlotte's bed and Stef copied her. They just sat there in silence for a few minutes and Charlotte was glad that they were there.
Soon snoring sounds came from Alice's bed which caused the girls to exchange looks as they giggled.

'At least she's getting her beauty sleep,' Stef snorted.

'Do you think she realizes how loudly she snores?' Gerty whispered.

'I think we should record it and play it back to her when she's irritating us.'

'Stef,' Gerty gave a disapproving look.

'What, I'm just kidding,' she smirked.

'Thanks guys but I think I'll be okay now. You two should go and get some sleep, just don't snore,' Charlotte smiled.

'Okay,' Stef stood up. 'If you need me you know where I'll be,' she said, before she headed across to her bed.

'Are you sure you're okay?' Gerty whispered to her.
'Yes thanks Gerty, I'm fine now.'

'It's scary isn't it how real dreams can seem sometimes. I once had a dream that my hair turned green and that whatever spell I used to try and turn it back to normal only made it greener. I checked the mirror about twenty times in a row when I woke up, just to make sure that it was still blonde,' she patted down her hair.

'Your hair looks lovely and in no way green,' Charlotte smiled. 'Thank you for looking after me.'

'That's what friends are for. Now, are you sure you'll be okay?'

'Yes thanks Gerty, I'm okay now,' she nodded as she looked at Gerty.

Gerty jumped up from the bed and half-walked, half-skipped over to her bed.

'It wasn't real, it was just a silly dream,' Charlotte whispered to herself, as she looked up at the ceiling.

She didn't want to close her eyes as she never wanted to enter that nightmare world ever again.

***

It took Charlotte ages to fall back to sleep and when she finally did, it had felt to her like the bell signalling the start of the day had rung out almost immediately.

She rubbed her tired eyes, got dressed and trailed behind the others towards breakfast, glad that there wasn't a fitness lesson this morning and hoping that eating something would make her feel less like a zombie.
'Are you okay?' Gerty stepped back and walked alongside Charlotte.

'Yes thanks, I'm just tired,' she forced a smile.

'You'll sleep better tonight, I'm sure of it.'

'Thanks Gerty, I'm sure I will,' she replied, not wanting to admit that falling asleep easily was what she was afraid of.

As soon as they stepped into the hall for breakfast Charlotte felt like she'd been transported back into her nightmare. Sitting at their table was a pretty girl with long blonde hair; it was Margaret. No one was sitting near her, but this didn't stop the rest of the students in the room from glaring over at her as they gossiped about her.

'What is she doing in my seat?' Alice grunted.

'Maybe she forgot that it was your seat Alice, she hasn't been at this Academy in a while,' Gerty said.

'As if,' Stef snorted. 'Margaret is many things but stupid is not one of them.'

'What do we do now?' Charlotte said, trying to hide the upset in her voice.

Margaret looked up from her breakfast and gave them an enthusiastic wave.

'It looks like we're going over there,' Stef gave an over-the-top wave back, before she grabbed Charlotte and Alice's arms and dragged them forwards.

'Hi,' Margaret smiled, as they sat down next to her.
'Hi,' Gerty said.

'Yeah hi,' Stef muttered.

'So you're back for good then?' Gerty asked, as she grabbed some berries off the plant in the middle of the table and put them into her bowl.

'Yes I am,' Margaret smiled back at her. 'I just hope there's no hard feelings between us, I would like a fresh start and it would be really good if we could all be friends.'

'Sure,' Gerty said.

'We'll see,' Stef rolled her eyes.

'You're in my seat,' Alice muttered.

'What was that Alice?' Margaret asked.

'Nothing,' she blushed as she looked into her bowl.

'I'm surprised you didn't sit with Demi,' Stef glanced over at the table where Demi and Destiny were sitting opposite each other, lost in conversation together.

'It appears that she's moved on,' Margaret gritted her teeth. 'Not to worry, as I said before, I'd love it if we could all be friends,' she smiled. 'What do you think Charlotte?'

Charlotte's eyes grew wide in horror. She didn't want to be friends with Margaret, she didn't want to be anywhere near her. This was the girl who nearly got her expelled and then turned her into a cockroach. She knew that there was absolutely no way that they'd ever be friends.

'I know that I was horrible to you before and I'm truly sorry about that. I just wanted to fit in and I thought that acting how I did would be the way to do that. I know that was daft and I was a cow, but I do want to be friends with you, if you'll forgive me?'

Charlotte didn't know how to respond but she knew that she needed to say something, as all of the girls around the table were staring at her.

'Sure,' she muttered, before she scooped up a huge spoonful of cereal and put it into her mouth so that she had an excuse not to say anything else.

'Great, I'm sure we'll soon all be the best of friends,' Margaret gleamed, the hint of a smirk on her face.

'So Margaret, you don't plan to be flipping burgers in your future?' Alice chimed.

Stef gave her an unimpressed look, before she kicked her under the table.

'Ow,' Alice groaned.

'No Alice, I don't,' Margaret held her smile. 'I plan to work hard and get good results so that I can have a successful career as a witch. Perhaps one day I will be running this Academy.'

An awkward silence fell across the table and Charlotte chewed on the side of her lip. She wanted to finish her breakfast and to get out of there, as being around nice Margaret was making her feel uneasy.

'I better get going, I'll see you in class,' Margaret gave them a wave as she stood up and left the room.

'Do you think we somehow fell into Charlotte's nightmare?' Stef said.

'I was beginning to think that I hadn't woken up,' Charlotte said and Stef leaned over and pinched her arm.

'Ow,' Charlotte uttered. 'Oh no, I'm awake.'

'It sucks to be us,' Stef sighed.

'Maybe Margaret meant what she said,' Gerty said.

'Gerty, I love how you always see the good in every situation but I fail to believe there is any good in Margaret,' Stef added.

'If she wanted to be nice she wouldn't have sat in my seat, she did that on purpose,' Alice said.

'We definitely need to be wary of her,' Stef looked at Charlotte and she nodded.

Charlotte remained quiet as they left the hall and headed towards their first class of the day. When Charlotte had appeared at their Save the Princess party she'd hoped that this had been a one-off visit. None of them had spoken to her then, not even Demi who'd run off into the Academy after seeing her.

No one wanted Margaret back, they'd all been getting on well together and the atmosphere was far better without her around. She was back though and it appeared that she wasn't going anywhere. Still, Charlotte knew that however overly friendly Margaret acted that it was highly unlikely that she meant it.

They walked into potions class to a waving Margaret sitting on a seat on the row behind them.

'At least she's not sitting in my seat this time,' Alice said, as she walked over to the front row.

'This is getting old,' Stef groaned. 'Keep your friends close and your enemies closer,' she grinned, as she waved back at Margaret.

When Charlotte had been five a girl had pushed her over in the playground and she'd grazed her knee. When Charlotte had told her mom what had happened she'd told her that tomorrow she should go up to the girl and ask her to play because no one was all bad. Charlotte didn't imagine that the girl could ever have been nice but she decided to do as her mom said, so the next day she went up to the girl and asked her to play. The girl didn't scowl or shove her over, instead she smiled. After that the two of them became friends and the grazed knee incident was never mentioned again.

As uneasy as Charlotte felt about Margaret's return she knew that she was here to stay and that she would just have to accept this. Maybe if she gave Margaret a chance then she would surprise her, after-all no one could be all bad, could they?

***

The next few weeks passed by in a blur of potions, lessons and books. The other students no longer stared and gossiped at Margaret as they passed her in the hallways or saw her at meal time. The routine of Academy life carried on and with it Margaret mainly kept to herself and remained friendly towards them. Charlotte was still wary of her but hoped that the nasty version of Margaret was gone for good.

All the first year girls were sitting on rows of seats in the great hall talking loudly amongst themselves. They had been instructed to all meet there, dressed in clothes suitable for the outdoors. Molly stood on the stage in front of them, her blonde hair pinned up into a neat bun and her wand gripped tightly in her right hand.

'What do you think we're here for?' Gerty asked, as she sat in-between Charlotte and Stef.

'I dunno,' Stef shrugged. 'I hope it's something good, like another school dance or something.'

'That'd be good Stef but there's only first years here and we aren't dressed for that,' Charlotte said.

'Maybe they're telling each year individually and they have another treat lined up for us afterwards, something happening outside?' Gerty said.

'Silentium,' Molly flicked out her wand.

Stef was moving her mouth to speak but no words came out. She exchanged looks with Charlotte and Gerty before she looked up at Molly. No one else in the room was able to talk besides Molly, however much they moved their mouths.

'That's better,' Molly smiled. 'You're probably wondering why you've all been called here? Miss Moffat is on her way here to tell you herself. All I can say is that you're all going to like it.'

Charlotte turned to face Gerty, she was about to ask her what she thought it would be? But as she opened her mouth to speak she remembered Molly's spell and closed her mouth.

The doors to the great hall swung open and Miss Moffat flew over the girls' heads on her broomstick. The girls looked up at her, transfixed by her every move. Their gazes followed her over to the stage where she landed next to Molly.

She stepped off her broom and with a click of her fingers made it float above her head.

'Hello first years,' she said, as she looked around the room. I have some exciting news for you, today there will be a picnic and a scavenger hunt with the first year boys from Alexander's College.'

Gerty and Charlotte exchanged excited looks before they looked back at Miss Moffat.

'Silence, how very odd. I was expecting far more excitement than that.'

'Oh,' Molly lifted up her wand and muttered out a spell as she gave it a quick flick.

The hall instantly filled with excited cheers and giggles.

'That's more like it,' Miss Moffat grinned at Molly. 'You will all be in groups of three and at the picnic you will be joined by a group of three boys. You can choose who you would like to be in a group with, so please, go ahead and pick,' she gestured across the room.

Gerty, Stef and Charlotte instantly grabbed each other's hands and the three of them giggled excitedly.

'This is so amazing,' Gerty said.

'I can't wait,' Stef said.

Alice burst into tears that reddened her cheeks. Charlotte looked from Alice to Stef and Gerty before she chewed on the side of her lip.

Stef looked directly at Charlotte and shook her head but Charlotte ignored this.

'It's okay Alice, you can take my place,' Charlotte reluctantly stood up.

Alice wiped her nose onto the back of her cardigan sleeve and beamed as she took Charlotte's seat.

'Do you think we could have a group of four?' Gerty said.

'I doubt it,' Stef huffed as she crossed her arms. 'Besides, we had a great group of three a minute ago.'

'It's fine Stef, I'll just join another group,' Charlotte said.

'You shouldn't have too,' Stef muttered.

'Right girls, if any of you aren't in a group of three please step out to the front,' Molly said.

Charlotte moved past the other girls and walked out to the front, along with a girl called Cindy, who gave an awkward smile to Charlotte before she pulled on one of her brown-haired pigtails.

Charlotte was wondering how it would work if there were only two of them left, when she heard footsteps coming from behind her and turned to see Margaret walking towards the front.

'Great, you three can make a group,' Molly smirked.

'I can't wait,' Margaret looked at Charlotte, her smile forced.

Charlotte gave a faint smile back, knowing that she was stuck in this group now so she had no choice but to get on with it. She thought about Charlie and how she'd hopefully be able to see him soon and her smile grew wider.

'It's so great that the three of us are in a group together, I can't wait to get there. I hope the boys in our group will be cute, do you think they will? I hope we win the scavenger hunt, what do you think the prize will be?' Cindy spluttered out. 'This is so exciting, we are so lucky to be in a group together and I cannot wait,' she said without pausing.

Charlotte smiled at Cindy but Margaret just rolled her eyes and looked away.

Chapter Two

They had followed Molly on their broomsticks until the Academy was out of sight. This was the furthest that most of the girls had even flown before and they felt a mixture of excitement and nerves. Charlotte made sure to keep a strong grip on her broomstick and not to sway too much.

Eventually Molly began to descend and signaled for them to copy her, as she swooped down towards a mass of green. They all landed relatively smoothly, apart from Alice who landed too abruptly and fell head first onto the grass. She instantly stood up and brushed down her grass-stained tights.

Behind Molly were different colored blankets that were spread out across the park. Charlotte looked around for the boys but they hadn't arrived yet.

'It appears as though we are here first. Please can each group go and sit on one of the blankets and await the boys,' Molly said.

Gerty and Stef gave Charlotte a wave as they walked over to a white blanket with blue and red polka dots on it. Charlotte wanted to sit on the blanket next to them but Margaret had walked straight past it.

'This one, purple is my favorite color,' Margaret smirked, as she knelt down on a dark purple and black squared blanket.

'I like purple too,' Cindy said, as she sat down next to Margaret.

'Great,' Margaret said snidely.

Charlotte looked back at Stef, Gerty and Alice who were only just visible from across the park, before she reluctantly sat down on the blanket.

There was a woven picnic basket in the middle off the blanket. Cindy opened it and took out a handful of chips, shoving them one-at-a-time into her mouth.

Margaret pulled the basket towards her and swung back the lid, revealing a basket full of savoury foods and fancy cakes. She picked up a slice of pizza and nibbled on the end of it, before she pulled an empty mug out of it. She picked up her wand and was about to use it…but before she could a sweet smelling liquid bubbled up in the mug, complete with whipped cream and mini marshmallows on top of it.

'Is that hot chocolate? That's so cool,' Cindy pulled on one of her pigtails before she yanked the basket away from Margaret.

'I've not finished with it yet,' Margaret snapped, as she snatched the basket back.

Charlotte looked over at Gerty, Stef and Alice longingly. She imagined Stef stuffing her mouth with cakes as Alice made some comment about how they weren't as good as the cakes she had handmade for her back home, whilst claiming all the strawberry-iced ones.

When Margaret and Cindy had both taken what they wanted from the basket, Charlotte took out a yellow-iced cake and a mug.

She watched as it filled itself up and then blew on it before she took a sip. The milky taste of chocolate filled her mouth and for a couple of seconds she forgot where she was. That was until Margaret sniggered at something Cindy said and the realization hit Charlotte...she was in the park waiting for Charlie but she wasn't sitting with her friends. Instead she was sitting with a girl who tried too hard to impress others and a girl who had turned her into a cockroach.

There was a flash of light, so bright, that Charlotte shielded her face with her arms. She cautiously lowered her arm and looked out across the park. The bright light had vanished but the boys had arrived.

'Look, they're here, they're here,' Cindy grabbed onto Charlotte's arm.

'Yes they are,' she forced a smile, as she gently tried to pull her arm free.

They all peered excitedly over at the boys and Charlotte scanned her eyes over them until she found a cute boy with brown hair and wide eyes.

The boys went off in different directions and joined the girls on their blankets. Charlotte saw a group of boys sit down on Stef, Gerty and Alice's blanket and she could tell from his neat black hair that one of them was Benjamin, the boy that Alice liked.

Charlotte could just make out that Nick, the boy that Stef liked was also sitting with them and she hoped that Gerty would get on with the other boy.

Charlotte felt herself tense up as a group of three boys walked towards their blanket. She kept a smile on her face, although she tried not to make eye-contact with the boys as she didn't want them to sit with them, instead she wanted Charlie to see her and come over.

Charlie spotted Charlotte and smiled over at her as he gave her a wave. She gave him a wave back and Margaret saw the exchange between them both and couldn't hide her smirk. The group of boys were nearly at the blanket now and on seeing this Charlie weaved his way around the blankets and over to theirs, his wand raised and he was just about to cast a spell but Margaret beat him to it.

'Cadent,' Margaret discreetly flicked her wand at the nearest boy from the group of three that were heading towards their blanket. The boy slipped backwards and caused the two boys behind him to tumble too, like standing dominoes.

Charlie whizzed past the fallen boys and quickly knelt down next to Charlotte.

'Hi,' he smiled at her.

'Hi,' she smiled back.

'Hey, we were clearly going to sit with them,' one of the fallen boys said, as he stood up and glared at Charlie.

'Sorry Doug but I got here first. Although there are still two spaces left.'

'No thanks,' Doug snarled, before he followed his friends over to the blanket where Patricia was sitting with Victoria and another girl.

'Denis, over here,' Charlie shouted over to a frumpy boy, who wheezed as he walked over to them.

Once Denis had caught his breath he proceeded to high-five everyone on the blanket and Charlotte saw Margaret wipe her hand on a napkin after her high-five.
'Hi, I'm Denis,' he said, his accent English.

'Hi, I'm Cindy,' she smiled at him, as she tugged on one of her pigtails.

'Hi Denis, I'm Charlotte.'

'Charlie, you've definitely picked the prettiest girls,' Denis blushed.

'I know,' Charlie grinned, as he looked straight at Charlotte.

'Charlie isn't it? I'm Margaret,' she said, as she knocked into Charlotte's side, extending her hand out to him.

'Yeah, it is. Nice to meet you Margaret,' Charlie shook her hand.

'We're a boy short,' Cindy said, as she looked around her. 'He's cute,' she pointed to a boy standing by himself as he looked for a free spot in a group.

Charlie whistled over at the boy and waved his arm.

'Hey Harry, over here,' he gestured him forwards.

The boy looked relieved as he hurried over to them, only he didn't seem to get any taller as he grew nearer to them. He didn't come up much taller than the rest of the group and they were all sitting down.

'Am I relieved to see you, I thought I was going to be the only one without a group. That would have been more embarrassing than the time I turned my hair blue in potions class,' he grinned and Cindy and Denis laughed.

'You should change your hair to purple, that's my favorite color,' Cindy said and Margaret groaned as she rolled her eyes.

'Anything for you,' he smiled, before he flicked his wand at his hair. 'Purpura tempus.'

Harry's hair instantly turned bright purple and the rest of the group laughed.

'Suits you,' Cindy blushed.

'You look like you belong in a rainbow,' Denis chuckled.

'Or as a candy wrapper,' Charlie grinned.

The purple began to fade until Harry's hair went back to its normal shade of brown and he ruffled his hand through it.

'Is there cake in there?' Denis pointed at the picnic basket.

'Yep there is, oh and I recommend the hot chocolate,' Cindy replied.

'Great,' Denis leaned over the basket and inspected what was inside. 'The cake is great,' he said with a full mouth, so that bits of cake flew out at the others.

'Ew,' Harry shielded himself with his arm. 'Close your mouth Denis.'

'Sorry,' he gulped down the rest of the cake, before he took a bite out of a slice of pizza.

'It's okay, I needed a shower anyway,' Harry grinned. 'Now pass me some of that pizza.'
Denis held a slice of pizza out to him and they both laughed.

'Do you want one?' Denis asked Cindy.

'I'll have one of those little pastries,' she blushed as she pulled on one of her pigtails.

'One of these?' he held an oval pastry out to her.

'Thanks,' she popped it into her mouth.

Charlotte and Charlie weren't taking much notice of what was happening on their blanket as they couldn't stop staring at each other.

'It's good to see you,' he said to her.

'It's good to see you too,' she smiled.

'I like that,' he pointed to the red clip that was in her hair. 'It's pretty, just like you.'

'Thanks,' she blushed. 'I borrowed it from my friend Gerty.'

'I'm so glad I reached you before Doug and his cronies did,' he stared into her eyes.

'I'm glad you did too,' she stared back into his.

'Do you want anything to eat?' he quickly glanced at the picnic basket.

'No thanks, I'm not hungry,' she beamed.

'Me neither, which is a good, as I don't think there's much left.'
Charlotte chuckled, her eyes not leaving his.

As nice as Denis seemed and as funny as Harry was...Charlotte couldn't keep her gaze away from Charlie. She couldn't stop smiling at him and he felt the same, barely taking his gaze off her, a fact which hadn't gone unnoticed by Margaret who folded her arms and smirked to herself.

'Payback time,' she muttered under her breath, a devious look on her face.

Chapter Three

All the groups gathered around Molly and a tall, dark-haired boy from Alexander's College. Charlie was standing next to Charlotte and they kept on exchanging smiles with each other.

'For those of you who don't know me I'm Molly and I'm head girl at the Miss Moffat's Academy. This is Dale, he's head boy at the Alexander's College,' Dale gave them all a wave. 'Each group will be given a list,' she held up a piece of paper. 'And a pen to tick off each item,' she held up a pen.

'Can't we just use magic to tick off the items?' Alice asked.

'Just use the pen,' Molly rolled her eyes, as she began to hand out the lists to the groups.

'As you can see, there are a number of items on your lists, your group's aim is to find them all and get back here first. Whichever group does that and has the most correct answers wins the scavenger hunt,' Dale said.

'What do we win?' a boy asked.

'Win and you'll find out.'

'Are you all ready?' Molly asked the groups, as she stood back by Dale.

There were excited murmurs and nods in reply and Charlie reached out and grabbed Charlotte's hand, which caused her heart to jolt and she couldn't hide the huge smile from her face.

'I said are you all ready?' she said and the crowd responded with loud cheers and whoops.

'Go on then,' she shouted, as she shooed them away.

All the groups instantly hurried off in different directions and Charlotte was led along by Charlie who was still gripping her hand.

'Where first?' he asked Margaret, who was holding the items list.

She looked at his hand wrapped around Charlotte's before she gave a large fake smile at them.

'This way,' she spun on the spot and knocked into Charlotte, causing her to let go of Charlie's hand.

'Sorry,' she said, as she rushed off across the park.

Charlotte longed for Charlie to grab her hand again but instead he just gave her a smile as he walked alongside her.

'Which item are we doing first?' Denis puffed out.

'You have to find the leprechauns house and borrow a cup of sugar,' Margaret read the first item off the list.

'What does a leprechaun's house look like?' Cindy asked.

'Well it isn't going to be a mansion is it?' Margaret rolled back her eyes.

'I reckon it'll be a small house that's even shorter than I am,' Harry grinned and the rest of the group giggled, including Cindy who made sure that she was walking next to him.

'Let's try through here,' Margaret led them towards the forest area that was at the end of the park.

That'd make sense,' Harry said.

Charlotte was wary about entering a forest with Margaret, but at least she had Charlie with her. She hoped that Margaret wouldn't turn her into a cockroach in front of the others, although she couldn't fully rule it out. Margaret may have been all friendly towards her but Charlotte was still unconvinced, although she hoped that she really had changed as being civil with her was much more preferable than having her as an enemy.

'What's that,' Charlie ran over to a tree and bent down.

'It looks like a door,' Denis puffed out.

'Well spotted Charlie,' Margaret smiled.

'Thanks,' he grinned back at her.

Charlie knocked on the little red door and waited for an answer.

It was then that Demi and her group appeared and Demi shoved her way over to the leprechaun's door and pushed Charlie out of the way just as the door opened.

A leprechaun in a green suit and a large green hat appeared and looked up at her.

'Please can I borrow a cup of sugar?' Demi asked.

The leprechaun muttered something under his breath as he disappeared inside the tree. He appeared back with a tiny cup of sugar held out in his hand and nodded as Demi took it, before he slammed the door shut.
'Wait,' Charlie shouted. 'We need a cup of sugar too.'

'And we were here first,' Margaret huffed, as she glared at Demi. 'You cheated.'

'There is nothing in the rules to say we have to be polite,' Demi smirked, as she barged past Margaret and back over to her team.

'Game on,' Margaret glared at her with folded arms.

'Whatever,' Demi rolled her eyes. 'Got it,' she held the cup out in front of her team.

'That's tiny, it's no bigger than your thumb,' one of the boys on their team said.

'Let's get out of here,' Destiny said.

The other team ran off into the forest and Charlotte's team remained by the leprechaun's house feeling frustrated.

Charlie knocked on the door again and waited for a response. Eventually the little door opened with force and the grumpy looking leprechaun stared up at them.

'What d'ya want?'

'A cupful of sugar please.'

The leprechaun slammed the door shut and Charlie looked up at Charlotte.

'Do you think he's coming back?' he asked.

'I hope so, as I refuse to be beaten by Demi and that girl she's found to replace me,' Margaret sighed.

'Don't worry Margaret, I think we'll win,' Cindy said but Margaret turned her back to her.

Eventually the leprechaun appeared and half-gave, half-threw the minute cup of sugar at Charlie.

'Thanks,' he replied, just as the leprechaun slammed the door in his face.

'I thought leprechauns were meant to be cheery old fella's,' Harry said.

'Not this one,' Charlie grinned, as he carefully grasped the small cup of sugar.

'The leprechauns we have at the Academy are always friendly,' Cindy said.

'Yeah, the ones at our College are too. They serve us the best steak and mushroom pie ever, it's even better than my mom's, erm, don't tell her I said that,' Denis said.

'Mrs Jackson, I'm afraid your steak and mushroom pie just isn't good enough,' Harry put on a posh English accent.

'Cut it out,' Denis play hit Harry's arm and nearly knocked him over. 'Sorry,' he very gently patted Harry on the shoulder.

'It's okay buddy, you've got some muscles on you there,' he smiled and Margaret let out a snigger.

'When you've quite finished we have a scavenger hunt to win,' Margaret announced.
'Yeah, sorry, what's next?' Denis asked.

Margaret looked over at Charlotte and saw that Charlie was still standing next to her, they were both staring at each other and it was as though no one else existed.

Margaret clutched tightly onto her wand and gave a mischievous look.

'What's next?' Harry asked.

'Find a gnome and ask them how do a gnome kiss?' Margaret replied.

'Okay, let's go!' Cindy began to walk forwards but paused when she saw that Margaret wasn't moving.

Margaret shooed her forwards and let all of the group pass her, including Charlie and Charlotte who were too busy smiling at each other to notice that Margaret hadn't moved. Now that she was at the back of the group she held out her wand and aimed it towards Charlotte's back.

'At the mention of their name ventus,' Margaret said, smirking as she hurried past them.

'Which direction do you think we should take Charlotte?' she asked.

Charlotte let out a loud fart which seemed to echo around the group. Her face went the shade of beetroot, desperately hoping that no one realized that it had been her.

'Who did that?' Harry laughed.

'That's horrible,' Cindy flapped her hand in front of her nose.

'Well it wasn't me,' Denis said.

'You know the saying, whoever smelt it dealt it,' Harry grinned over at Cindy.

'It wasn't me,' she said defensively.
'Who do you think it was Charlotte?' Margaret asked.

Charlotte instantly let out another loud fart and this time everyone knew that it had been her.

'Sorry,' she blushed.

She couldn't bring herself to look at Charlie, worried that he wouldn't like her any more.

'See, it wasn't me,' Cindy said.

'Or me,' Denis said.

'No, it was Charlotte,' Margaret smirked as Charlotte let off another loud fart.

Charlotte was more embarrassed than she could ever express. She wanted to run off into the trees and be far away from the rest of the group, then she wanted a beautiful white pegasus with a glossy mane and feathered wings to fly down and flick her onto its back. She wanted to be flown high up into the clouds and away from this situation.

As much as she wanted to escape she knew that she couldn't, instead she was stuck here with Charlie who most probably thinking she was disgusting. She felt warm fingers curl around hers and looked up to see that they were Charlie's and that he was smiling at her, so she smiled back.

Margaret was furious, she didn't understand how Charlie could still like Charlotte. She decided that there was only one thing for it, she'd just have to repeatedly say Charlotte's name until Charlie's smile faded.

'Charlotte, I think you should look over there,' Margaret pointed to the side of her as Charlotte immediately farted.

'Go on Charlotte, before the other teams beats us Charlotte.'

Charlotte didn't understand why she couldn't stop farting but going by the smirk on Margaret's face she predicted that she had something to do with it.

She followed Margaret's instructions and hurried off, glad to put some distance between her and the others, although she still found herself glancing back at Charlie. Sweet, caring, super cute Charlie, she knew that he liked her for her and that whether she farted or not wouldn't put him off. She smiled to herself as she stepped over a large white spotted red mushroom.

'Watch it!' a squeaky voice said.

She peered around to find the source of the voice but couldn't see anyone there.

'Down here,' the voice said.

Charlotte carefully knelt down and looked at the ground, before she spotted a gnome with rouge cheeks and a blue waistcoat standing beneath the mushroom.

'Oh, hello there,' Charlotte smiled at him. 'I'm sorry to disturb you, I was just wondering if you could perhaps answer a question for me.'

'I guess I could, if you promise to take more care where you're stepping in future.'

'I will,' she smiled.

'I was wondering if you could tell me how do you kiss?'
'Kissing hey,' he chuckled. 'I can't tell you that.'

'Please, you said that you woul-'

'But I can show you.'

Charlotte nodded, she lowered her head and closed her eyes, waiting for the kiss from the gnome. Only the gnome didn't kiss her lips, instead he rubbed his nose against hers.

'Now if you don't mind I'd like to be left to my thoughts,' the gnome said, as he hurried back under his mushroom.

'Thank you,' Charlotte waved at him, as she hurried back over to her group. 'I found a gnome and got the answer.'

'That's great,' Harry said.

'Well done,' Cindy said and the rest of the group, except for Margaret, all clapped and cheered.

'About time,' Margaret said under her breath, as she rolled her eyes.

'What's next on the list?' Cindy asked, but Margaret ignored her.

'Come on, we've got to find a pot of gold at the end of the rainbow and take one gold coin out of it,' Margaret said, as she rushed forwards. 'Hurry-up, she shouted back to them.'

'Good one,' Charlie said, walking alongside Charlotte. 'I knew you'd find the gnome and get the answer, you're as smart as you are cute.'

'Thanks,' Charlotte blushed.
'So, what what did he say the answer was?'

'He didn't tell me, he showed me.'

'Oh, well now I'm jealous of that gnome,' he gently grabbed her arm to stop her walking and they both stared at each other.

They both leaned in closer to each other until they were so close to each other that Charlotte could feel his breath brush against her face. Charlotte closed her eyes and pursed her lips, as she waited for Charlie's lips on hers.

'Charlotte, Charlotte, Charlotte,' Margaret whispered and Charlotte let out three loud farts.

Charlie pulled away from her and couldn't hide his laughter. Charlotte covered her face with her hands before she rushed forwards. She had been touching distance away from her very first kiss and it'd been ruined. She wanted to cry, scream and hide all at the same time and she longed for Stef, Gerty and even Alice to be here to cheer her up and give her advice.

Margaret was the first to spot the rainbow and they all followed her to the pot of gold. Charlotte trudged behind them, watching as Charlie caught up with Margaret and chatted to her.

'Are, y-you, okay, Charlotte?' Denis puffed out, as he stopped walking to catch his breath and she farted on queue.

'Sorry,' she blushed. 'It seems as though that keeps on happening to me today.'

'It's okay, it happens to be too, especially after I've eaten beans,' he grinned.

She gave a weak smile and chewed on the side of her lip. Suddenly a realization clicked in her head and she grabbed onto Denis's arm.

'Say that again.'

'W-what, that beans make me fart?'

'No, no, not that. My name. Say Charlotte,' she farted.

'Okay Charlotte,' he replied and she farted again.

'Exponentia remotio,' she said, as she turned her wand on herself.

'Denis, can you say my name again please?'

He nodded and then coughed to clear his throat.'

'Charlotte,' he smiled at her.

'Did you hear that?'

'What?'

'I didn't fart. Charlotte, Charlotte, Charlotte.'

'You think someone put a spell on you?'

'It would appear so.'

'Who would do that?'

'I have a good idea,' she folded her arms and looked over at Margaret.

'Will you both stop flirting with each other and hurry up,' Margaret shouted over to them.

'Catch you in a bit,' Charlotte smiled at Denis, before she stormed forwards, slowing down behind Margaret and discretely aiming her wand at her.

'At the utter of their name eructate,' she said quietly, before she hurried forwards until she was walking alongside Charlie.

'Charlotte, the end of the rainbow is up there,' Margaret smirked, until she realized that Charlotte hadn't farted. 'Charlotte,' she repeated.

'Why don't you lead the way Margaret,' she smiled back, just as Margaret let out a loud burp. She immediately covered her mouth with her hands and ran off.

'Hey,' she smiled at Charlie.

'Hi,' he smiled back.

They all reached the end of the rainbow where a large bronze pot lay beneath a patch of overgrown grass. It was so overfilled with glowing gold coins that Margaret had to pick one up cautiously so that she didn't knock any over.

'Wow, there must be hundreds of coins in there!' Cindy exclaimed.

'I doubt they'd notice if we took more than one,' Harry grinned.

'We are not getting disqualified because of your greed,' Margaret snapped.

'Alright calm down, I was only joking.'

'There are no times for jokes, we have a scavenger hunt to finish,' she huffed, as she held the list up.

'I'd rather spend time with you than have a pot of gold,' Charlie whispered to Charlotte.'

'Same,' she nervously giggled back.

They finished off the rest of the items on the list and then hurried to the finish line, where Molly and Dale were waiting.

The picnic blankets had been moved together to make one giant blanket that resembled a patchwork quilt and there was a long table filled with yet more sandwiches and fancy cakes.

'Wow,' Denis said, as he veered off towards the food.

'Ahem, we haven't finished yet,' Margaret huffed out, as she grabbed his arm and yanked him forwards, his gaze lingering on the table.

Charlotte turned her head to see Demi and the rest of her team running towards them.

'We need to hurry,' she pointed to the oncoming group.

'There's no way that I'm losing to them,' Margaret began to run, her grip still on Denis's arm and he let out a yelp as he was dragged forwards.
As they ran in sync alongside each other Charlie reached over and took Charlotte's hand.

'Come on guys, remember that the whole team has to reach us for it to count,' Molly shouted.

Charlotte and Charlie reached Molly and Dale just after Harry and Cindy had. They all looked over at Margaret and Denis and cheered them on. Denis was hunched over, his hand clutched to his side.

I...can't...stitch,' he puffed out.

'We are not losing,' Margaret shouted, as she yanked at his arm. 'Pull yourself together.'

'It hurts.'

'If we lose because of you then you have my word that every time I see you I shall turn you into the most hideous toad imaginable.'

Denis swallowed, a frightened look on his face before he nodded and forced himself onwards.

Demi had nearly reached them now and she pulled out her wand and aimed it at Denis's back.

'Don't even think about it,' Margaret held out her wand.

Demi grimaced as she put her wand down by her side but she continued to run, barging past them both and racing over to Molly.

'Come on,' she shrieked over to the rest of her team, who were all gaining on Margaret and Denis.
'I'm not being beaten, least of all by them,' Margaret huffed, as she pulled Denis forwards.

Denis continued to clutch his side but he knew that he had to keep on going, he didn't want to let his team down and he also didn't want to be turned into a toad.

'Come on Denis,' Charlotte shouted.

'Not much further now, then you can raid the picnic,' Harry said.

Margaret kept on yanking at Denis's arm until he fell onto his knees in front of Dale. The rest of the group cheered as they wrapped their arms around him, except for Margaret who stood there smirking over at Demi.

'Well done, you're the first team back,' Molly said, after they had let go of Denis.

'What do we win? Margaret asked.

'Maybe there is no prize, you just get to bask in the knowledge that you won.'

Margaret's face fell and she found herself clutching tightly at her wand.

'Just kidding,' Molly grinned. She pulled a pile of golden medals out from behind her back and placed the medals around each of their necks before she cheered the rest of the incoming teams on.

'Shiny,' Cindy said, as she held the medal up to look at.

'I suppose this will do as a prize,' Margaret said.
'Well done Margaret, we wouldn't have won if you hadn't helped Denis,' Charlie smiled, as he placed his hand on her shoulder.

Margaret didn't burp on her name being used so Charlotte took it that the spell had worn off. She chewed on the side of her lip and tried not to feel annoyed, after-all Charlie was just being nice, a trait which she liked most about him.

'Yeah, well done,' Charlotte smiled.

'Thanks,' Margaret ignored Charlotte and looked directly at Charlie.

A loud sizzling sound came from behind them and they turned to see that Molly had turned the end of her wand into a sparkler and was holding it up in the air.

'It looks like all the teams are back. Well done to all of you, especially the winning team,' she smiled over at Charlotte and Charlie. 'They are the ones wearing the gold medals if you want to congratulate them.

Anyway, it's time to feast, so help yourselves,' she pointed over to the long table. 'Although if all the cherry slices go before I get to them, I will not be pleased,' she smirked.

As most people hurried over to the food table, Stef and Alice rushed over to Charlotte and wrapped their arms around her.

'Well done Charlotte,' Gerty smiled.

'I like your medal,' Stef lifted it up to look at it. 'It's a shame we didn't all get one really, seeing as we all took part. They could have given an extra prize to the winning team.'

'We'll just have to win next time,' Gerty said.

'We might stand a chance if we have Charlotte on our team instead of Alice.'

'Stef,' Gerty gave her a stern look.

'Well it's true, a snail would have been quicker than her. All because her shoes were rubbing her feet or something,' she rolled her eyes.

She wasn't that bad.'

'Pfft, that's a matter of opinion.'

'How's it going with Charlie?' Gerty changed the subject.

'Yeah, okay,' Charlotte gave a wide smile. 'Well, apart from Margaret trying to ruin it for me.'

'How so?' Stef asked.

'Someone cast a spell on me so that every time my name was said I farted,' she blushed.

'What a cow,' Stef chuckled. 'Sorry, it is a tiny bit funny though.'

'Yeah I suppose it is a bit, but it wasn't at the time.'

'What did Charlie say?' Gerty asked.

'He was sweet about it but it was super embarrassing.'

'He clearly likes you Charlotte.'

'Yeah, he's looking over at you now,' Stef waved over at Charlie, who was stood by Harry and Denis at the food table.

Charlie waved back, his gaze settling on Charlotte and they exchanged smiles.

'You should go over to him,' Gerty said.

'We should all go,' Charlotte grabbed both of their arms and pulled them forwards.

'I'm not saying no to that, I want an egg sandwich before they all go,' Stef said.

'The sandwiches are always the last thing to go,' Gerty said.

'That's rubbish, I always go for them first.'

'Well then you're the exception.'

'I want a cake, although I think I'll stay away from the cherry slices,' Charlotte grinned. 'How's it going with Nick?' she looked at Stef.

'Okay,' she couldn't hide her smile.

'I'd say it was going better than okay,' Gerty giggled. 'It seems that it's going well for Alice too,' she looked over at Alice and Benjamin who were sitting close together on the blanket and chatting.

'At least it gives us some peace,' Stef said.

When they reached the table Gerty and Stef went off to get food and Charlotte walked over to Charlie. They both smiled at each other and she tried to think of something to say but her mind was blank, all she could think about was how sparkly Charlie's eyes were.

'Do you want a cake?' he continued to smile at her.

'Okay,' she smiled back.

'I recommend the strawberry cupcakes with the vanilla icing,' he picked one up and passed it to her.

'Thanks,' she took it off him and nibbled at the icing.

'It's not as sweet as you,' he took her hand and smiled at her.

Margaret folded her arms as she looked over at Charlotte and Charlie. She was determined to have ruined things for them by the time this picnic had finished, however many spells it took.

'Flumine of in sudore,' she discreetly flicked her wand at Charlotte.

One minute Charlotte had felt fine and the next she'd began to feel hot, so much so that the armpits of her sweater were dripping with sweat and a mass of it glistened on her forehead. She could feel how sweaty her hand was and quickly pulled it away from Charlie's.

'Sorry,' she muttered, as he wiped his hand onto his trousers.

'It's fine,' he smiled. 'Can I get you a cold drink?'

Charlotte nodded before she took a bite of her cupcake and Charlie rushed over to the end of the table and picked up two glass flutes that were filled with different flavoured layers of fruit juice.

'This should cool you down,' he held the glass flute out to her.

'Thank you,' she took the glass off him and studied the layered colors.

'The orange layers are my favorite,' he smiled.

'I like orange too,' she cringed as soon as she said it.

'Haven't you ever had one of these before?'

'No,' she shook her head. 'We don't have these at the Academy.'

'My mom makes them every Christmas and for special occasions, I always drink too many of them, they are irresistible, much like you.'

Charlotte giggled before she took another sip of her drink.

Margaret looked over at them, not understanding how he could still like her, even after the spells she'd cast on her. She smirked as her mind recalled a perfect spell and she aimed her wand at Charlotte.

'Summa cupiditas,' she flicked her wand.

Charlotte took another bite out of her cupcake and then another one. Soon the whole thing was gone but she was still hungry, so she turned to the table and picked up sandwiches and chips.

'You must be hungry,' Charlie said.
Charlotte wanted to stop eating but her hunger was just too strong. She found that she couldn't stop, instead she had to keep on eating. She began to shovel food into her mouth and then she picked up a chocolate cupcake and squashed it into her mouth.

'That foods not just for you,' Molly appeared by her, her arms folded and her gaze unimpressed.

'Exponentia remotio,' Margaret said quietly, as she aimed her wand at Charlotte.

She immediately stopped eating and quickly grabbed a bunch of napkins off the table and spat the food left in her mouth into them.

Charlotte looked at Charlie who couldn't hide the look of disgust on his face.

'Sorry,' she muttered.

It was then that she felt the nausea rise in her stomach and the tears began to cloud her eyes so she turned and ran off, not wanting the boy she liked to see her be sick whilst crying at the same time. Molly sighed before she followed her, muttering 'first years,' under her breath.

Margaret waited until Charlotte was out of sight before she walked over to Charlie.

'Do you think I should go after her? I didn't mean to upset her, it's just she was eating so much food and-'

'It's not your fault Charlie, the problem runs deeper than that,' she feigned worry. 'Charlotte's my friend and all, but she's got issues, ones I've told her to address but...' she shrugged.

'What is it?' he asked, concern in his voice.

'She'd be sooo mad if she knew I'd told you.'

'I won't tell her you said anything, I just want to help her. I should probably go and check if she's okay,' he started to walk away but Margaret grabbed his arm.

'Well, you saw how she stuffed her mouth with all that food? That's what she always does every meal time and then she runs off to be sick. Sad really but she's been doing it ever since I met her, it makes meal times at the Academy awfully messy. So you can't go after her because if you saw her being sick she'd be so embarrassed and I know how much she likes you.'

'She likes me?' he smiled.

'Well yeah, like way too much. She mentions you like all the time and she writes Charlie hearts Charlotte in all the covers of her books. She talks as if you're already dating, in fact she's always talking about you. I've told her to calm down but she says that you're soul mates and that she's going to marry you and have twenty children.'

'Right,' Charlie said.

'I know a boy like you would never be interested in her. I mean what with all her eating problems and the way she gets weird over you and everything. Still, she's my friend so please let her down gently,' she placed her hand on his and smiled at him.

When Charlotte had stopped being sick, she cleaned herself up and then hurried back to the picnic to find Charlie, only when he came into sight he was deep in conversation with Margaret. She took a deep breath and walked towards them, not wanting to give in to Margaret.

'Are you feeling better?' Charlie asked.

'Yes thanks,' she nodded.

'You look very pale, I think you should go and lay down as you don't want to infect us,' Margaret smiled.

'I'm fine thanks Margaret.'

'I'm just worried about you Charlotte,' she couldn't hide her smirk.

On hearing her name Charlotte let out a loud, long fart. She blushed bright red and looked at Charlie who was trying not to laugh.

'Like I said, I don't think you're very well,' Margaret patted her shoulder. 'I think you should go and get some rest before you stink us all out.'

Charlotte was annoyed at herself for not noticing that Margaret had put the farting spell back on her.

She wanted to scream at her and to tell Charlie exactly what Margaret was like. She wanted to cast a spell to turn Margaret into a balloon and watch her float off so that she was left to talk to Charlie without any interruptions. There were so many things that she wanted to do but instead she found herself walking away from them.

'Is she okay?' Charlie asked Margaret.

'Yeah, she will be fine, she just needs some time to herself,' she leaned in closer to him. 'She always gets terrible wind after her food binges.'

Charlotte looked back at Charlie and let out a sigh. He was so close to her yet he seemed so out of reach.

'Are you okay Charlotte?' Molly asked, and Charlotte let out a fart.

'Sorry,' she looked at the ground. 'Please can I be excused, I don't feel very well.'

'Okay,' she couldn't hide her smile. 'I'll get Sonya to fly back with you to the Academy. Wait here while I go and find her, I know I saw her around here somewhere.'

Charlotte nodded before she looked over at Charlie. Margaret may have won this time but next time Charlotte was determined not to let her ruin it.

'Exponentia remotio,' she turned her wand towards herself.

Soon Sonya walked over to her, both of their brooms in hand and she passed Charlotte's over to her.

'Sorry for taking you away from the picnic,' Charlotte said.

'It's okay, I've had enough sandwiches anyway.'

Charlotte took one last look over at Charlie before she got onto her broom and followed Sonya up into the air.

She thought about her nightmare, the cupcakes, sweat and the farting. All those things had been in her dream and they'd happened today. This didn't make any sense, it was as if she'd subconsciously known what was going to happen to her. Had her dream been some sort of premonition or a warning?

She noticed how everyone looked so tiny from up there, like dots on a map. The truth was that they were all small in comparison to the world but this didn't make them any less important.

Charlotte knew that she mattered, just as all of the dots beneath her did. The next time she met Charlie she was going to prove to him that even though she was quieter than Margaret and not as cunning or as good at spells, this didn't mean that she wasn't just as important as all of the other dots that were down on the ground.

She knew that she was a kinder, fairer, more caring person than Margaret and that she was the dot for Charlie.

Chapter Four

Charlotte landed next to Sonya in the yard of the Academy. A group of second years were having a fitness lesson with Miss Dread, who was twisting herself into a variety of positions and encouraging the girls to copy them. A few of the girls looked over as they landed but most of them were too busy concentrating on their positions to take much notice.

'Do you want me to walk you back to your room?' Sonya asked.

'No thanks, I'll be okay,' Charlotte forced a smile.

'If you're sure?'

'Yep, I'll be fine,' she nodded.

'Okay then, you should go and rest in your room and then hopefully you'll feel better soon.'

'Yeah hopefully,' Charlotte sighed.

'Don't worry, you'll see that boy again soon,' she said and Charlotte blushed. 'I saw you talking to him, he's a cute one.'

'Yes and thanks.'

'Anyway, go and sleep off your bug.'

'Thanks Sonya.'

'No problem, although I hope I get back before Molly eats all of the cherry slices,' she grinned.

Charlotte waved at her and then watched as she flew up into the air until she became a tiny dot in the sky.

'Come on Clarissa, your left leg needs to come up higher,' Miss Dread said.

'I can't, get it up there,' a girl with long red hair said, as she tried lifting her leg up behind her and ended up toppling onto the ground.

Charlotte clutched onto her broom as she walked through the empty halls. She still felt sick from all the food she'd eaten and she couldn't get the taste of vomit mixed with cake out of her mouth. On the walk back to her room she found that she couldn't stop thinking about Charlie. His hair, his eyes, his smile. Everything about him had her smitten and she couldn't seem to shake him from her mind.

She walked into her room and closed the door behind her. Part of her was glad to be alone but the other part of her wanted a hug from Stef, Gerty and even Alice, even though she'd probably go on about how it was messing her hair up. On thinking about them she found herself smiling, they were her friends and she knew that they'd always be there for her.

She brushed her teeth, changed into her pale pink pyjamas and got into her bed. She buried herself beneath the covers as she thought about the warmth of Charlie's hand on hers, winning the scavenger hunt and how Margaret hadn't changed at all.

Swirling around in her mind was the nightmare, which she couldn't stop thinking about. Had she really had a premonition or had it been a fluke? Thoughts of her sweat covered skin, frosted cupcakes and a constant vortex were spinning in her head until her mind switched off and sleep claimed her.

***

'Charlotte, are you okay?' gentle hands shook her.

'W-what?' she blinked open her eyes and saw Gerty and Stef peering over her.

At first she thought that the scavenger hunt had just been part of her nightmare and she felt relief.

'Sorry for waking you, we just wanted to check that you were okay?'

'Um yeah, fine,' she placed her hand over her mouth as she yawned.

'We looked for you at the picnic but Molly said you'd left,' Gerty said.

Charlotte bolted upright, the nausea feeling in the pit of her stomach returned.

'The picnic,' she muttered. 'It really happened, it wasn't a dream?'

'Yeah it happened, your team won, remember?' Stef asked.

'Oh yes,' Charlotte lay back down in bed.

'Are you sure you're okay?' Gerty asked.

'Yes thanks, I'm just tired.'

'More like someone spiked your drink with forgetful powder, it happened to my uncle once, he couldn't remember where he'd placed his best hat for a week afterwards, my aunt was the least bit pleased,' Alice said, as she searched through the draw beneath her bed.

'More like your uncle just forgot where he'd put it,' Stef snorted.

'You won't be laughing when someone uses it on you and you misplace your broom for a fortnight,' she huffed.

'How'd it go with Charlie?' Gerty asked.

'Terrible,' she mumbled out, before she sank further into her bed and closed her eyes.

'Charlotte, what happened?' Gerty asked her.

'Let's leave her alone,' Stef whispered to her, before she led her away from Charlotte's bed.

'Who's stolen my robe, the one with the lilac trim?' Alice folded her arms and glared at Stef and Gerty.

'Why would I want your itchy old robe?' Stef replied.

'I'll have you know that is a designer robe.'

'You could show some manners, Charlotte is trying to sleep.'

'Alice we haven't got your robe, I'm sure it's somewhere. I'll help you look for it,' Gerty said quietly, as she walked over to Alice and knelt down next to her before she began to look through her draw.

'Maybe someone used forgetful powder on you?' Stef sniggered.

Charlotte tried to block out the noise from the room and get back to sleep but it was no use. Soon silent tears were streaming down her face and as much as she tried to wipe them away they continued to drip down her cheeks in clear blobs.

'Is this it?' Stef took a lilac robe out of her draw and threw it over at Alice.

'I knew you'd stolen it.'

'I did no such thing, I was merely looking for my PJ's and I found that monstrosity. I reckon you put it in with my laundry so that you didn't have to wash it yourself.'

'You're a thief,' Alice huffed.

'It doesn't matter Alice, you have it back now.'

'I suppose so,' she glared over at Stef, before she put her robe on over her cream satin PJ's.

A knock at the door caused them all to fall silent and Gerty hurried over to it, opening it to see Margaret standing there.

'Hi Gerty, I was just here to check on how Charlotte is feeling?' she smiled.

'She's sleeping,' Stef shouted.

'She's okay but she's resting right now but I'll tell her that you came by,' Gerty said.

'Thank you Gerty, please tell her that I'm thinking of her and that I hope she feels better soon. Also make sure that she knows that I kept Charlie company in her absence so that he didn't feel lonely.'

'I bet you did,' Stef muttered under her breath.

'Thanks Margaret, I'll pass on your message.'

'Goodnight Gerty, Stef, oh and Alice, I didn't see you there but I love your robe, I'd like to borrow it some time,' she gave an exaggerated smile and a single wave in Alice's direction.

'Of course you can borrow it, any time,' Alice shouted over to her.

'Night Margaret,' Gerty smiled, as she closed the door.

'What a load of rubbish,' Stef sneered.

'I think it was nice of her to check by,' Gerty said.

'Yes, she didn't have to do that. I think she's changed,' Alice said.

'You're only saying that because she likes your stinky old robe,' Stef rolled her eyes. 'Besides, she cast a farting spell on Charlotte to embarrass her in front of Charlie, so it's clear she's the same old Margaret.'

'We don't know for sure that it was her who put that spell on Charlotte. She didn't have to stop by and check on her, I think that was a really sweet thing to do.'

'Whatever,' Stef rolled her eyes again. Gerty and Alice might have been fooled by Margaret's words but she wasn't so easily convinced.

***

The Academy's grandfather clock chimed twelve times yet no one stirred, no one that was except for Charlotte who couldn't seem to find sleep. The clock stopped chiming and silence returned, uncomfortable silence. Even Alice wasn't snoring! Charlotte couldn't decide if this was a good or bad thing, as annoying as it was…at least it broke the deathly quiet.

She wondered if Charlie still liked her and what lies Margaret had told him? She wondered how her dream had been so accurate and she wondered why she couldn't stop over-thinking these things and just go to sleep?

On realization that sleep wasn't going to come any time soon a thought flashed into her head.

'I wonder,' she said under her breath.

She carefully pulled the cover off and crept out of bed. She paused briefly before she knelt down and as quietly as she could, pulled the draw out from under her bed.

'Lux,' she held out her wand and the intricate carvings on her wand glowed orange, along with the yellow light that appeared at the end of it.

She rooted through the draw and held up the small vial of fairy dust that she'd won in Miss Scarlet's class. She had been saving it until she believed that she truly needed it and now seemed like a good time to use it.

Remembering what Miss Scarlet said about using it sparingly, Charlotte took the lid off the vial and gently knocked a small amount into her palm. She blew the glittery silver substance into the air and watched as it sparkled before her. Suddenly the sparkles disappeared and in their place appeared a male fairy, with pale skin and purple hair.

'Hello Charlotte, I'm Zonta and I'm here to help,' he said cheerfully.

'Hello,' she smiled back.

'What would you like to ask me?'

'Erm,' Charlotte said, realizing that she had no idea what to ask.

She chewed on the side of her lip as she hurriedly tried to think of something to ask, something helpful.

'What is wrong with me?'

'I can assure you that there is most certainly nothing wrong with you.'

'Really?' she smiled.

'Yes, in fact you are very special.'

'I am?' she gave a confused look.

'Yes, you possess an ability that few others have.'

'What kind of ability?' she whispered.

'Charlotte my little witch friend. You can read minds.'
'No I can't,' she said louder than she intended and then
quickly placed her hand over her mouth.

'Us fairies do not lie, I suggest you try it tomorrow.'

'But how do I read minds?' she asked, but Zonta had
vanished.

She carefully shone her wand around the room to check that
he'd gone, before she buried the vial of fairy dust back in her
draw of clothes and then she crept back into bed.

She found herself over-thinking even more than she had
been before she had met Zonta. His words repeated in her
head and she contemplated using more fairy dust to bring
him back and ask him how she was meant to mind read?

She decided against this, as she had to at least try to mind
read for herself before she wasted more of the fairy dust.
Also Miss Scarlet had told her to use it sparingly so she
didn't want to risk overusing it.

Thoughts were swirling in her head in a confused ball until
finally and unknowingly she fell asleep.

***

Charlotte woke-up first, about an hour before the bell was due to ring. She used the bathroom before a queue grew for it, got changed into her sports kit for fitness training and then stretched out on her bed and thought about what Zonta had said.

She'd read an article in the paper once about this man who took up boxing for a hobby and a week later had won a major championship. Maybe she really did have this hidden skill and she just needed to figure out how to use it.
The bell went off and the others woke-up and began to get ready for the day. Charlotte looked at Gerty and tried as hard as she could to read Gerty's thoughts; nothing.

'You're up early?' Gerty smiled over at her. 'I hope you're feeling better today?'

'I like waking up early, it means I can have the bathroom to myself without feeling rushed,' she grinned. 'I'm feeling better thanks, my head feels somewhat clearer today.'

'Good point and I'm glad.'

'Did you hear Margaret stop by last night?' Stef asked.

'Yeah, I did.'

'She's faker than the fake designer handbag my cousin Belinda takes with her everywhere.'

'Ew, why would anyway buy a fake designer bag?' Alice shuddered.

'Because not everyone is as rich as you Miss Moneybags. Although the bag Belinda has is faded and peeling off at the seams and the zip keeps getting stuck. She's actually told us all that it's the real deal, as if!'

'I think she was being sweet,' Gerty said.

'Gertrude Baggs, you are the nicest person that I've ever met but when it comes to Margaret you are deluded.'

'I'm with Gerty on this one,' Alice said.

'Don't get me started on you, it's far too early for this,' Stef sighed, before she disappeared into the bathroom.

'I was about to go in there,' Alice huffed.

'Gerty, is it true that fairies can't lie?' Charlotte asked.

'Yes, fairies never lie, ever. They are generally kind in nature but their truth telling has been known to offend some people. In fact, legend has it that they seldom come to this realm because centuries ago the ruler of the magical world asked a fairy if they thought they were a good leader? The fairy told them that they weren't and the ruler became bitter with anger and banished all of the fairies from his land.'

'So they can't tell any sort of lies whatsoever?'

'She's already told you that they can't,' Alice snorted.

'Alice, I was just making sure,' Charlotte replied.

'Nope, they can't lie at all. Not even a tiny little lie. Why are you so curious about fairies?'

'Oh, it's just that I read something about them and wondered if it was true.'

'I like fairies, they are so cute. If I was the ruler I wouldn't banish them, even if they told me that I was the worst ruler in the entire universe.'

'You'd be an amazing ruler,' Charlotte said.

'Aw, thanks Charlotte, I think you'd be a great ruler too. We could rule the land together and fill our kingdom with fairies,' she smiled.

'There would be glitter everywhere, imagine the mess,' Alice said.

'I like glitter,' Gerty said.

Charlotte tried to discreetly look down by the side of her bed and saw specks of silver and purple glitter. She got off her bed and knelt down by it, pulling the draw out as a distraction as she used a clean-up spell on the glitter. She tried not to look as it flew up into the air and was swept across Alice and Gerty's heads and into the trash can at the far side of their room.

'I think fairies are misunderstood, much like Tinkerbell was in Peter Pan. She shouldn't have betrayed Peter but she only did it because she was so afraid of losing him. Besides, she turned out good in the end.'

'I do believe in fairies,' Charlotte grinned.

'What on earth are you going on about?' Alice looked bewildered.

'You've NEVER heard of Peter Pan?' Gerty looked stunned.

'I grew up in the wizarding world, we are far too superior to delve into silly fairies.'

'It's a book and a film, oh and also I saw a stage play of it once.'

'Yeah, we performed it at school, I was one of the Lost Boys,' Charlotte said.

'You played a boy?' Alice looked horrified.

'There were more boy characters in it,' she said, remembering how she had secretly longed to be Wendy.

Gerty was still going on about fairies as Stef came out of the bathroom and Alice huffed at her as she hurried into it.

'What are you on about?' Stef glared at her.

'Tinkerbell,' she replied, before she cast a spell so that her bed made itself.

Zonta had said that fairies didn't lie and Gerty had said that they didn't lie either, so surely that meant that unless they'd been some sort of mix-up, then Charlotte could read minds.

'I believe that I can do this,' she thought to herself, before she looked over at Gerty and tried to dive into her mind.

'I stay out too late, got nothing in my brain. That's what people say, mmm-mmm. That's what people say, mmm-mmm,' Gerty sang.

Charlotte stared hard at Gerty, she was still singing but her mouth wasn't moving.

'Strange,' Charlotte thought as she rubbed her head.

The bathroom door swung open and Alice stepped into the room. Gerty smiled at her before she hurried into the bathroom.

'She could have asked me if I'd finished with the bathroom,' Alice moaned.

'What! like you asked me?' Stef snorted.

'It is absolutely ridiculous that we have to share a bathroom.'

'I'd like to flush her down the toilet,' Stef's words sounded in Charlotte's head. Charlotte looked over at Stef who was ignoring Alice as she lay out on her bed and fiddled with her wand.

'Did you say something Stef?' Charlotte asked.

'Huh?' Stef replied.

'Sorry, it's just I thought I heard you say something,' her words trailed off.

'Baby, I'm just gonna shake, shake, shake, shake, shake. I shake it off, I shake it off,' Gerty sang as she came out of the bathroom, only she wasn't singing out loud, instead she was singing in her head.

'I can do it,' Charlotte said louder than she intended to.

'What can you do?' Stef asked.

'Oh, nothing,' Charlotte blushed.

'I hope Charlotte's okay, she's acting odd,' Stef thought.

She could really do it, Zonta had been right, she could read minds. She felt as though she'd suddenly developed a superpower and she imagined herself in a shiny pink leotard with a sparkly mask on.

'Super Charlotte,' she said to herself, as she shook her head. 'No, it can't have my name in it as everyone would know it's me. Erm, how about Mind Girl?' she thought.

She shook her head as she chuckled and Stef glanced over at her.

'Thought Thrower,' she smiled as she said it to herself.

Charlotte looked over at Gerty who was standing in front of the mirror.

'Will my chest ever grow or will I be totally flat-chested forever?' Gerty thought.

Charlotte looked away from Gerty but still, Gerty's thoughts continued in her head.

'I hope it does grow else I'll look like a little kid forever. It's hard enough being the youngest here.'

There was a part of Charlotte that wanted to go over to Gerty, tell her she looked great just the way she was, and to give her a huge hug. She didn't do this though, because she didn't want Gerty to know that she could read minds. The last thing she wanted was for her friends to be wary around her, so she knew that she needed to keep her mind reading skill to herself.

They left their room and headed to breakfast, passing Molly in the corridor.

'He is so gorgeous, I wish I could spend the day with him instead of looking after these little snot noses,' Molly thought, as she smiled at Charlotte.

Charlotte smiled back, although she wasn't impressed at being called a snot nose.

'I wish I looked like Molly,' Gerty thought.
'I wonder if Molly would swap rooms with me for a week if I let her borrow my designer shoes?' Alice thought.

'I hope Margaret's not sitting at our breakfast table, I'm not in the mood to act nice around that cow,' Stef thought.

As these thoughts popped into her head Charlotte found herself looking from one girl to the next. As they walked down the stairs and passed more people, more and more thoughts filled her head.

'If she says one more horrible thing to me today I will turn her as red as a beetroot,' a fourth-year girl thought.

'I shouldn't have stayed up so late studying,' a second-year girl thought, as she yawned.

'Hi girls,' Miss Scarlett said, as she passed them as she walked into the great hall. 'Only five-weeks, three-days and two-hours until the holidays,' she thought.

Demi and Destiny walked alongside them and they exchanged acknowledging waves and hi's.

'They are so lucky that they don't have to share a room with Margaret. I would rather put up with Alice than her. She's so controlling, just when I'm getting in with the good kids she turns up to ruin my life,' Demi thought.

'They should have put me in with the second-year girls. I look as old as they do, I'm sick of being in the baby class, although at least I have Demi around, so this place doesn't totally suck,' Destiny thought.

Charlotte was enjoying spying on people's thoughts, she saw it as harmless fun and she was developing her new found skill at the same time. At least that was until she walked into the main hall and her head was instantly overwhelmed with hundreds of thoughts.

She put her hands over her ears and stopped herself from screaming. It was too much and she didn't know how to stop them.

'Charlotte, are you okay?' Gerty asked her but Charlotte didn't hear her over all of the thoughts.

She sat down at their breakfast table and closed her eyes tightly, telling herself to block out all thoughts but her own. When this didn't work she began to count back from ten in her head and by the time she'd got to one all other thoughts had gone. She let out a sigh of relief before she took a sip of her grapefruit juice.

'Are you okay?' Gerty gave her a concerned look.

Charlotte took a moment to work out if Gerty had just thought this or said it out loud.

'Yes thanks Gerty, I think I just need to eat something,' she took a syrup covered pancake off the large plateful that was placed in the middle of the table and placed it onto her plate.

'They look good,' Gerty looked at the pancakes.

'They aren't as good as the ones made for me at home,' Alice said, before she ate a forkful of her third pancake.

Stef rolled her eyes as she grinned at Charlotte and Gerty.

'My friends really are the best,' Charlotte thought.

She was glad that she had managed to block out the thoughts of her school mates and that the inside of her head was for now just her own.

Chapter Five

The Mistress of Spells was sitting with her huge spell book opened in front of her, her hair was down and she had a beautiful pearl headband holding her gorgeous hair away from her face. She wore a beautiful gold silk dress and her make-up was exquisite.

All of the girls stared at her transfixed, as they waited for her to break the silence.

The Mistress of Spells hummed to herself as she inspected the shelves crammed full of ingredients beside her. 'I must order some more sandalwood,' she said under her breath, before she turned around to face the class.

'Hello girls,' she smiled. 'Decisions, decisions. What spell do you think we should learn today?'

None of the girls said anything, as they all recalled the last time they'd chosen a spell and had ended up looking like nine-year-olds.

'Come on girls, surely you can come up with something?'

'It's not a spell as such but Miss Scarlet has told us a little about the Book of Dragons and we'd love for you to tell us more about it?' Destiny asked.

An awkward silence fell upon the room as the girls looked from Destiny to the Mistress of the Spells.

'We talked about it all the time back at my old school,' Destiny continued.

'Very well,' The Mistress of the Spells sighed. 'I suppose that it is only natural to be curious about this and if I keep it from you, your curiosity will only increase. It's a dangerous book and in the wrong hands the results could be catastrophic. I shall tell you about it, so that your curiosity is put at bay and so that you understand the perils that this book brings. It is not something to discuss frivolously so after this I don't want to hear it mentioned again.'

The girls nodded, as they tried to hide their excitement.

'I want you to take your mind back hundreds of years. The word was a different place then, fear and violence ruled and the weak were oppressed.

A powerful witch named Dabria ruled over the magical world, she ruled heartlessly, using dragons to impose her will over all witches and wizards. Those who dared to oppose her were killed by the dragons, who served her loyally, all of them obedient to her will.

'Where did the dragons come from?' Victoria asked.
The Mistress of the Spells glared sternly in her direction before she continued with her story.

'A thousand years ago there was a tribe called the Izu who lived in the harsh Arabian desert. The legend was that the dragons came from a different world, one many realms away from the one we live in.

One day when the leader of the tribe was out hunting he found a nest of eggs in a cave. Intrigued by them he took as many as he could carry back to his tent. That night he ate one of the eggs and instantly began to change, his skin cracked and grew as hard as leather. His tail bone lengthened and formed into a thick tail, his toes webbed and long teeth protruded from his mouth. So it is told that he grew so large that he ripped his tent apart. He wasn't human any more, instead he had turned into a dragon.

He was terrified at first but relieved to still be alive. He was consumed by confusion and anxiety, yet above all else he felt the overwhelming desire to fly and so he lifted out his arms. The skin had grown from his ribs out to the arms, forming wings.

At first he was unsure and unstable, finding it difficult to control his body. After an hour he felt comfortable and even enjoyed the freedom of flying. He flew over to the cliffs above the oasis where his tribe slept peacefully.

He sat there for hours, wondering how his family would react to him. Would they realize who he was or would they attack him in fear? He flew down and sat near the camp-fire waiting for them to awaken. Just as the sun began to rise above the horizon he felt himself softening and changing. He stood by the firelight and watched himself change back into a human.'

'Did he change into a dragon again?' Gerty asked.

'Yes, every night when the sun went down and darkness descended. When the sun rose the following morning he returned to his human form. He did not tell his family about this and protected the other eggs that he's taken, hiding them in a small cave high on the cliff face above the oasis.

After many moons had passed, the eggs began to hatch. Four tiny dragons clawed their way out of the eggshell and looked to him as their parent. He fed them, nurturing them as if they were his own blood and giving them as much comfort and love as he could muster. Over the following months he trained them to follow his instructions.

When he felt the time was right he gathered his people, telling them that he had something magical to show them. As the sun set they watched as his body transformed into that of a dragon. His tribe gasped in horror and fell to the ground begging for mercy, afraid that he would kill them.

He explained to them what had happened and reassured them that they had nothing to fear. His oldest and dearest friend was the first to rise and walk towards the dragon man. Touching his leather skin, he lowered his head and pledged that he would continue to love him like a brother no matter what.

They hugged and slowly other members of his family and tribe came to inspect and touch him.

Knowing that this was a shock to his tribe...he kept the other dragons a secret for a few more nights before he announced to his tribe that he had more news and then he introduced the four dragons to them.

They were still only small and very obedient and at first the people were fearful, but as their fear lessened, they rejoiced in the honor that had been cast upon their tribe. The people worshipped them and showed them only kindness and love. The dragons were only ever used for good.

The dragon man wrote down all the secrets on how to control the dragons in an old leather book. He called it the Book of Dragons, recording in it the secrets of the dragons forever-more. When he eventually died the dragons disappeared and the book was buried with the dragon man's body in a cave.

Eventually the stories of the dragons died off and were no longer passed down from father to son. The legend of the dragons was lost for centuries.

This all changed when a witch called Olga the Dark found the Book of Dragons. She summoned the dragons and now loyal to her they obeyed her every command. These were dark, dark times, ones which are best left in the past,' the sadness was evident in her voice, as she wiped away the tears that trickled down her cheeks.

'Eventually she was defeated by the White Witch, Gwenyth. The dragons were encapsulated within the Book of Dragons and it was sealed with a powerful spell.

To keep the book safe, it was entrusted to two wise and good hearted witches.'

***

'Why did they tell two witches?' Victoria asked.

'In case one died, as they didn't want the secret to be lost.'

'Do you know the witches who were told the secret?' Demi asked.

'Yes, it was Miss Moffat and myself.'

On hearing this the girls gasped, shocked at how powerful their teachers were.
Charlotte took in the Mistress of Spell's youthful complexion and had to remind herself that her appearance didn't reflect her real age. Charlotte had no idea how old she really was and what horrors she'd seen. The magical world was a fascinating and welcoming place but it sounded as though it hadn't always been this way.

'It is important for you ALL to remember just how dangerous the Book of Dragons is. The pain that it can unleash is more than you could ever imagine, so it is of the utmost importance that its secrets are never unleashed again.

Now, enough about this, it's time to commence the lesson and practice spells.'

No more about the Book of Dragons was mentioned during the lesson, although it remained on everyone's minds.

How I imagine the
Book of Dragons
looks like...

Charlotte chose to block everyone's thoughts out and focus on the floating spell they were doing. She decided that she would have plenty of time to listen in on people's thoughts after the lesson but during them she needed to be distraction free. She really wanted to become as skilled at magic as Margaret was and that would take a lot of time, concentration and effort.

The class came to an end and the Mistress of Spells dismissed the class in her usual positive tone. There was no mention of the Book of Dragons but Charlotte doubted that her classmates would have stopped thinking about it.

Charlotte trailed behind Gerty, Stef and Alice as they left the classroom.

'One day I will be the owner of that book,' Destiny said smugly, as she walked along the corridor with Demi and Melody.

Melody gave her an uneasy look and Demi couldn't hide her shock.

'It's going to happen but don't worry, I may let you borrow a dragon for errands, seeing as you're my best friend,' Destiny grinned.

'Gee, thanks,' Demi rolled her eyes.

Margaret appeared up the corridor and shoved past Melody so that she could stand next to Demi.

'Hi Demi, that was an interesting lesson wasn't it?' she said cheerily.

'Yeah, I guess,' Demi took a step further away from Margaret.

'Are you off to lunch?'

'Yes, WE are,' Demi grabbed Destiny's arm.

Margaret didn't say anything but Charlotte noticed that she had a sly grin on her face. Curiosity took over and as she continued to walk, she focussed her mind and counted to ten inside of her head. Nearby thoughts instantly filled her head and she continued to follow the others, careful not to draw attention to herself.

Charlotte grabbed onto the wall behind her, shocked at what she'd just heard. She stared at the back of Margaret, Demi and Destiny's head as they continued up the corridor.

'Are you okay Charlotte?' Melody asked, as she walked over to her.

Charlotte nodded, as she forced a smile and let go of the wall.

'Yeah, sorry I just went a bit dizzy but I'm fine now.'

'Let's go to lunch.'

Charlotte nodded again as she walked alongside Melody up the corridor.

'I hope there are meatballs, they haven't had them for the last week so we should be getting them soon.'

'Yeah, hopefully,' Charlotte muttered back.

Stef, Gerty and Alice were long gone, no doubt they were now sat in the great hall wondering where she was. It was her own fault for lingering behind them and listening in on people/s thoughts. Maybe she was better off not delving into minds, as she wouldn't always like what she heard.

'Why am I talking about meatballs, Charlotte's going to think I have an unhealthy addiction to them,' Melody thought.

'I hope there's rainbow jelly for dessert, we haven't had that in a while either,' Charlotte said and Melody gave her a large smile.

Margaret, Demi and Destiny were now out of sight but their thoughts were still vivid in her mind. Thoughts that Charlotte didn't know what to do with, thoughts that made her feel nauseous just thinking about them.

Chapter Six

Charlotte was sitting at one of the far tables in the library. She usually opted for whichever free table was the furthest away from the desk of The Mistress of Books, as their relationship was very much flawed since the 'Margaret incident'.

As she wrote down notes from one of the talking books, she found herself glancing over at the golden door where the Book of Dragons was kept. She wondered what the book looked like? Was it a grand golden book with moving images of dragons on it or a simple leather bound book? She wondered what spells were protecting it and the havoc that could be unleashed if it ever got into the wrong hands?

Charlotte quickly looked away from the door, not wanting the Mistress of the Books to see her looking at it. She chewed on the side of her lip as she looked down at her notes and pretended to read them. Margaret and Demi's thoughts were at the front of her mind and seeing the door made what they'd said feel more real. There really was a book behind those doors, a book that could change the magical world forever, a book that in the right hands could be used for good…but in the wrong hands could be used to carry out the cruelest of actions.

'They were just thoughts, I'm sure they didn't really mean them,' Charlotte thought to herself, as Margaret's smirk came back into her head.

Margaret may have been acting all sweet and innocent but Charlotte knew better than to fall for her façade.

'It will be okay,' Charlotte accidentally said out loud.

'Shh,' the Mistress of the Books glared over at her.

Charlotte sank down in her seat and took a quick look over at dragon handled door. She packed up her stuff and placed the textbook on the shelf that was by the door before she left the library and with it the book that she couldn't get out of her head.

***

The great hall was alive with voices and the clattering of spoons against bowls as the students ate their breakfast. Amongst the first years the hot topic was still the Book of Dragons, a fact which didn't sit well with Charlotte. She made the decision not to listen in on anyone's thoughts but this didn't stop most of the girls from talking about the book.

'Do you think anyone's ever broken the spell and got to the book whilst it's been in the library?' Stef asked.

'I doubt it, Miss Moffat and the Mistress of Spells are such accomplished witches that their spells would be virtually impossible to break,' Gerty said.

'Nothings completely impossible,' Alice said.

'Do you think something terrible would happen to the person who tried to get to the book?' Stef asked.

'Maybe their skin turns bright blue?' Gerty giggled.

'Or they turn into a pig,' Stef said.

'Oink, oink,' Gerty wrinkled her nose.
'They are far too sophisticated to cast such childish spells,' Alice said snootily.

Stef rolled her eyes and Gerty giggled, neither of them giving much care to Alice's comment.

'Charlotte, what spell do you think the Mistress of Spells has cast to protect the book?' Gerty asked.

Charlotte looked up from her bowl and shrugged. She didn't want to talk about the book, she was trying to block it from her mind.

'I don't know,' she muttered, before she purposely shoved a huge spoonful of cereal into her mouth.

'Come on Charlotte, I'm sure you can come up with something?' Stef said.

'I reckon any intruders would turn into ice statues,' Gerty said.

'Imagine the Mistress of the Books reaction if she found someone by the dragon door frozen solid?' Stef chuckled.

'She'd probably use them as decoration for the library,' Gerty chuckled.

'With a plaque beneath them reading disobedience will result in this.'

'As if that would be allowed,' Alice huffed, the hint of doubt noticeable in her voice.

'It was a joke, lighten-up,' Stef groaned.

'Well, it was stupid.'

'It's not my problem that you are too snooty to understand jokes.'

'It's not my fault that your family aren't privileged like mine are.'

'That's it,' Stef kicked Alice under the table.

'Ow,' she kicked back.

'Come on, quit it,' Gerty said.

'Whatever,' Stef muttered, as she stirred her spoon around her soggy cereal.

A flash of light exploded over by the teacher's table and silence fell upon the room as everyone looked over to see Molly standing there.

'Please can all first years stay behind for a special announcement,' she said.

There were cheers of excitement from the first years and groans from the other students.

Charlotte kept on looking at Molly, noticing how the ends of her hair had changed color from orange to a dark blue.

'I wonder what spell she's used on her hair?' Gerty asked.

'No idea,' Stef shrugged. 'Back to more important matters, such as what the special announcement could be?'

'I hope it's another picnic,' Gerty clapped her hands excitedly.

'I don't,' Charlotte said.

'I hope there's food,' Stef said.

'All you think about is food,' Alice said.

'You can't talk, I saw you smuggle those strawberry cupcakes the other day.'

'I did no such thing,' Alice blushed.

'Whatever,' Stef smirked. 'I hope we get to be in a group of three again and this time it won't get ruined.'

Alice's bottom lip quivered as she sniffed and tried to hold back her tears.

'Stef,' Gerty glared at her.

'Sorry,' Stef grunted. 'Hopefully we will get to be in a group of four this time, if there are groups.'

Alice gave a weak smile but she didn't say anything.

'Whatever it is, I hope it's good news,' Charlotte said.

'And that you get to see Charlie again,' Gerty said.

'Yeah and that. I need to fix things with him after our last disastrous meeting.'

'Do you know that Benjamin's parents own their own private yacht?' Alice said.

'That sounds great,' Gerty smiled.

'Yeah, brilliant,' Stef continued to stir her spoon in her mush of cereal.

Charlotte finished her breakfast and she took a few glances over at Demi and then Margaret. She didn't use her ability to listen to their thoughts as she knew better than to do that again in the hectic hall. Still, she found herself wondering what they were thinking and if the Book of Dragons was still on their minds.

***

Only the first year girls, Molly and Miss Moffat remained in the great hall. Miss Moffat had used a spell to remove all of the food, cutlery and tables from the room and to make the chairs form rows at the front.

'Hello girls,' Miss Moffat smiled. 'I am pleased to announce that today signals the start of the Half-Yearly Witches Test. The test will cover three areas that you have learned so far, flying, speed reading and fortune telling, and casting a spell.'

'Tests, great,' Stef quietly moaned to Charlotte.

'These tests are important but I don't doubt your abilities. Each and every one of you has proven that you are true witches in the making and I am very proud of you all. Now, the five girls with the highest overall result in the test will go on to challenge the top five boys from Alexander's College for the Golden Wand Trophy.'

On mention of the boys there were gasps of excitement from the girls and Gerty squealed as she again clapped her hands. Charlotte couldn't hide her smile at the thought of seeing Charlie again. Then doubt crept in, what if she had put him off so much at the picnic that he never wanted to see her again? She needed to make sure that she was in the top five girls so that she could hopefully talk to him and put things right between them.

She looked over at Margaret and focused on her as she counted back from ten.

'I hope Charlie makes the top five, although I'm sure he will. I can't wait to see him again,' Margaret thought.

Charlotte scowled, as she blocked out any more of Margaret's thoughts and concentrated on Miss Moffat.

'I thought that would interest you,' Miss Moffat grinned. 'But it is also important that you all try your best. Also it would be lovely to have the Golden Wand Trophy in our awards cabinet, which we all know is where it belongs.'

'Even though Alexander's College won last time,' Molly added.

'Yes, thank you for that Molly. The boys may have won last time but that doesn't mean that they won't be beaten this time. I have my faith in my girls and their clear ability to show those boys how skilled we are.

'The first test will begin in two days, so until then my advice would be to practice as much as you can. Don't just focus on your strongest area, as to make the top five you will need to get a high overall score. Remember that a true witch never stops learning and always seeks to find knowledge wherever they can.'

'Don't forget that I expect the top five girls to bring home the trophy, there is a gap in the cabinet that it would fill perfectly,' she smirked, before she gripped onto her broomstick and flew over the girls' heads and out of the great hall.

'Okay girls, I suggest you hurry to class,' Molly said.

All the girls stood up and hurried across the room, none of them wanting to get on Molly's dark side.
'This is so cool,' Gerty jumped on the spot. 'I hope I make the top five.'

'I don't see why you won't,' Charlotte said.

'I hope we all make it, how great would that be?'

'Of course we'll make it, although I'm not so sure about Alice,' Stef said.

'Ahem,' Alice folded her arms.

'Joking,' Stef grinned.

'If we all practice lots and test each other then we'll all make the top five. This is going to be so great,' Gerty looped her arms through Charlotte and Stef's.

'Yeah, it is,' Charlotte replied, unable to hide the doubt from her voice.

She hoped that Gerty was right and they would all make the top five, preferably without Margaret. Then all her friends would be happy and she could hopefully try and fix things with Charlie.

As much as she tried to remain positive there was a hole of doubt positioned in her gut that seemed to be increasing in size the more she thought about it.

***

The next two days were filled with endless practice. By the time the first test had arrived Charlotte had clocked up hours of flying practice, gone to Miss Zara's after school fortune-telling lesson and cast at least a couple of hundred spells. Her hands, mind and wrist all ached, yet she found herself worrying if she had done enough.

The last two days had proven to her just how much she wanted to make the top five, not just for Charlie (although she couldn't deny that she longed to see him) but most of all for herself. She saw this competition as a good way of proving to everyone that although she was brought up oblivious to the magical world, this didn't mean that she didn't deserve to be here.

The test day arrived and a spell of cold weather came with it. All of the first year girls stood in the flying arena, in front of a cheery looking Miss Firmfeather.

In front of them where the rest of the arena should be was a vast whiteness of nothing. At first Charlotte didn't know what was going on but them she came to the conclusion that a spell had been put onto it.

It was a particularly cold morning and frost sparkled on the ground. Charlotte had her warm quilted jacket on over her zip-up top and jogging pants, yet she still felt the cold.

'Waiting in this weather is ridiculous, If I get pneumonia I will make sure my parents sue the Academy,' Alice said. 'You should have put a coat on like the rest of us then,' Stef replied, as she stared at Alice's flimsy tracksuit.

'I'll have you know that this tracksuit is designer and I am not covering it up with a common coat.'

'Well then you can't moan that you're cold.'

Molly and Miss Moffat flew into the arena, Miss Moffat's long black fur coat trailed on the ground as she walked off with Miss Firmfeather.

'Cold enough for you?' Molly grinned, as she jogged on the spot.

'Are we starting soon? I can't feel my toes,' Patricia asked as she shivered.

'Hopefully. And it's a good job that you don't need toes to fly,' she smirked.

Charlotte looked over at Miss Moffat and Miss Firmfeather who were still in deep conversation with each other, before she looked over to the small crowd of students that had gathered to watch. Although there had been a buzz about this competition throughout the Academy, most of the students from the other years were in classes or didn't fancy braving the cold to watch.

Miss Moffat and Miss Firmfeather stopped talking and headed back over to Molly.

'Girls, it is important that you don't let this sudden appearance of cold weather make you lose your focus,' Miss Moffat said.

'Hello girls,' Miss Firmfeather smiled. 'The flying arena has been transformed into a thrilling obstacle course for you all to compete in. I'm sure you're all wondering where the course is, there is an invisibility spell surrounding it that will be lifted once I signal the start of the test. We aim to keep things exciting for you,' she winked.

'I'd advise you to leave your coats here as you will get hot flying around but if you choose to keep them on then that is indeed your choice. Please mount your brooms and you can begin on my whistle.
Remember, you are all aiming to finish in the top five as only these people will receive points for this test.'

'Good luck girls,' she gave them a wide smile, before she placed the whistle that hung around her neck in her mouth.

Charlotte took off her coat and placed it on the ground, she tried to ignore the cold as she got onto her broom and waited for the race to start.

When Miss Firmfeather blew the whistle bright lights whizzed out of it and exploded in the sky in a mass of colors. The whistle continued to echo until of all the girls had cleared the invisible shield, which then vanished so that the spectators could see what was going on.

Hundreds of prickly, tall cacti were zig-zagged in front of them. Margaret was the first to whiz towards them and to begin to weave around the cacti. Alice and Victoria were more hesitant, lingering back on their brooms.

Charlotte exchanged looks with Gerty before they both took off in different directions, swooping their way around them.

Stef had made her way through the zig-zig path quickly and with ease. She hadn't been prickled once and she wasn't far from the front.

Margaret turned her head and saw how close Stef was behind her. Smirking she flew around the corner and stopped, Stef swooped around the corner just as Margaret swung her broom into the side of her, causing her to tumble backwards into a cactus. Stef screamed out as dozens of prickles embedded themselves into her arm.

'I'll get you for this,' she shouted.

Margaret was quick to fly off and leave Stef there, as she bravely pulled the prickles out of her skin before she got back onto her broom and hurried after Margaret.

As the girls began to clear the cacti, a large, arched, stone bridge came into view. Charlotte wasted no time in zooming towards it, there were several girls in front of her and she knew that she needed to get a move on if she was going to finish in the top five.

There was fencing above the bridge and a black outlined, yellow arrow pointed downwards. Charlotte swooped down and began to fly beneath the bridge, carrying on in a straight line until the signs of daylight in front of her grew clearer.

Suddenly the silhouette of a large moving shape came into view and a troll appeared, growling as it swiped at the girls. Charlotte managed to weave past it and fly out from beneath the bridge. Gerty didn't react quickly enough and the troll grabbed onto her leg and refused to let go. Gerty tried struggling free but the troll was too strong.

'Help,' she shouted but the rest of the girls zoomed past her, none of them stopping to assist her.

'Sorry Gerty,' Patricia said, as she whizzed past her.

Gerty didn't understand why no one had helped her, as she would have stopped and helped them if they'd been in her place. She fought back tears as she again tried to free her leg. The troll continued to growl and wail as time ticked by and Gerty's chances of finishing in the top five grew slimmer.

An idea came into her head and she gripped tightly onto her broom with one hand and with her other hand she went to pull her wand from her pants pocket.

Suddenly the troll shook her and she watched in distress as her wand fell through her fingers and clattered onto the ground.

'Please can you let me go, I really don't want to lose this test?' she pleaded with the troll.

The troll looked at her before it stuck its long, white covered tongue out at her and then chortled to itself. Gerty sighed on the knowledge that she wasn't going anywhere soon.

A forest of silky white cobwebs was the next challenge, Alice flew straight into them and squealed as she tried to swipe and shake the cobwebs out of her hair.

'They are only webs Alice, they can't hurt you,' Stef chuckled as she passed her.

Destiny found this challenge easy and had managed to pass Margaret and go into the lead.

'Parvus turbo,' Margaret flicked her wand out at Destiny.

A mini tornado whirled its way around Destiny, causing her vision to be blurred and causing her to fly straight into a giant golden orb spider's web. The tornado cleared and the spider became visible as it crawled towards Destiny, she let out a loud shriek and struggled to free herself from the web. Margaret smirked as she flew past Destiny, happy that she was now firmly in the lead.

Charlotte and Alice were the next ones to pass Destiny, who was holding her broom out in front of her as a barrier between her and the spider. Eventually the spider scuttled up its web and Destiny hopped back onto her broom and flew off after them.

The cobweb forest ended and the girls found themselves entering a hall of mirrors. Dozens of reflections surrounded them, making them feel giddy. Charlotte had to grip on extra tightly to her broomstick as she began to feel disorientated. She was no longer sure if she was flying upright or upside-down. it was only when her head began to throb that she realized she was upside-down and turned herself around. She rubbed her head as she tried to find her way through the mirror maze.

Demi became so disorientated that she misjudged what was mirror and what wasn't and she flew straight into one of the mirrors and bashed her arm. She groaned under her breath as she rubbed her arm, grateful that she hadn't broken the mirror, as her uncle Syd had done that once and seven-years of bad luck had followed him.

Alice flew past Demi, using her as a guide to dodge the mirrors as she flew around the corner. Demi was quick to fly off after her, although this time she took more care when turning to work out what was mirror and what was space.

Margaret was still in the lead, although Charlotte, Alice and Demi weren't far behind her. She flew around a corner and saw a huge ornate mirror at the end of the mirrored corridor, the word 'exit' was written above it in bold, flashing letters.

She stopped abruptly in front of it and looked around to try and find where the exit was.

Alice and Demi were next to appear and on the mirror with the sign above it they both stopped by Margaret. It was then that Charlotte appeared, she saw Margaret and the others but she also saw the sign, so she took a deep breath before she flew straight at the mirror.

'No, Stop,' Alice shouted.

'Don't do it,' Demi shrieked.

Charlotte ignored them and closed her eyes as she reached the mirror and kept on flying. The glass didn't break, her body didn't bruise, instead she'd flown safely through the mirror and was now in a field full of green-leaved apple trees. It was as warm as a day in late spring and she felt glad that she'd left her coat behind.

The apples were a variety of colors, from dark red to bright orange.

On the ground in front of her were woven baskets and a sign that read: 'To win the test and be the best, pick six apples and in this basket they should rest.'

Quickly she lifted up the basket closely to her and flew off towards the closest tree.

Margaret was furious, she should have known that the mirrored exit was an illusion and not paused in front of it. Now Charlotte was ahead of her and she was stuck with Alice and Demi. As soon as Charlotte had disappeared through the mirror she had quickly followed her, determined to make sure that she didn't beat her. Margaret was desperate to not only come first in the top five but also to make sure that Charlotte didn't finish in it. This time she wanted Charlie all to herself!

Charlotte had already put her first apple into her basket but as soon as she'd touched the bright green apple the rest of the apples on that tree had vanished. She moved onto the second tree, her sights set on a lilac apple.

Margaret flew after Charlotte, a smirk on her face as she lifted her wand.

'Sempiterno foramen,' she flicked her wand in Charlotte's direction.

Charlotte reached for a second apple and threw it into her basket, she glanced down at it and that's when she double-looked. Her basket was empty and there was a large hole in the bottom of it. She looked over at Margaret who was now on her second apple and knew that she was responsible.

'Reficere,' she pointed her wand at the basket; the hole remained.

'Mutare,' she tried.

The hole remained and worse still, Margaret was now on her fourth apple.

Charlotte bit on the side of her lip as she desperately tried to think up spells that would help her.

'Alice,' she said, as she saw her whiz near her.
Alice was too busy concentrating on collecting apples and she didn't notice Charlotte and flew straight past her.

Charlotte continued to try spells but still the hole remained in her basket. She looked over and saw that Margaret had just flown over the finish line, closely followed by Demi.

One-by-one the rest of the girls crossed the finish line. Charlotte continued to try spells on the basket, even though she knew that she wasn't going to finish in the top five on this test.

'Magicae novis,' she tried.

She looked down to see that the bottom of her woven basket had been restored. Quickly she whizzed from tree to tree, grabbing an array of colorful apples.

After she had crossed the finish line the crowd became visible to her and she could hear the clapping and cheering. She looked at Patricia who was crouched over regaining her breath and then to Alice who was going on and on to Melody about how it was unfair that she hadn't won. Her gaze fell on Margaret, who was looking straight back at her, a devious smirk on her face.

'What happened. You were in the lead then when I crossed the finish line you weren't here?' Stef asked, as she walked over to her.

'A hole mysteriously appeared in my basket,' she sighed.

'No prizes for guessing who was behind that,' Stef looked over at Margaret.

'Where's Gerty?' Charlotte asked.
'Molly had to rescue me from the troll's bridge because you all flew off and left me,' Gerty said, as she walked over to them, with folded arms and dirt smudged cheeks.

'Sorry,' Stef muttered. 'I didn't see that you were in trouble.'

'Patricia did, she flew straight past me.'

'Maybe she didn't realize that you needed help?' Charlotte said.

'Maybe,' Gerty huffed. 'It doesn't matter, I'm sure I'll do better in the next two tests.'

'Of course you will,' Charlotte smiled.

'You both will,' Stef said.

'You didn't finish in the top five?' Gerty gave Charlotte a confused look.

'There was an issue with my basket during the last section of the task.'

'Oh, okay. I'm sure you'll make up for it in the next test, you're a skilled witch.'

'Thanks Gerty, I think that you are a great witch too,' she smiled. 'And you are too Stef.'

'We're all good and we're all going to finish in the top five,' Stef said.

'Course we will,' Gerty smiled.

'I hope so,' Charlotte said under her breath.
'Girls, girls, gather round,' Miss Moffat gestured them forwards. 'A marvellous effort was put in by each and every one of you but as you all know only the first five placed girls will receive points. In fifth place with a score of one point is Destiny.'

Demi cheered and the other girls clapped but Destiny just gave a forced smile. Charlotte took this opportunity to read her mind and found out that Destiny was thinking about how unfair it was that she hadn't come first.

'In fourth place with a score of two points is Stephanie.'

'Well done Stef,' Charlotte patted her on the shoulder.

'Third place with a score of three points is Alice, second place with a score of four points is Demi and taking first place with a score of five points is Margaret. Well done to the top five and for those of you who didn't quite make it, I hope that the remaining tests will show your true potential.'

'Third,' Alice huffed. 'How could I have only come third?'

'Stop moaning, you finished in the top five so I don't know what you have to complain about,' Stef grumbled.

'Third is great Alice and so is fourth,' Gerty smiled at Stef.

Charlotte let out a shiver, as her body suddenly remembered how cold it was out here. She was about to walk off and find her coat when Gerty put an arm around her.

'You'll ace the next test,' she whispered to her.

'Thanks Gerty, so will you.'

Charlotte walked over to her coat that had been placed in a floating pile. She rummaged through the coats and pulled hers free, as she put it on she found herself worrying about the test and how she had managed to mess up the first one. She had been positive around Gerty but she wasn't sure if she believed her own words. She longed to make the top five but she was afraid that she wouldn't and that her chances of seeing Charlie at the competition would completely fade away.

She looked over at Margaret who was standing by herself as she twirled her wand in her hand. Charlotte couldn't resist reading her mind, as she longed to know what she was thinking about.

'It's Thought Thrower time,' she said to herself.

'I'm going to win and I'm going to see Charlie again. He won't be able to resist me and I will claim him as my boyfriend. She doesn't stand a chance,' Margaret thought, as she feigned a smile in Charlotte's direction. 'There's no way that she will make the top five so I won't have to worry about her sticking her nose in.'

'Well done Margaret,' Charlotte forced a smile, as she walked past her.

Charlotte was determined to make the top five and she wasn't going to give up. To stand a chance of making the top five she knew that she had to finish as highly as she could on the next test. She wasn't going to stand by and let Margaret get the better of her and she wasn't going to let her steal Charlie from her.

'Bring on the second test,' she said under her breath.

She walked back over to Stef and Gerty, making sure that she had blocked out all thoughts. She didn't need to read their minds to know that they were her friends and that they would always be there for her. Margaret would always be as smart as she was spiteful, but Charlotte knew that she had something that Margaret would most likely never have.

Charlotte had the best friends that she could have asked for and she knew that with them on her side she would be just fine.

That afternoon the great hall was set out ready for their second test. Sitting on one side of the long tables were adults that none of the girls had ever seen before.

'As you can see we have some special visitors at the Academy. These are friends of the Academy but they are also normals, they have kindly agreed to take part in this test.

You will each go over to a section of one of the tables where a row of three of our guests are sitting and your challenge will be to read their fortunes. Miss Zara is here to explain the rules more clearly,' Miss Moffat said.

'Thank you Miss Moffat,' Miss Zara took a step forward. 'Each of our guests has a crystal ball in front of them. I vant you to look into it and to find out vhat their current job is, vhat their hobby is and vhat they vill be doing in a year's time. Go ahead girls but remember to vait for the signal before you start, as this is a speed race,' she signaled with her hands for them to move.

The girls moved over to the tables and sat behind the first adult in the row of three. Charlotte and Alice both went over to the same long table and sat down next to a different line of normals. Molly was at the head of the table close to Charlotte, her hair braided and fixed into a neat bun.

'Each girl will have someone watching them and you have me,' Molly said to Charlotte, before she waved to Silvia who was stood at the other end of the table near Alice. 'Remember that you need to find out their job, hobby and what they will be doing in a year's time. The aim is to do this accurately and quickly, if you get an answer wrong then you will hear a gong. You can choose to try again or to move onto the next question or person, good luck.'

Charlotte gave her a smile before she looked at the normal woman sitting in front of her. She was about forty, with chin length poker straight hair and she was dressed smartly in a navy suit.

Charlotte made sure that she had blocked out all thoughts as she wanted to win this test fairly, also their thoughts would have been an added distraction. She knew that the best way to get the answers she needed was to find them in the crystal ball.

The sound of a squawking bird filled the room and caused dozens of the normals to jump in alarm. Molly gave Charlotte a nod and she quickly placed her hands over the crystal ball and focused on it. An image appeared of the woman, she was stood in front of a classroom with equations written on the blackboard.

'Math teacher,' Charlotte said, smiling when the gong didn't sound.

She looked back into the crystal ball and saw the woman sat in the front row of a theatre.

'Going to the theatre.'

Lastly she saw the woman dressed in leggings and a waterproof jacket, she was carrying a backpack as she walked up a mountain.

'This time next year she will be in Wales, England where she will be visiting family. This day next year she will be climbing Mount Snowdon.'

The normal woman gave Charlotte a smile and she smiled back, before she hopped onto the next seat where a young man was sitting in front of her. She wasted no time in looking into the crystal ball and finding the answers that she needed.

'Chef,' no gong sounded. 'Skiing,' again no gong sounded. 'He will have just bought his first house with his fiancé Christina.'

Charlotte hopped onto the third seat and quickly read the elderly normal gentleman's fortune. Once she had finished Molly made a golden spark shoot out of her wand.

Charlotte looked over at Alice who was reading her second normal's fortune.

Alice said something and the gong sounded, Alice paused briefly before she moved onto the next seat and peered into the crystal ball, desperate to get the answers she needed about the middle-aged woman who sat in front of her.

No one else was even close to finishing and now that Charlotte had finished concentrating on her normals, all she could hear were the other gongs that were sounding off all over the hall.

Gerty was next to finish, she had only made one mistake. She'd seen the man sat on the toilet reading a book and said that his hobby was reading. It turned out that this wasn't really his hobby, he just liked to hide in the bathroom to escape his wife's nagging, his real hobby was taking his grandson to watch their local team play football.

Fortune telling didn't come naturally to Margaret but she'd somehow managed to work out some of the answers from the blurry images she'd conjured up in the crystal ball.

'She's a cleaner,' she said, as she looked up at the smartly dressed woman that was sitting in front of her. The gong sounded and the normal woman gave an insulted look.

'I do apologize,' Miss Moffat said to the woman, after she had rushed over to her. 'Margaret, this is Mrs Davenport, she is head of the normal's university.'

Margaret muttered an apology and blushed before she looked back into the crystal ball.

When the test had finished all the girls gathered in front of Miss Moffat to hear the results.

'Firstly I would like you all to join me in giving a huge thank you to our guests who took time out of their very busy schedules to join us here today,' Miss Moffat flicked her wand and clapping sounds erupted in the hall, which were soon joined by the other girls' claps and cheers. 'Now, for the results. In first place and with one-hundred-percent accuracy,' she arched her eyebrow. 'And who will receive five points is Charlotte.'

The hall erupted in more cheers and Charlotte saw Molly wink at her.

'In second place with ninety-seven percent accuracy and receiving four points is Gertrude. In third place with eighty-percent accuracy and receiving three points is Alice. Fourth place with seventy-three-percent accuracy and receiving two points is Stephanie and finally in fifth place with sixty-five-percent accuracy and receiving one point is Margaret.

Well done to the top five, and to those of you that are disappointed, don't forget that there is still one more test to go. For now, go off and have some free time and may I suggest that you practice your spells. The final test will take place in the yard tomorrow morning straight after breakfast. After this test, our top five will be revealed, which is very exciting. I am eager to observe the final test and to find out which of you girls will be representing the Academy,' she smiled at them before she walked over to the normals and started talking to them.

As the girls followed Molly out of the hall, the sweet smell of hot toffee filled the room. Charlotte glanced back to see that one of the tables was now filled with colorful cakes, snacks and warm drinks for the normals.

'Well done,' Stef said.

'Thanks, you did great too.'

'Third, how could I have come third again?' Alice moaned.

'Third is great Alice, it means that you are in a strong place going into the final test. And you are currently in joint first place with Margaret,' Gerty said.

'I should have come first in both tests,' she muttered, before she walked over to Melody to grumble about her placing to her.

'We are the comeback kids,' Gerty smiled, as she linked arms with Charlotte.

'We sure are.'

Margaret barged past them, an annoyed look on her face.

'Watch it,' Gerty said.

'Whatever,' Margaret snapped.

'I suppose she's just annoyed at her placing,' Gerty shrugged.

'Yeah, probably,' Charlotte replied, unable to hide her smile.

Charlotte and Gerty were currently in fourth and fifth places, they just needed to do well in the spell test and they stood a good chance of making the top five.

Charlotte was one step closer to proving that she was an accomplished witch and one step closer to hopefully getting a chance to sort things out with Charlie.

***

It seemed as though the whole school was out in the yard to watch the final test. Lessons had been cancelled for the morning and a floating row of bleachers had been positioned on all sides of the yard.

The first year girls were all lined up on one side of the yard, each of them had a wooden horse in front of them. Across the yard were two large flags with the Academy's crest of two crossing brooms below the letters MMA on them.

'As you can see, you each have a horse in front of you. For your spells test you have to ride your horse over the finish line,' Molly pointed over to the flags. 'To do this you will need to cast a spell on your horse. Begin when you hear the bang of my starter gun, good luck.'

Charlotte and Stef exchanged anxious looks as they waited for the test to begin. Charlotte tried hard to think up a spell to use on her horse but she wasn't sure which one would work best.

BANG, echoed loudly across the arena, followed by hundreds of bats that flew off across the yard.

'Paulo Equus,' Charlotte aimed her wand at her horse.

A small, greyish-brown animal with a short mane and long ears appeared in front of her.

'Eeaw,' it said, before it nudged its head against her arm and began to chew on her sleeve.

'My sweater's not food,' she shook her head, before she climbed onto the animal.

'Eeaw, eeaw.'
She gently kicked its sides to try and get it to move but it remained where it was.
'Nice donkey,' Margaret snorted over at Charlotte, before she trotted off on a pretty white pony.

Charlotte tried to ignore Margaret and instead patted the donkey.

'Please don't be stubborn, I need to do well in this test.'

'Eeaw,' it said, before it bucked her off.

'What am I going to do with you?' she sighed, as she got back up onto her feet.

The donkey once again moved its head towards her sleeve and as she moved her arm away from it she thought of an idea. She got back onto the donkey and then held out her wand.

'Natantis carota,' she said and a floating carrot appeared in front of the donkey.

The donkey immediately began to move, trying to bite the floating carrot which remained just out of its reach.

At first Demi turned her horse into a rocking horse. She tried to block out the laughter that was coming from the crowd and cast another spell on her horse but this time wheels appeared on her rocking horse. She jumped on it and tried wheeling it forwards, before she cast another spell and this time the wheels spun quickly by themselves, transporting her across the yard.

Alice had turned her horse into a cute Shetland pony but it's little legs were struggling to go very fast.

'Hurry up,' Alice shouted at it.
Destiny had turned her horse into an elegant black stallion and on seeing it the crowd cheered. Once she'd jumped onto it Destiny found that it was far too powerful for her to control and it wandered over to a nearby patch of grass and refused to move from there.

Margaret finished with ease, crossing the line long before anyone else. Next was Alice, who was still shouting at her pony.

Demi whizzed past Stef who was on an angry grey pony, she kicked the pony to get it to move and it flared its nostrils and stopped abruptly, causing her to fall forwards onto its mane. Demi finished in third place and Stef managed to get her pony moving again and finished in fourth.

Charlotte's donkey was still trying to reach the carrot, it was moving forwards but not at a very fast speed. She saw that Gerty was close by on a Spanish dancing horse, which was trotting her the long way around the arena with its head held high.

'Please, come on,' Charlotte said to the donkey but it carried on forwards at the same pace.

Gerty wasn't far from the finishing line now but her horse had stopped and held its head into the air.

'Please move,' Gerty asked it nicely but it remained still.

Victoria whizzed past Charlotte on a zebra and was just about to cross the finishing line when the zebra got spooked by the cheers and shouts close by. It reared back before it spun around and ran off in the opposite direction, with Victoria clinging onto its mane in fright.

Charlotte passed Gerty just as her horse began to move. She closed her eyes and chewed on the side of her lip as the donkey placed one of its hooves across the finishing line at what appeared to be the same time as Gerty's horse had.

The rest of the girls crossed the finishing line, apart from Destiny who was still trying to move her horse away from the grass. They all gathered around Miss Moffat and excitedly waited for the results.

Charlotte was both excited and nervous. She had the fingers on both of her hands crossed as she eagerly waited for the results. Margaret looked over at her and scowled and Charlotte looked away from her. Still, she could feel Margaret's gaze boring into her.

'I know I'm going to win,' Alice said.

'Get over yourself,' Stef rolled her eyes.

'Congratulations girls, I am most impressed with your progress over the past six months. Today you have demonstrated your abilities and skills and let me tell you that we are impressed...with most of you,' Miss Moffat smiled. 'Remember that only five of you will represent our Academy. And the top five are...in first place is Margaret.'

Margaret squealed in excitement as she jumped on the spot, before she rushed over to Miss Moffat and hugged her. Miss Moffat pulled back and brushed down her coat.

'There's no need for that,' she said and Margaret blushed, before she walked back over to where she'd been standing.

'Second place is Alice.'

'There must be a mistake, surely I came first?' Alice said loudly.

Miss Moffat frowned before she waved her wand at Alice. She carried on trying to talk but no words came out of mouth, so she clasped her hands over her mouth and looked at the ground.

'Third place is Demi, fourth place is Stephanie and lastly in fifth place, with only a fraction of a hoof in it, is...Charlotte. Well done girls, you have shown true promise and skill and I don't doubt that you will do this Academy proud when you compete against the wizard's college.'

Charlotte and Stef hugged each other excitedly but then they looked over at Gerty, who couldn't hide her disappointment.

'I'm sorry Gerty, it was so close,' Charlotte said.

'You still did well, your horse was really good,' Stef said.

'Thanks guys,' Gerty forced a smile. 'But it's okay, you both did great and deserve to be in the top five,' she hugged them both.

They pulled apart and stood in silence for a few moments.

'Hopefully Charlie will make the wizard's team too,' Gerty winked at Charlotte.

'Hopefully,' she smiled.

'I'm positive he will, although you can't go all gooey-eyed as there's a trophy to be won,' she grinned.

***

The day of the competition arrived and the five girls to make the team flew with Molly over to Alexander's College.

Dale was there to greet them and he led them through the hallways of the castle and into the empty hall. There were seats set out on each side of the stage and Dale gestured for them to sit there.

'It's very quiet, when do you think the boy's will arrive?' Stef whispered to Charlotte.

'Why am I sitting on this end?' Alice huffed. 'They will think that I came last.'

'Who cares,' Stef replied, rolling her eyes.

Alexander appeared on the stage in a royal blue suit.

'Molly, always a pleasure,' he leaned over so that he could kiss her hand.

'Alexander, Miss Moffat sends her regards and hopes that you won't miss the trophy too much,' Molly grinned.

'Well, we shall see about that.'

'Girls, no doubt you are wondering who you will be competing against? Well wonder no more,' he whistled and five boys wearing long black capes and floppy wizard hats appeared on the stage.

Charlotte looked eagerly at the boys but she couldn't tell if one of them was Charlie.

'The first member of our team,' Alexander gestured to the boy on the end of the row...'
Charlotte held her breath as she watched the boy take off his hat.

'Is William.' Polite applause greeted this decision.

'In second place...is Patrick. ' Once again, people clapped their hands.

'Third was John.'

'Fourth place goes to Michael.'

Both Charlotte and Margaret were shocked, their chins dropped at the thought of missing out on seeing Charlie.

'And the final competitor to face the girls is'...he seemed to take an eternity to say the last name... 'Charlie.'

On seeing his brown hair and sparkling eyes both Charlotte and Margaret jumped out of their seats and cheered loudly. All eyes in the room turned to the two girls.

Charlie looked over at Charlotte and smiled, then he winked at Margaret.

'Well, this is going to be interesting,' Stef whispered to Alice.

***
Continue with the second half of this series
in Witch School Part 2

Witch School
Part 2
Books 4, 5 & 6

Katrina Kahler

***

I hope you have enjoyed the Witch School series

as much as I enjoyed writing it!

If you could leave a review that would be wonderful!

And please tell your friends about Witch School.

Have a magical day!

Katrina xxx

Some other books you may enjoy...

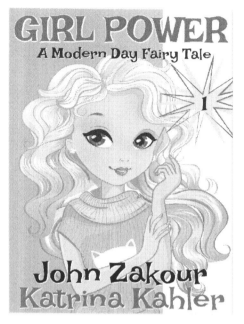

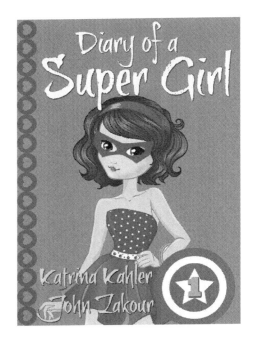

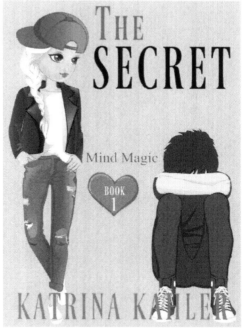